SIGN & BREATH

Voice & the Literary Tradition

Also by Shanta Lee

Do Words Dream Themselves Into Silence Told in Riddles?
(Harbor Editions, 2026)

Close Is…& Hopscotch Between the Living and the Dead
(Two chapbooks, one volume)
(Diode Editions, Fall 2024)

This is how they teach you to want it…the slaughter
A Field Guide for the Hunted & the Hunter. The dead-alive.
The live-dead ones, The…(Harbor Editions, 2024)

Black Metamorphoses (Etruscan Press, 2023)

GHETTOCLAUSTROPHOBIA: Dreamin of Mama
While Trying to Speak Woman in Woke Tongues
(Diode Editions, 2021)

Also by Philip Brady
Poetry

The Elsewhere: Poems and Poetics (Broadstone Books, 2021)

To Banquet with the Ethiopians: A Memoir of Life Before the Alphabet
(Broadstone Books, 2015)

*Fathom (*Word Press, 2007)

Weal (Ashland Poetry Press, 1999)

Forged Correspondences (New Myths, 1996)

Non-Fiction

Phantom Signs: The Muse in Universe City
(University of Tennessee Press, 2019)

By Heart: Reflections of a Rust – Belt Bard
(University of Tennessee Press, 2008)

To Prove My Blood: A Tale of Emigrations & The Afterlife
(Ashland Poetry Press, 2003)

Edited

Poems and Their Making: A Conversation
(Etruscan Press, 2015)

Critical Essays on James Joyce's Portrait of the Artist as a Young Man,
co-edited with James F. Carens (Twayne, 1998)

SIGN & BREATH

Voice & the Literary Tradition

Edited by Shanta Lee and Philip Brady

Etruscan Press

Etruscan Press
Wilkes University
84 West South Street
Wilkes-Barre, PA 18766
(570) 408-4546

www.etruscanpress.org

Published 2025 by Etruscan Press
Printed in the United States of America
Cover design by Lisa Reynolds
Interior design and typesetting by Aaron Petrovich
The text of this book is set in Iowan Old Style.

First Edition

17 18 19 20 5 4 3 2 1

Library of Congress Cataloging-in-Publication Data

Names: Lee, Shanta editor | Brady, Philip, 1955- editor
Title: Sign & breath : voice & the literary tradition / edited by Shanta Lee and Philip Brady.
Other titles: Sign and breath
Description: First edition. | Wilkes-Barre, PA : Etruscan Press, 2025. |
Summary: "Sign & Breath is a new critical anthology that takes a different approach to exploring these questions: What is poetry? What defines voice? Featuring a range of contemporary artists, many of whom work across different mediums and genres, Sign & Breath introduces the reader to one page that sings in any genre - prose, fiction, poetry, spoken word, hybrid forms, and song - across diverse traditions. Rather than define poetry as a genre with conventions, traditions, codes, and modalities, this book features poetry as a faculty that thrums in all written and spoken art. Readers are introduced to a text followed by a discussion with the author about creating the piece, ties to creative lineage, and the definition of voice through their practice. This anthology contributes to the dialogue among genres which will reframe understanding of poetry as an aesthetic experience of language. With one page that sings in any genre, Sign & Breath presents a new, inclusive perspective on poetry while two questions remain: Do we have a clearer understanding of what defines poetry? Do we have a clearer understanding of voice?"-- Provided by publisher.
Identifiers: LCCN 2025020100 | ISBN 9798990767812 paperback acid-free paper

Subjects: LCSH: American poetry--21st century | Creative nonfiction, American--21st century | American fiction--21st century | LCGFT: Poetry | Creative nonfiction | Short stories
Classification: LCC PS507 .S536 2025 | DDC 810.9/006--dc23/eng/20250425
LC record available at https://lccn.loc.gov/2025020100

Please turn to the back of this book for a list of the sustaining funders of Etruscan Press.

This book is printed on recycled, acid-free paper.

In Memory of Jerome Rothenberg (1931 – 2024)

Table of Contents

Acknowledgements

Many hands and hearts went into making *Sign & Breath*. For their work transcribing and editing the recorded interviews, we thank Jon Lawrence, Allison Maher, Tommy Mihalopoulos, and Natalie O'Brien. Our talented designers, Kari Bayait, Aaron Petrovich, and Lisa Reynolds, worked tirelessly to produce this beautiful codex. For marketing and publicity, we are indebted to Elizabeth Cunningham, Talbot Logan, Jess Van Orden, and Wyatt Steltz. We owe the enticing book trailers and teasers to Shanta Lee and Damon Honeycutt. For technical support, Justin Bodnar is always on the spot. And for guidance and support, Albert LaFarge has been invaluable throughout. The Maslow Family Creative Writing Program and their Director David Hicks have been endlessly generous. Thanks to Youngstown State University for a Research Professorship and subvention. The Oristaglio Family has supported this book and the press from the start. Finally, to the great team at Etruscan Press, Amanda Rabaduex, Bill Schneider, and Pamela Turchin—you're the best!

About This Anthology:
A Conversation Between the Co-Editors
(Not Your Usual Introduction)

SL: Yayyyy, we get to talk about *Sign & Breath* as co-editors.

PB: Yes, we've been working together on this project for 18 months or so. We have solicited "one page that sings" in any genre and we've recorded 48 interviews about that page and about the dual nature of poetry as written and spoken language. *What is voice?* we've asked. *How does it relate to and engage with the literary tradition?* So, Shanta, what has been your experience conducting all these interviews? What common threads do you see?

SL: Oh, man, it's been so interesting. There are lots of unique themes that attempt to arrive at an answer to this very question: how do we even get into voice? Is it the thing that we hear or that we experience on the page? How does it begin in the body, right?

I have also experienced individuals talking about how human memory shifts, discussions about culture, and writing to deconstruct the conceptions we have about what we believe a writer's life would look like. There were some themes that surfaced connecting to ghosts and the ancestral coming through in many voices...there were so many amazing contributions.

What I love about this anthology is the diversity. It's not just about the literary, but also what happened to be translated into the literary by these various, multi-faceted artists. The conversations were had with individuals who came from backgrounds that range from embodiment through dance, choreography, performers, orators, spoken word artists, and visual artists to individuals who talked about how the engagement between the body and the act of riding a horse informed the rhythm within their work.

What I appreciated most across all the interviews was being left with a feeling of "To be continued."

I want to toss the same question to you. What did you notice about some of the threads and what have you learned from the interviews?

PB: One of the things I find most interesting is what we're doing right now. In the normal course of writing a book, the editors would draft their introduction. Here we are doing this interview, which we haven't rehearsed.

SL: Right.

PB: As you pointed out in your interview, we're giving space to something ephemeral. To attest to that space in a codex—which by its very nature is a rebuke against the passing of time—creates this enormous tension. Recording these interviews and curating them on the Etruscan website points to the dual condition of poetry as a written and oral art. And I feel that in many of our interviews these writers come to a heightened awareness of the fact that poetry is perhaps the only art that has no native means of apprehension.

So, poems come in two species. They come heard, and then they come seen. And in both, something is missing; no single iteration encompasses the whole experience of the poem. This absence is poignant and nearly palpable—the absence itself is part of the experience. You were saying earlier that you could not define voice. Here, we asked every interviewee to try to define it. And everyone wanted very much to address that essential question, and yet, everyone, at the same time, expressed a resistance to defining voice.

SL: I think that's very true. And when you were talking about the ephemerality of performance, there's also the piece of what is in between the space on a page, whitespace. One thing that I'm always interested in is what is in between what is not said and what is said, even in this editing process, which leads me to another question. Sign and breath. Breath, you can't see it necessarily, I mean, you only can see it in certain circumstances. If it's too cold, you see breath. It's almost the same way when it's really hot on the horizon, you see heat, right? But overall, you can see a sign, you can only, at least mostly, feel breath. So, my question is a curiosity about the title, prior to me coming onto the project which I was honored and thrilled to join.

What does sign and breath mean to you? Also, in this editing process, what does sign and breath come to mean? Where did it begin and where does it end, if it does end, for you?

PB: I wanted to avoid using the word "poetry" because once you use that word you drag along—like Marley's ghost—all the chains of conventions and expectations inherent in a particular practice or discipline. We've included work that doesn't fall under a conventional rubric of poetry. We've broadened our scope to include work that sings, in any genre. As H. L. Hix has it, "Nothing attested, everything sung."

I think we're asking whether poetry and prose are driven by the same energy and merely follow different sets of conventions. Or are they completely different art forms that are joined by the technology of the alphabet? The poets and novelists and other artists that we have interviewed have taught me that poetry offers insight into stillness and the lyrical moment. Stillness opens into a sense of infinity, as Blake says—eternity in an hour, a world in a grain of sand. While the impulse of prose may be to tell the story, delineating character and plot, no sentences worth their salt are bereft of music. So, our anthology addresses this question of what is poetic. What is oral? What is voice? We come to the question from an inclusive point of view, not merely relying on the conventions of one particular genre but instead, the artistic expression of human impulses.

SL: It's funny, the H L Hix quote makes me think of a historical foundation for a video game. Most are familiar with *Assassin's Creed* as a video game, but it's tied to the history of actual assassins. Anyway, the quote is, "Nothing is true, everything is permitted." And so, there's something about these questions—What is voice? What are signs? What is the unsayable? Or thinking about the in-between—when in fact, everything is fair game! We get to decide those things. At the same time, one of the things that I've enjoyed about poetry, what draws me to really good poetry, are things that I just really can't get, no matter how many times I'll reread it. No matter if I hear it, or look at it many times, there's a deep mystery. There's a wall. There's something I must keep returning to.

Is it like...what's the name of it? There is a sculpture, Kryptos. I believe it is outside of the CIA building. There's a riddle, a structural riddle, on this sculpture. Many people have been trying to solve the whole riddle, and I've been fascinated by that. There's something about that concept that poetry is tied to. My favorite work is work that just kind of leaves something. It doesn't really give you all the answers. You've got to figure it out. And even in breath, even that demands that you listen to it. Even within that listening, you may not decipher fully what that is.

PB: We talked earlier about the noise in the background of a few interviews—sound of school bells or city sirens or someone shuffling papers, and it reminds us that when we listen, we can't discriminate. We don't get to tune out the parts that we don't want to hear. The visual has a little bit more control—we can close our eyes or turn away. And I think that the visual imagination may be more tied to a linear sense of the world. The aural imagination is immersed in a cacophony.

We're on Zoom. I'm in one place, you're in another. But we both listen to the environment as it surrounds us. You and I have witnessed many performances where that noise—the "music of what happens" as Finn MacCumhal puts it—whether it could be traffic, or the espresso machine, or a cough, or a baby crying–this is all part of the experience and it's almost the signature of authenticity, to say this is happening in the world that we know.

SL: It's very John Cage. Very *4:33*, which is a brilliant piece where the whole composition is Cage sitting at a piano, not playing it. Whatever is in the environment is the composition. That is the piece, and it is very fascinating.

PB: Jerome Rothenberg, one of our contributors who very sadly just recently passed away, invited us to consider all work—our own and that of others—with the same creative attention. He says, "I write those poems which I have not found elsewhere and for whose existence I feel a deep need." In this anthology we invite all of us to dissolve that barrier between our work and the work of others because that's originally how the oral tradition worked. Poems did not belong to a certain person—Homer, for instance, is probably just a name that we assigned to a whole phenomenon. We've talked about the political repercussions—the fact that we're now entering an age where authorship is again going to come into question with AI. We are questioning the relationship between the individual and that which is somehow universal and expressed without ownership.

SL: This also raises the question of humanity, and how we define ourselves. I'll ask this last question. I'm curious, if you were to name three or four things that you hope readers take away from the anthology, what would that be?

PB: One of the things that has come up over and over are attempts to come to terms with this one word: voice. What does it mean? How is it expressed? As you pointed out, it can't really be defined. The minute you try to say it's one thing, it turns into something else. Another thing I've been amazed by is the range that is represented in terms of culture, genre, and approach. It feels expansive. We have touched upon people at many different stages of their career. So, this anthology doesn't represent a canon. It is as if we stood with eyes closed by a river and dipped our fingers in the stream. We don't know the length or direction. But we know the flow and temperature.

SL: I love that. The things I've been thinking about, this is somewhat along the same vein, I'm hoping that it invites more conversation, and also through that conversation, it becomes an expansion about language and its transmission. I hope we continue to think about that, and instead of the either/or we see it as and, and, and, and, and beyond the *and* that we can't think of. Also, I would say entanglement, like the way that for every one of the individuals who contributed, it's almost like you get to see just one sliver into their world, into the individual, and we are still experiencing one side of it. I'm hoping those things are what individuals take away and even beyond that, what we can't imagine.

PB: Very much so. I also love the fact that this experience has several forms: you can experience it here or by watching the videos and reading comments.

SL: Actually, one of our interviewees, Professor D'Aguiar—who writes across so many genres—also suggested a playlist. He suggested that perhaps we get a favorite song from each contributor to put together a playlist that accompanies the anthology! So, that will be another dimension that people can experience sign in breath.

PB: That sounds great. And as you pointed out, this book is really just about creating an ongoing conversation. I know that you and I will continue to encourage and join in that conversation.

I.

"...who's writing poems that no one has asked him to write."

Michael Waters

Christal Brown

"Day 14: Outside In"

I have one biological sibling. We are eight years apart. I am the youngest. We basically grew up as two only children. We perceive our parents and our upbringing from extremely different vantage points.

Because we're so far apart in age and because my father and mother had their own battles, I spent a lot of time alone. I became pretty independent early in life. I entertained myself, did my own hair, and could make a few things in the kitchen. But what I couldn't do was give myself love and attention. I found love and attention outside of our home through friends, the parents of my friends, my great aunts, dance teachers, and unofficial mentors.

The love I began to recognize was based on accomplishment through academics, dance competitions, pageants, or track. This early understanding of conditional love became an impediment along my self-love journey.

My upbringing, paired with a twenty-year career as a performing artist, wove a complicated entanglement in my heart and mind between acceptance, love, and authenticity.

But somewhere between becoming someone's mother, becoming an orphan, and turning forty, I began to understand that all the love I had been receiving from the outside needed to be internalized.

I had to learn how to accept my gifts, talents, differences, and desires in order to experience the true love I had always desired. I fell in love with myself and began to see myself as others had seen me: clear, beautiful, powerful, graceful, and free.

SL: Why did you choose this page? What was it about this specific page that you chose? What does this piece represent about your practice across all the things you do?

CB: This is an excerpt from a 30-day devotional, *30 Days of Growth with Grace*, and each of the pages inside this devotional end with a series of questions for the reader. For me, this page traverses what we are all looking for, which is self love. Right? Everything we do is either an act of self love, learning to love others, or trying to get love. Especially the love required to forgive. In my practice, I teach clients that we are usually tasked with forgiveness when people make an unskillful request for our love.

What I wanted to do in sharing this excerpt was to give the trajectory of how I came to this understanding of self love. I came to the place of loving myself by disconnecting from an unending cycle of conditional love called success. I use my experience to give people an entree into authentic freedom which is built through self love.

SL: I think that's embedded in that would have to be voice, right? How does voice play a role in your composition? How do you relate to voice as someone who has choreographed, danced, and as a coach? Can you talk to me about those different iterations of voice for you?

CB: When we think of voices, we think about people wanting to be heard, but we're often heard in so many other ways. We're heard by our body language. We're heard by the way we enter a room. We're heard through the silence of our own discontent. Rather than saying, "Oh, I'm going to use my voice to tell you how I feel," we're often showing people how we feel. As a choreographer, I am tasked with translating written language or ideas into a visual language that speaks through the body. Inside the creative process is often where I find true understanding. The balance of language on the page, no matter how finely tuned or crafted, is always missing something; the body.

If we're thinking about the choreographic process, how do we bring a story to the now and somehow give it such a physical embodiment that people can not only see themselves in it but also see themselves beyond it? People come to watch dance not because they can do it in their living room, but because the bodies in front of them are doing something that they've thought about or imagined or experienced in a different way. In my choreographic process, I'm often taking and translating the feeling of language into the embodied practice of choreography, which then becomes a language of its own, a storytelling that gives voice to the human experience.

SL: How do you see your work different on the page versus performance? Do you compose with performance in mind? How is this different for you working across your different mediums of dance and writing?

CB: That's a great question, the common thread is intuition. The voice that I have to listen to across all of my work is my intuitive voice. In my coaching practice, we talk about how to hear the still small voice, the voice within. How do you get to that place where you trust that intuitive voice so much that it becomes the directive of your next action? A lot of times, if we look at this from the field of dance, we would call that improvisation; musicians, actors, and comedians may call it the same thing. But that level of improvisation requires a deeper level of saturation. What that means is that I've been saturated in words as a writer, I've been saturated in movement as a dancer, I've been saturated in people as a coach. Therefore, when my intuitive voice bubbles up for the next right thing to say, do, or be, I trust it from experience. Trusting my intuition comes from that understanding comes after experience. Experience can bring my subconscious mind into alignment with my wealth of experience to create moments of embodied, written, and relational understanding. For many of us, lived experiences have eroded trust in our own intuition. We move in patterns of scarcity or systems of success that do not require that we listen to our own voices.

SL: What is your posture towards conventions in the traditions as connected to the different mediums that you work across? Are you someone who is deeply rooted within the different traditions that you work within? I often call myself a practitioner of entanglement and I see you as a fellow practitioner of entanglement bringing all these different things together. Or are you trying to break beyond tradition, especially because you bring such a knowledge and skill of embodiment?

CB: Maybe you've heard me say this before, but I have two core values: love and trust. I don't do anything I don't love, and I don't work with people I don't trust. I find that many people stop themselves from following the intuitive voice that's inside because they're not an expert at something. I have to think about that in the same way, right? I've wanted to write and be a writer since I was nine years old. I also wanted to be an accountant, that was the first entanglement. Even publishing this book, this 30-day devotional, I had to find a format that felt honest to me, so that it didn't feel like I was trying to imitate a writer. I had to take the expertise away, and I had to be really honest about sharing stories that help people rather than focusing on the best story. I wanted to tell stories that allow people to see themselves inside the work, the same standard I have with my choreographic work. I don't want to make dances that are so high art that most people don't know what they're [the choreographed dances] talking about. I want to make dances where people can see themselves in them, walk away from the experience with a deeper understanding of themselves, and a kind of peripheral view of the craft of dance—making. When I think about the depth of all the things that I love, I'm pulling from an authenticity of experience rather than a need to be an expert. Because as we know from Zen Buddhism, in the beginner's mind, there are many possibilities; while in expert's, there are few. I always want to see the things I love with the mind of a beginner.

SL: What is voice given everything you're talking about—authenticity, self love, reaching into the stillness of life? How do you define voice, especially as someone who's engaged your whole body across your careers?

CB: For me, I think I would define voice as any medium that gives you the courage to share who you really are, and what you really know, without second guessing your experience. That's how I would think about voice. It is the offering of the deepest version of ourselves, the clearest version of ourselves, without hindrance or judgment. Within a deep amount of courage and willingness lies the permission to be whole and to be real, regardless of right and wrong. There's right, there's wrong, and there's real. The entanglement of the intuitive, the lived, the human, the embodied, however that comes out. If it comes out through your mouth, if it comes out through a glance at someone human to human, or if it comes out through a hug, that is your voice. You're giving voice to the depth of emotion, feeling and experience that you've had, and that takes courage.

Christal Brown *(Mother|Artist|Educator|Disciple|Coach) is the Founder of INSPIRIT, Project: BECOMING, the creator of the Liquid Strength training module for dance, an Associate Professor of Dance and Director of the Anti-Racist Task Force at Middlebury College, and the CVO of Steps and Stages, LLC.* ***"Day 14: Outside In" is an excerpt from Christal Brown's*** **Steps and Stories: 30 Days of Growth with Grace** ***(Trilogy Christian Publishing, 2023).***

Dante Di Stefano

"My Favorite Things"

Why am I always querying myself into a single endless couplet repeated in note after note of a poem that does not want to lineate itself in the language of the electrocardiogram || I will continue to pour my discourse into the river of blinking cursors at this document's imagined edge || place two fingers on my wrist & listen for the mountain brook as it recites an unseen horizon || there will never be enough time to say all the words contained in the galaxy of whitespace pinwheeling around this comma || , || & every golden phoneme that ghosts my throat is || *yes* || & || *love* || & the way the wind jaws the boughs of a linden tree in my memory || the eyelashes of my newborn son opening in an unending blue hour as a star whose name I don't know blinks through the living room curtains|| my four-year old daughter's hand clamped onto my own as she falls asleep listening to the dull edge of a once-upon-a-time I déjà vu us into each night before bed || the dog a doodle of sunlight curled on the couch in the afternoon portending grace as a pat on the muzzle || my wife in any season unhusking the vowels that echolocate the verbs flying in my knuckles & transform them into psalms || all this reaching against time & railing against death & singing truculently & mellifluously into the numb maw palpitating decay in the hundred hundred hearts of the residuary worm || what I mean to say is: all the poems I've ever written leaf to life right here & tell you I am alive || & I love you || these poems || little metropolises of pain & joy || dioramas of so much longing & striving & being || restorative utterances on the verge of unsaying || all these misprisionings of the half-known & the intuited & the holy holy holy inscrutable palpable brokenness that binds one (you and me) to the volta of the moment || any moment a poem these poems || & || I hold them out greenly || & dumbly || & frailly || & fiercely || my hand in your hand become two sparrows banking against an overcast sky || & I keep holding forth the poem's ark the poems' arcs for you || for you || for you || for you || for you || for you || for you || for you || for you || for you || for you || for you || for

PB: Dante, how did this piece come about? Why did you choose it for this project?

DD: Well, when you asked me to be part of the anthology, I immediately thought of a poem that I wrote called "A Love Supreme," which is written in a similar form, and has similar poetic concerns and aesthetic considerations. But that poem was way too long. So, I wrote this poem yesterday and this morning. And obviously, the title evokes John Coltrane, who is the artist I admire most, and whose work has taught me so much about writing. It's amazing how in the twelve years of his recording career he could create a body of work as impressive as any artist in the history of the world. And there's something about the spirituality and the questing and the effusiveness within the restraint of his music that, to me, is instructive for a poet and for poetry. Because poetry is all about negotiating the tension between restraint and effusion, between structure and surprise, and really when you listen to how Coltrane transforms a Rodgers and Hammerstein show tune into this incredible work of art, that kind of alchemy is what I'm after with the word, with these interior fluencies that I'm attempting to bring out into the world. That's what you call voice, I guess.

Voice is the adjunct to a continually multiplying set of interior fluencies that you try to transcribe.

PB: I have not seen you use the technique you use in "My Favorite Things" before. Tell me about this technique, and why you chose it.

DD: I'm just interested in understanding poetry as a variegated field and not as a monolith. So, I've always been drawn to form, but it strikes me that every choice one makes in a poem is a formal choice, a means of constraint. This particular poem is a prose poem written in a textbox style with full justification on Microsoft Word (where all lines in a paragraph are expanded so they butt up against both the left and right text margins and the prose looks like a block). The poem employs caesura marks, which would be used in scansion, instead of traditional punctuation. In the past ten years or so, many poets have been employing virgules in their prose poems. And, you know, that is definitely a metapoetic gesture. "My Favorite Things" is metapoetic and a kind of Ars Poetica. The prose poem itself is a form and a tradition that questions the boundaries of form and asks, "What makes a poem a poem?" When you write a prose poem, you put your poem in dialogue with all the other prose poems that have ever been written, just as when you write a sonnet you open up a dialogue that extends back through the centuries to Petrarch. As a prose poem, "My Favorite Things" connects with the experimental tradition: the David Anton talk poem, Jack Kerouac's *Old Angel Midnight*. Ultimately, though, as with any poem, this one has a strange pedigree that I don't really want to quantify. As Harvey Hix would remind us, all genre, all form, is artificial, right? A means of categorizing and imposing order on something (poetry? voice? breath? inspiration? imagination?) that skitters on the edge of consciousness.

For me, poetry lives this tripartite life. One part of that life is in the body. There is something palpably visceral about poetry before you even get to the moment of invention, or before you dwell in the space of composition. The poems are there vibrating with an intensity, circulating in your heart (as a muscle, not as a metaphor), in your lungs, and in your body. But poetry also lives a second life on the page in a particular way, in the arcane topographies of alphabet, ink, font, blank space, blinking cursor, the glowing white on a computer screen, margin, the pulp of dead trees, all the other innumerable physical realities and modes of transcription. And lastly poetry lives what, in popular speech today, might be called its "best life." Poetry's oldest and ultimate life is in the air as a spoken thing, as a heard thing, an utterance meant to be listened to, as a matter of what is most necessary in music. I'm always cognizant of those three manifestations of the poem.

PB: Many paths. Is this the first time that you have voiced this poem for others? What did that feel like?

DD: Well, when I'm writing I'm always reading it aloud. That's one thing, I write the first draft of it, reading aloud as I do, and then I keep reading it aloud as much as I can after I have a draft down. Then, I have to do things like put my four-year-old to bed, help my wife with the baby, teach during my school day, or whatever else I have to do. So, I'm kind of reading and revising around all these obligations and interactions. And I think people probably think I'm a very eccentric person because whenever I can, I'm reading, reading, reading, and talking to myself.

So, right now was the first time somebody else has heard this poem, but it's been spoken as much as it possibly could be spoken aloud in the time between yesterday and today. After my wife and I put our daughter to bed and the baby was asleep, I just sat in a chair and said it ten or fifteen times before I went to sleep. Then in the morning, I revised it and riffed it into what it is now. And again, read it many times throughout my school day (when I had an empty classroom, which wasn't that often, but I have a couple free periods). So, you know, the poem got a good workout before it came to you. But that's kind of my process no matter what poem, and with this poem, I discovered by reading it aloud that the caesuras are meant to be a kind of score that indicates how you should read it. And to indicate the length of a breath. In the poem, there's these long loping passages, and then there are these short intervals too.

And again, that's something I'm learning from Coltrane, dwelling in these repetitive structures, these riffs that go on chorus after chorus, and then you're searching really, and you're risking a great deal by doing that, because it could all collapse. I think this poem works as what it is, but there's a big risk inherent in the structure. Nevertheless, you should always be willing to put yourself out there and not be afraid to sound ridiculous, otherwise, without that risk, you'll never be able to translate all those interior fluencies that you feel in your knuckles and that you are attempting to set down on the page with the hope that they will ascend from there into the arena of aria, psalm, prayer, song, and breath.

Dante Di Stefano *is the author of five poetry collections and a chapbook, including, most recently, the book-length poem,* The Widowing Radiance *(Bordighera Press, 2025). He co-edited the anthology* Misrepresented People *(NYQ Books, 2018) and lives in Endwell, NY with his wife and two children.*

Michael Waters

"Shark River Bridge"

That spot in the center of the bridge
Where the seam splits metal, where
The two leaves of the span part
For tuna boats—their 7' rods
Rigged high as though trolling for God—
That spot above the gray waters of the inlet
Where Avon-by-the-Sea arcs into Belmar—
That's where I'll jump some wintry predawn
Once dementia has commenced, before it seeps
Deeper into my brain & swerves me
From my purpose, protects me from self-harm,
Makes my death dependent
Upon those whose love will stay their hand.
I'll wear my black woolen overcoat, its pockets
Jangling with silverware, & wash down
With a tumblerful of vodka
The long-amassed tablets of Ambien
Before leaping toward oblivion.
Watching our elders deepen into dementia,
We rehearse escapes, our exit fantasies.
I will not gaze like my mother beyond the son
Who visits the memory care facility, will not
Pluck incessantly a ghost-hair off my tongue
Or spin & spin again the buttons of my cardigan
Only to focus suddenly on his face & whisper—
Those glinting hooks descending—"I want to kill you."
No. I will not.   I've picked my spot.

PB: When I started reading the poem, Michael, I did not have any clue that it was going where it goes. Obviously, this poem originates in deep personal experience. What does it feel like to craft and then say this poem?

MW: Like you, I wasn't sure where this poem would go. I began with a description. Almost every day I walk a few miles on the boardwalk from the tip of Asbury Park, NJ, south through Ocean Grove, Bradley Beach, and Avon-by-the-Sea, then cross that bridge into Belmar before returning. My mother had been diagnosed with Alzheimer's a few years before, and I had been watching her deepen into that disease, and thought, as we all do, that I would not let that happen to me. When it begins, I thought, well, here's what I'll do.

I would stop each day on that bridge and gaze into the water. Occasionally, the bells would ring, and I'd have to get off the bridge so that the span could open to allow the outgoing tuna boats with their tall, propped-up fishing rods to pass. I'd watch them and connect them with my mother in her dementia. On one hand, there was that visual sense of upward movement, weirdly aspirational, with the poles; on the other hand, there were the huge hooks that would be descending into darkness.

Suddenly, this split verticality seemed an apt metaphor, as did the horizontal split of the span opening. My horror at watching my mother deepen into Alzheimer's, along with my own fear, worked its way into the poem, and the diction, in its flow, took me where the poem wanted to go.

In 1971, in London, I attended a series of lectures by Jorge Luis Borges, and something he said in one of those lectures struck me and stayed with me. He said that Walter Whitman was a homosexual newspaper reporter who one day dreamed the idea of Walt Whitman the poet, and who then spent the rest of his life trying to write poems that only Walt Whitman the poet could write. Then Borges paused and asked, "But who can write poems like Walt Whitman?" I was twenty-one and must have asked myself, "Who is this Michael Waters who's writing poems that no one has asked him to write? Who will care if he stops writing them?" There must have been some idea, though, of the poet I wanted to be, and for the past fifty years I've been trying to write poems that this poet would write.

This may be where the notion of voice comes in. Whose voice is this? There's *his* voice as I imagine it, but which I can never quite attain. And there's my voice, which is where craft enters. I struggle with my limitations, and try, poem by poem, to transcend them, to manage a poem that comes close to the poem I can almost hear. When I do manage that, I wonder why I can't do it all the time. I think, this is what I would like to write. I just wrote this. *How* did I do it? Why can't I write another one? Then depression sets in, because the more I learn about craft, and the more I deepen into it, the harder it becomes to get the poem right.

PB: As I listened to your reading, I thought, how can this man read these lines having also lived them? You were composed as you read the poem. I'm curious about what that felt like for you.

MW: I read the poem aloud for an audience for the first time last week, and I'm still navigating its cadences. My poems are written in lines, not sentences, although the lines compose sentences, and I've insisted before that the line is the integral unit of the poem, as opposed to the sentence which is the integral unit of prose. Each line should function as a unit unto itself, and full attention should be given to its beginning and end, to how it *sounds*, how its syllables clamor against each other. Each line should be the fulfillment of the lines that have preceded it and anticipate the lines that follow. I want the narrative to be cohesive, but sound work can also offer cohesion. Good free verse doesn't give up the formalities and rhymes found in traditional forms, but instead relocates them as the poem shapes itself.

How the poem is said is as important as what the poem says. That's where craft enters. I want my poems to have a rich musical surface that might make them memorable. Often, I find myself having memorized, unconsciously, poems by Emily Dickinson, for example, or by John Logan or Richard Wilbur: "Edgar Degas purchased once / A fine El Greco which he kept / Against the wall beside his bed / To hang his pants on while slept." It's like a Taylor Swift song, an earworm! You can't get it out of your head.

I love how you responded to my poem because I respond to certain poems that way. They just kill me. I'm so struck by them, though it's never simply the story that strikes me, but the diction that conveys it. If I remember only the story, it may as well have been told in prose. If the diction's right, if the lineation's effective, the poem will lodge itself within me and be hard to shake loose.

In terms of voice, I want to be that poet who has read and absorbed everything, who then starts winnowing. I want to articulate to myself the reasons that I like or dislike a poem, until what comes out of all the voices is a singular voice that may be my own, the voice of the Michael Waters whom I envision writing poems. It's a voice that responds to the tactile quality of words and to their sensuality. It's a voice that jibes with my own obsessions which have to do, especially in recent work, with sensuality and transgression and sin.

Finally, I've dodged your question by focusing on aspects of craft. How did it *feel* to write this poem and then to read it aloud? Good. In a way that may be almost cruel to myself and to anyone who reads or hears it, it felt good.

Michael Waters *is the author of numerous books of poetry, including* Sinnerman *(Etruscan Press, 2023),* Caw *(BOA Editions, 2020), and* The Dean of Discipline *(U Pittsburgh P, 2018). He has been the recipient of fellowships from the Guggenheim Foundation, the National Endowment for the Arts, and the Fulbright Foundation. He lives without a cell phone in Ocean, New Jersey.*

Bruce Bond

"Peacock"

Geoffrey Hill is dead, and still, now, as I read his words,
his voice keeps crossing over. And a woman at a nearby
table says to her companion, *I am so many people these days—*

mother, child, whore—I feel exhausted. And as she laughs,
her unlit cigarette keeps making little circles, and the other
woman listens. I want to say, *I know the feeling,* when I know

I cannot. I want to break through unspoken boundaries.
I cannot write of Nobody, says Hill. *No one to narrate this.*
But then his writing, with all its ferocity and plumage, turns

from an image of the self as a peacock to praise the bird's
bare corrosive scream. I cannot speak for no one. I try.
Some laughter belies the cutlery inside it. But what I see

in the author's portrait is his namesake, a rock, withholding
and thereby held. What I hear is a woman and her broken
English, the many selves lonely for the one who talks of them.

Her companion says, *yes*. The unlit cigarette rises and falls.
And as I bow my head, I read a little deeper. *Names live alone*
their separate lives, says Hill. *Yes*, I say. And softer still, *yes, yes.*

PB: Why did you pick this poem for our anthology about voice, Bruce?

BB: I picked this poem for this particular anthology because it's obviously so much about voice. It's about what voice can accomplish and what it cannot. That's a subject dear to me. Voice can be critical in a poem in creating a sense of personhood, but that sense is always failed. That's not to say that all failures are the same. These failures are relative, and the relative nature of failure is absolutely essential to understanding what a poem is and how it works.

You could see that the woman in the poem is struggling with the idea of representing herself accurately. She's so many different selves. And that dissonance, or that distance between representation and the actual authentic self, which is withheld, is important to understanding the distance between any kind of identity construct and this unrepresentable aspect of the self that is more interior.

I sometimes bemoan the fact that we have conflated the issue of identity with the issue of selfhood so much. If we can see flaws and identity constructions, if we think then there's no more real out there to access, that confusion can become tragic if not problematic in this age when there's so much emphasis on self-performance, facilitated by social media and the internet. It exacerbates the problem whereby people busy themselves curating their constructed selves, and there's less talk about how that construction can be either faithful or performed in bad faith.

I don't think there's such a thing as a credible poem without this horizon that we call authenticity. But to conflate it with the idea that a poem is a crystallization of the authentic is unfortunate. It opens the door for New Conceptualism and dismisses the idea of authenticity because there's so much fabrication online. We are bombarded with insincere representations. If a performance can be phony, there must be one that dares to be relatively authentic.

But that's not to say the real can be constructed. Goeffrey Hill provides an example, because here he is writing a poem about a peacock praising a bare interior beyond the ostentatious display. And yet, his verbal constructions can sometimes be formidable. They tend toward the highly rhetorical, and the fact that that rhetoric pays off is a tribute to his genius. I would say he's in the category of someone like a Hart Crane, maybe a Hopkins in that they've created voices that are quite clearly to my ear artificial. And yet, there still is a sense of necessity about them. They aren't just full of ornaments.

So, I picked him as an example in part because there is this framing paradox in his particular poem about a peacock where he seems to be critiquing the very thing that he is so clearly associated with, which is a kind of high rhetoric. This quote, "names live alone their separate lives," provides an admission that poems have a reality that is not our personal possession. You're entering a public forum. Language is very much that place where the public and private meet and often conflict and this is no more evident than in the world of poetry. We associate it with interiority, and that's its strength.

Metaphor is our best means out there for representing inner life, which is hugely important in this day and age. Interiority is unfairly under attack as a kind of bourgeois luxury or illusion, a kind of withdrawing from a moral engagement in the world. But I don't see it that way. First of all, our interiors are deeply invested in the world. There is no interior without a world to engage. It is our way of humanizing that world, of expressing why it matters. But also, you've put together this wonderful anthology on this issue of voice, which is so closely wedded to music in my mind. Obviously, it's oral. But there's a relationship between musical phrasing and the way that we use language, the way that syntax inflects timing, pitch, stress. I'm an instrumentalist, but I recognize when I improvise, a relationship between musicality and singing, the way the voice works, the way it breathes and phrases.

When I think of voice, I think of this evanescent quality in a poem: the part that evaporates, the musical quality, the performative quality that is there and gone. And that's always in dialogue with the trace that's left behind. So, there's a sense of a poem as always both a process and a thing. I would never want to exclude one of those things from the equation, which is why I'm drawn to poetry that has an auditory dimension because it's so associated with a voice, it's associated with a human presence. But also, it's associated with the brevity of that presence. I find that deeply moving.

There's a quote from Robert Bly where he says, "from the ear to the heart, from the eye to the mind." It's very quotable. It's very short. It's not always true. But there is some truth to it. The experience of weeping just hearing a piece of music is pretty common. The experience of weeping before a painting is uncommon. So that says something. I think it might have to do with a number of mysterious things that I can't even talk about. But also, it has something to do with the fact that music is so much about time, and so it embodies so much of our existential anxiety. It's very much about becoming, not just being, right?

Its evanescence is part of its power. It's making friends with time, which is the source of so much fear in us. And now we see it turned into something beautiful. I think there's something intensely compelling about that: the redemptive power of music to take this element of time and make it beautiful.

Bruce Bond *is the author of several poetry collections including* Rise and Fall of the Lesser Sun Gods *(Elixir Press, 2018) and* Dear Reader *(Free Verse Editions, 2018). His book* Radiography *(University of Michigan, 1997) was the winner of the Natalie Ornish Best Book of Poetry Award. He is currently a Regents Emeritus Professor of English at the University of North Texas.*

Shara McCallum

"May 2018: for grandmother"

When the dead return
they will come to you in dream
and in waking, will be the bird
knocking, knocking against glass, seeking
a way in, will masquerade
as the wind, its voice made audible
by the tongues of leaves, greedily
lapping, as the waves' self-made fugue
is a turning and returning, the dead
will not then nor ever again
desert you, their unrest
will be the coat cloaking you,
the farther you journey
from them the more
distance will maw in you,
time and place gulching
when the dead return to demand
accounting, wanting
and wanting and wanting
everything you have to give and nothing
will quench or unhunger them
as they take all you make as offering.
Then tell you to begin again.

SL: Tell us about this page, why did you choose it? How does it represent your practice?

SM: I've long been a poet interested in speaking to the dead and for the dead, and *No Ruined Stone* is no exception—though this book is comprised almost entirely of voices that are not my own. Over the years I've written many dramatic monologues in contemporary vernacular, persona poems in which I am adopting a character and speaking in first person as someone else. For the majority of this book, that's what's going on. But in this poem, which comes at the very end of the book, I am speaking as myself. Regarding where the poem is placed in the book, it reflects my desire to layer voices throughout this collection. All the personae that have come before are inflecting the voice here, even when I am ostensibly speaking as the poet, as Shara, in a more unmasked manner in this moment.

Some of the voices of the dead that populate this book are enslaved people. One of the main characters is a mixed-race woman, Isabella, who is descended from enslaved African women and Scottish plantation owners and overseers. Obviously, there are aspects of her story that bear a striking resemblance to my own, namely that we both can pass for white. But there is a crucial difference, even so. I wasn't born in 1806 into slavery. Isabella passes for white to escape slavery, which creates a very different existential imperative for her voice when she is speaking about her history. There are many things that interest me about voice, particularly when writing a dramatic monologue. For instance: Where does my own point-of-view end and the character's begin? What is the character/persona asking of me, as the poet and as a human being, trying to bring aspects of who they are into a poem and into the present?

SL: I am curious, in engaging with dramatic monologue or persona, do you feel like you are a conduit to these voices and persona? It feels like it also can perhaps be a sort of channeling. How does that work for you? And do you feel like you have to sometimes separate your voice from those voices within that flow?

SM: We are an amalgam of many personae, I believe. I often ask students to analogously consider, when I teach this form, the Shara who does grocery shopping is not exactly the same one who writes or who is in front of them teaching. As writers, we draw from and often isolate one part of ourselves, in order to create a singular voice on the page. So, yes, threads of who we are being 'channeled'—I fully agree with you, and I like that word and image! But I would simply point out that we've chosen which ones we are going to include—and exclude—which parts of ourselves to magnify. What we leave of ourselves on the page is what helps to create voice in our writing.

I'd also add that voice is almost entirely, in my view, made manifest in diction. Our personal lexicon, and even our syntactical tendencies, drive character and colour, voice and tone; the attitude of the speaker of the poem toward the situation at hand.

Other things I think about when writing 'persona poems': the dramatic monologue is a pronounced speech act and, figuratively, the voice of the poem is standing on a stage when speaking. The form also often employs apostrophe, or direct address—the speech being delivered to someone in particular and arising out of a tense, precipitating moment. When, in life, are we inclined to monologue? Generally, when someone has provoked us, right? The urgent need to address (and hopefully redress) a grievance charges the voice we hear in many persona poems.

SL: How do you define voice? When you're composing your work, do you think about how it feels on a page versus engaging it as provoked speech on a stage? Talk to me a bit about those differences.

SM: I think when I begin composing a poem, I typically hear a line, which I follow, to see where it will lead me. When I feel compelled to begin a poem, it isn't typically that I have an idea for a poem, it is that I hear someone speaking to me, in my mind. Sometimes this speaking voice, in the drafting stage, is simply a string of aurally resonant and imagistic language (I don't yet know much about the character of the voice or her backstory). I am also interested in bringing in demotic language and blending it with the former, which we tend to refer to archaically still as 'poetic diction.' I write in Jamaican Patwa, at times, and I think one of the reasons is because I find in Patwa various registers of language—musical, metaphoric, and quotidian—to which I'm drawn as a writer, all coming together.

When I want to revise, that's when I start to ask myself questions that will allow me to flesh out the voice of the poem. For instance: Who exactly is speaking here? Where is she, in time and place? What does she care about? How will I bring her concerns to light? By asking such questions, I'm able to expand and deepen the poem's voice during the revision process. I think of writing a poem as an act of world-building, one in which I am trying to give the voice I hear a dwelling.

With Isabella, the white-passing mulatta who speaks in the second half of the book, I know someone like her would have existed in the 19th century. Yet she doesn't show up as an agent in the annals of recorded history. And when she shows up in literature, I find I often hate how she's represented: She's a tragic figure who can belong to neither the Black nor white world and must often literally kill herself as a result. A good bit of my motivation for shaping the narrative the way I did with *No Ruined Stone* was to revise this plot and suggest a different possible outcome for Isabella. It's not that there isn't tragedy aplenty in her life in this book, but I didn't want death to have the last word.

SL: You are so right about what happens when we meet these voices and these figures and literature versus the agency. As we wrap one last question, I'm curious if there is something you have not done with a voice on the page that you might be interested in exploring in your work?

SM: I think I've tried to approach polyvocality for a long time now, but the written word is limited to what it can do in this regard. The poem—whether we are writing or reading—is bound by linear time. We have to read one line, or phrase, then the next.

To try to disrupt this, I've moved things from the left margin and worked with the 'field of the page', at times. At times, I've employed fragmentation and juxtaposition, some of the tools of literary modernism. These techniques might have arisen, as is often argued, in response to the poet's loss of faith in the utility of the first-person voice and in the construct of the self. But, for me, they are merely another set of tools to try to make multiple voices audible in a poem, rather than signaling an arch aesthetic position I'm taking as a poet.

At the end of the day, I know it is not possible to sound multiple voices in a poem at exactly the same time–as opposed to music, in which we can receive the effect of many singers, instruments, chords, melodies, notes, etc. coming together in one moment in our ear. I know I will never be able to reproduce this effect, but I like trying to work with a larger sense of voice in a poem, nonetheless. This is for philosophical and ethical reasons, as much as any aesthetic inclinations I may have. While I believe wholly in the value of the "I", I think all of us are a product of many voices and selves that precede us. Those include in my life my ancestors, those known to me when they were alive, as well as those I never met but whose stories I have learned and feel a responsibility to carry forward, as a person and writer, both. My DNA, as a poet, is also composed of every poem I've ever read and loved (and even those I've hated!). Thus, my voice as a poet is not only my own.

From Jamaica and born to a Jamaican father and Venezuelan mother, ***Shara McCallum*** *has published six books in the US & UK, most recently,* No Ruined Stone, *winner of the 2022 Hurston/Wright Legacy Award for Poetry. An anthology of her poems in Spanish,* La historia es un cuarto, *appeared in 2021 in Mexico. Awards for her work include a Guggenheim Fellowship, a Musgrave Medal, an NEA Fellowship, among others. McCallum is an Edwin Erle Sparks Professor of English at Penn State University and on the faculty of the Pacific University Low-Residency MFA.*
"May 2018: for my grandmother" is from the collection, **No Ruined Stone** ***(Alice James Books, 2021).***

Tim Seibles

"Come Home, Lady"

for Natalie

Without you, the seconds limp
like sad millipedes
in hard shoes. Minutes sag
like bad lectures
in the late afternoon. Like old men
out of smokes, the hours
itch and fidget
but soon

your smile—that shard of shooting star,
that softly candling chandelier
will take my room. Your hips
slick wheels for a hot race!
When I see you, my soul
is a sous chef—my heart

rubs itself a zest
worthy of your mouth.
Your kiss: April clarinet
for this grim November, big
Orange Crush for my
dust-bunny life.

O, let me be that one
come-hither morsel, that
savory flavor and shine
on your lips: what's sorrow
but a grown man
stuffed in the trunk
of his worry?

Your legs! Lady,
your legs—long as an Alaskan
summer day! That easy gait:
your velvet thighs, your deeply
wise and wicked ways—

when I see you
we will dance like bumper cars
on rubber streets, like lazy ducks
on crazy lakes, like hippos and hobos
in toe-shoes!

PB: Tell me about your process of composition, Tim. How does the dual role of being an oral poet and poet on the page affect your work?

TS: When I'm writing, I'm often saying the lines aloud. Even if no one can hear them. I may be sitting in a public place, I'll be muttering them just loud enough so I can hear them, which allows me to get a sense of rhythm, or a sense of the assonance and consonance if I'm really playing heavily with it. It gives me a sense of how those devices are actually working. In my mind, I always think of poems as being spoken. I've read many poems and loved many poems just on the page, but in the ideal world (in my mind) poetry would be read and heard. There's another kind of life in the actual utterance of the poem, and that's the thing I lean on quite a bit.

Beyond that, I think my process is probably like yours or any other serious poet. You're trying to get it said right. So you write and rewrite, and you rethink, and you rewrite some more. I don't think there's anything particularly unique about that. Perhaps the idea that I hear poems in my head when I'm writing them is different. Some people say they see the words in their head, and that's not my experience. I hear the words in my head and that's partly why I always think of poems as being said.

People ask me why I read the way I do. I try to read the poems the way I hear them. I hear them in my head a certain way, so I'm really trying to mimic the voice in my head.

PB: Your chosen poem is in one way very typical of the poems that are going to be in your new book *Voodoo Libretto: New & Selected Poems*, in the sense that it involves a celebration of people. There's a lot of people in your poems, yet at the same time you can also be cuttingly critical as in those "Villanelles for George Bush." What's the role of people, and celebration, and cultural criticism that you bring to your poems?

TS: Our lives are, of course, informed by people. People populate our worlds outside and inside. So many of the things I think about are memories of people, places I've been with people, or people I've met. People I've been friends with, been in love with, people who bore me with enmity. People are all over my mind.

When I write, I was saying earlier I hear the poems in my head. Maybe I should say more specifically I imagine speaking poems to people or to someone. I think of poems as part of an ongoing conversation throughout human history. We're just talking. I'm certainly talking to my time and people that I know. But I'm also talking to people like Langston Hughes, Pablo

Neruda, Walt Whitman, Anne Sexton, Lucille Clifton, and of course my many contemporaries. I always feel like I'm in this conversation. It may not be a specific call and response exactly. For example, I'm hearing your work; I'm listening to how you work music. I'm listening to the plain kind of speech William Stafford might use. Some of the really bitter images that Sexton might employ. The super compression that Lucille Clifton uses in her poems. I'm talking indirectly in many cases to these people who have affected the way I think about poems.

When we step back from the people who influence us, our contemporaries and historical influences, we're also talking to the people of our time. When I read a poem aloud in front of an audience, I am hoping they are hearing me as a citizen of the world. Like they are. I'm talking to *you*, and you may not be talking back directly but the conversation is hopefully ongoing in their heads.

I think if you're lucky enough to be literate, and you're lucky enough to have developed an art, then you have to use it to talk about what you see. That's a way of engaging life of course, and a way of encouraging or inviting your fellow citizens to see what you see, or at least to follow your perceptions as far as they can. They may say "No, no, I don't think of the world in those terms at all." But even in the moment that they disagree with you, they have been obliged to think in a way that they hadn't before. Certainly that has been true for my own life when I'm reading someone. I may not necessarily like their aesthetic all the time, or I may see the world in terms that are more raging, more sensual, or whatever. I still am obliged to think along with them as I read.

That's really what I want with poems that assail racism, assail war machinery, or poems that criticize a president. I'm trying to say essentially, "Isn't it like this?" "Do you see what I mean?" "Isn't this thing I see true?" Of course, people can certainly disagree and say "No, Seibles, you're a lunatic! You crazy liberals don't know anything!" But the idea is that if this is a democracy, we should be shouting. Brandishing our fists spiritually and saying "Dammit! I think this!" I think to the extent we have a vibrant literary community we have the potential to have a vibrant general citizenry, if we can get people to read. If we can get people to listen to poems and come to readings. I think it really changes the dynamics of a society.

This may sound like fantasy but nonetheless it's what I think.

PB: It doesn't sound like fantasy to me Tim. It sounds like a program. What must be done. Before we were recording, you had visited a school. Tell me about your interaction with young people and poetry. What do you find?

TS: Well, that's among my favorite things as a writer and a teacher. Oftentimes, teenagers, or students who are too young to have had any opportunity to study poetry with a poet, like yourself, have only heard poetry treated like a unit in a class. They had to learn iambic pentameter, make sure they got all the symbols right.

Oftentimes young students have a pretty narrow idea about what a poem can be. One of my favorite things is to be able to say "Here's a poem. Check out this poem. Check out this poem." Bit by bit, sometimes the lights will go on and they'll think "Oh, so a poem can talk like that? A poem can say these things? This doesn't sound like Robert Frost." For a lot of young people that's all they know. What's that Frost poem? The one about the horse and the snow?

PB: Whose woods these are I think I know...

TS: Yes! Yes! That one! God! That's all they know, and Frost should be insulted by that being the only poem of his they know. The primary thing I love is that maybe poetry becomes a living thing for them. They suddenly think "Oh! I could write a poem," or, "I wouldn't mind reading a poem," or "If someone wants to read a poem, I'll listen because I think poetry might be kind of cool." My main thing in high school is to get students to expand their idea of what a poem is, so that they'll be receptive to the information and the music and the news that only poems can carry. If I feel that has happened when I leave a classroom, I feel pretty good. Doesn't mean they're going to be reading poems every day, but (hopefully) a few of them take poetry to heart in a way that they may not have otherwise.

Tim Seibles' *latest book is* Voodoo Libretto *(Etruscan Press, 2021). He is the author of five previous collections, including* Fast Animal *(Etruscan Press, 2012), which won the Theodore Roethke Memorial Poetry Prize and was nominated for a 2012 National Book Award. Seibles' honors include fellowships from the NEA and the Provincetown Fine Arts Work Center, as well as an Open Voice Award from the National Writers Voice Project. In 2013 he received the PEN Oakland Josephine Miles Award for poetry. Seibles lives in Norfolk, Virginia. From 2016 to 2018, he was the state's poet laureate.*

Claire Bateman

"Mystique Academy"

The first thing they taught us is that hair isn't dead.

An exotic state of matter, it's composed primarily of discontinuities, retracting at an average rate of a quarter-inch a month.

We learned that a child may become tearful or agitated on the occasion of her first hair-lengthening, and how to distract her.

We learned to identify and respond to the singular tone each follicle emits as we chanted out the strands.

We committed to memory the esoteric names of the various knots, tangles, and convolutions we'd encounter.

We were examined on the circumstances under which the separate emptiness of those knots' vital cores might, without our intervention, first stellify and then opacify into spinning inversions.

We were tested in dim rooms and assessed in harrowing glare; we were questioned underwater and evaluated in our sleep.

And don't we now tremble at our stations, wielding the sacred torches on behalf of those whose hair is finally long enough for apotheosis?

There's nothing more paradoxical than our work—red burns the slowest, then blonde, then brown.

But black goes up in a flash, as though darkness excites the flame.

*

PB: Tell us about this page. Why did you choose it? How does it represent your practice?

CB: In both reading and writing, I'm drawn to inclusive, expansive poems with sprawling lines; that territory is this piece's natural habitat.

Though I wrote for decades from versions of the "lyric I," lately I've found myself writing from collective voices with their tonal surges and undercurrents, so this piece is more connected to my recent practice than others I could have chosen, even ones that might be even more expressively melodic.

And this poem has an intimate, incantatory quality evocative of trance (I envision the hair salon academy students as a kind of mystic sisterhood) while at the same time it plays with the terminology of quantum physics and engages with the mundane as it inverts a cultural rite of passage and mythologizes the trappings of daily life (haircuts, fretful children, the exigencies of vocational training); I think that the tension between the scientific, the esoteric, and the ordinary complicates voice and tone, creating simultaneous disorientation and a sense of the familiar. I'm energized by that kind of complication.

PB: How does orality, or voice, play a role in composition?

CB: My journal pages are filled with two kinds of fragments:

1. phrases that come to me through a kind of voice (not an audible voice, but something like the inner voice that, for instance, quietly speaks a name or a word I've been trying to recall)

2. mental images or image-clusters waiting to be described/unpacked. The journal itself is usually on the large side to provide lot of space for voice and ideas to roam around and get lost in; the one I've got now is 12.5-x-10.75-inches with 600 pages—It's so heavy you could probably kill someone with it, which is a bit of a problem for portability, but I've become quite attached to it.

Part of my process has to do with creating connections between these audible and visual fragments/extrapolations so that they become inextricable in the poem, the words from the auditory imagination fusing with the images from the inner eye.

This poem came from combing through several pages of such fragments, messy and accretive, followed by the subtractive part of the work as I sculpted an implied narrative (the ordeals of a collective educational journey), determined which phrases and images didn't quite fit, and arranged the sequencing.

PB: How is your work received differently on the page and in performance? Do you compose with both in mind?

CB: I've noticed that audiences seem to prefer simpler narrative poems and can have trouble taking in the image-dense, complex pieces that are my favorites, so I do find myself mentally dividing my work into page poems and performance poems, though not until a poem is finished. I see this poem as a crossover piece—it has some density, but there's a narrative structure, so I would probably include it in a public reading.

When I'm composing, I tend to be very inwardly focused, listening for the mental voice, watching for images, combing through stacks of old journals, taking walks. I don't aim toward either page or performance. Instead, I follow what the poem seems to want to become, and it's only then that I place it in one category or the other according to what I think an audience can process in one hearing.

I don't see a "page poem" as being deficient in voice, however—the voice in the head, the reading voice, can be just as galvanized as the audible voice, if not more so.

PB: What is your posture toward the conventions and traditions of the genre to which your work has been assigned?

CB: I almost always work within the free verse tradition in which of course one can generally find echoes of the formal.

I think that "Mystique Academy" has some resonance with Shakespeare's Weird Sisters in Macbeth, with the Fates and Muses, and the Norns of Norse mythology.

In terms of the various frameworks Michael Theune presents in his book *Structure & Surprise*, this poem takes the turning associated with the descriptive-meditative structure—it presents a scenario with its history, then closes with a shift toward phenomenological reflection as the trainees contemplate their elemental labor with human nature, darkness, color, fire, etc.

Thematically, the poem plays with the age-old motifs of initiation and innocence/experience. Also, one can imagine hair in this poem as a metaphor for thoughts springing out of the brain, so the academy students' function is a sacred one, helping to release manifestations of consciousness itself with all its wildness and unpredictability.

PB: Claire, how would you define voice?

CB: The classic definition is that voice is the combination of tone and point of view conveyed through syntax, diction, and various rhetorical devices, but I prefer to say that it's the felt presence of what Avery F. Gordon calls "complex personhood." In *Ghostly Matters, Haunting and the Sociological Imagination*, she says, "Complex personhood is the second dimension of the theoretical statement that life is complicated. Complex personhood means that all people (albeit in specific forms whose specificity is sometimes everything) remember and forget, are beset by contradiction, and recognize and misrecognize themselves and others. Complex personhood means that the stories people tell about themselves, about their troubles, about their social worlds, and about their society's problems are entangled and weave between what is immediately available as story and what their imaginations are reaching toward." She also says this (it's about social visibility but serves as a fine description of the vicissitudes of human voice with its range of the spoken and the withheld): "Visibility is a complex system of permission and prohibition, of presence and absence, punctuated by apparitions and hysterical blindness."

Claire Bateman *is the author of ten collections of poetry/prose poetry/fiction/flash fiction, most recently,* The Pillow Museum *(FC2),* Wonders of the Invisible World *(42 Miles Press, 2023) and* Scape *(New Issues Poetry and Prose, 2016). She has received two Pushcart awards and a NEA grant and is the Poetry Editor of Hubris. She is also a visual artist.* ***"Mystique Academy" was first published in the*** **Bacopa Literary Review** ***and appears in*** **Wonders of the Invisible World.**

Dominique Christina

"Josephine Baker"

America, as it turns out,
Is a country for white folks so
I go where the music of my blackness
Can shimmy like it does

Somebody said "France"
And a bird
Fell out my mouth
Steepled and cobbled
Wine toppled and sugared over

I let my hipbones slip and
The steam and funk of
Midnights without apology
Know what to do with me.

Paris is no place for I'm sorry.

Look at this twirl
I rouge my breasts
Costume my thighs
White feather,
Red lipstick war paint

People come to watch me *woman*
And I give it to 'em-
Black Pearl (they say)
Do that thing you do

So I spin and dip
I bring it down and
Snatch it up

Paris! 1939 and all is glitter and sex-
As it turns out I am free here
If you don't know about hunger
You can't sing these songs-

Bring me a shot glass and a rose, sweet baby

In the morning I'll tell you my name.

SL: Let's talk about orality, voice, and how you think about it within your composition of words? How does orality work within your work?

DC: People have heard me say this many times, but language is a culture keeper and a way-maker. Depending on the user and the usage, language can also be a destroyer and an inhibitor. There's an insistence in language. There's a call to action in language.

There's provocation in language. I entered somewhere around being educated in these really intensely homogeneous environments in which there weren't many people who looked like me, and certainly none reflecting back my experiences in any way. I learned the King's English and I was getting pretty good at it. I started to realize in adulthood that I had an opportunity, an obligation, to own the language that I'm using; to allow that language to be a liberating thing for me and for others, which often feels rooted in radical truth telling. Being the one willing to interrupt the dinner party to say the hard thing. That's how I show up and approach writing. I think there's an insistence and an urgency in it, particularly if you are a melanated person trying to create, there's an urgency in it because it's not just you speaking.

It's also the people who preceded you. It's the grandmother who was wildly talented, who never got the platform you have. It's my grandfather's deferred dreams. He got to be a teacher, but he wanted to be a doctor. Black men weren't permitted to do some of the things that my grandfather imagined for himself. The voice and orality is, for me, an urgent and insistent ritual that is rooted in ancestral logic that calls us to action.

SL: I love that because what you're really talking about is the way that language goes beyond the seen to unseen hands, and it goes beyond the singular "I." When you think about how your work is received or how you've experienced it on the page versus performance, does something change or shift for you depending on where the work—or the voice—is showing up?

DC: I think that a whole lot of folks think there's some big shift between page and stage, and in fact, sometimes there *is*. There are performers who I've seen live and was underwhelmed. However, when I read their work, I was completely captivated. There are also performers that I am enamored with in real time, on stage, whose work falls flat for me on the page.

One of my mentors, an elder named Jack Hirschman, told me when I was in the fledgling stage of my writing, that he saw me as a writer who was both page and stage. He noticed that I didn't do a lot of shapeshifting in between those two modalities. As I write it, I want that truth to be made flesh when I'm on the stage. I want that same truth to be made flesh if you are sitting quietly in your living room reading it. I need the words to be enough. I don't want a shtick. I don't want some sleight of hand trick that I'm doing on stage that has people enamored in the moment but when they interact with the writing later, they can't feel the same enchantment.

So, I don't have a different approach. I'm a very willful writer, and a very experimental performer. In my writing, I'm trying to move myself, my ego, and even my own agendas out of the way to see if there's somebody who has something to say. Some ancestor who has something to say, and they *always* do. That process isn't entirely my own. It's a collaborative effort between me and my people, a shared experience. I have an obligation to get it right; to author it or to pen it the way they need it to be penned. Because it does not belong to me singularly—the writing—I spend a lot of time thinking about the language that I'm using, making sure that I'm owning the words by the time the poem is being born and I feel like it's a complete thing. The utterance of it on stage is, for me, is the act of motioning for the old ones to come on in because I'm giving it sound. Word-sound is power. I don't want there to be some vast difference between how people experience me on the page versus how they experience me on the stage.

I'm a good performer, and I know that. I got it from my grandmother. She drilled into me when I was really young that, *"If you're ever given the opportunity to say something to an audience, you better hold that room."* That's a heavy thing. So, I come from that, and I take it very seriously. I worked really hard before I am seen on that stage, to make sure that those words line up with what I think the people I borrow bone and blood from want me to say, if that makes any sense.

SL: That makes a lot of sense. It's almost like you show receipts or back it up in some way that there's a mutual respect between the languaging and the language itself.

DC: That's right.

SL: One last question before you share your piece. What is your posture towards any conventions or traditions? I don't want to assume that you consider yourself primarily in the genre of spoken word. How do you see your work within a genre? Is it within or beyond genre? Are you trying to break tradition?

DC: I think I reside comfortably in the realm of spoken word because, again, I know that word—sound is power. I know that our rituals are rooted in an agreement around that principle. That's why we pray and meditate. That sound is somehow restructuring things in the room and calling things forward. At my core, a *writer*. I think I'm interested in the ritual of it because I do feel folks show up to speak, and I do feel my grandmother enter the room. She was a music teacher, so stage performance was a big deal for her. So, I'm okay with that category or that classification of spoken word artist because it's no different than what some of the most urgent folks in our history have done for us. They gave word—sound power, and in doing so, we found ourselves or we owned ourselves more widely or more fiercely. Or we came to grips with something, particularly, again, melanated folks we just, I think, have a way of making the words mean *more* and getting the old ones to listen...getting God to listen.

I don't know if that comes from want, our complicated history, how much blood is involved within that history, or how many bodies are underneath our feet. I don't know. I just know that we seem to be expert at finding the power in language and sound. When we are willful about it, intentional, and we use it for our greater good, we really do save lives. We usher people out of the darkness. That's why black folks go to church, we're listening for the Underground Railroad. We're listening for the keys. We're listening for the breadcrumb trail. Something that calls us home. Something that reminds us that we belong, that we matter. Something that keeps starch in our backs.

***Dominique Christina** is an award-winning poet, author, curator, conceptual installation artist, and Arts Envoy to Cyprus through the U.S. Department of State. She holds five national poetry slam titles in four years, including the 2014 & 2012 Women of the World Slam Champion and 2011 National Poetry Slam Champion. Her work is greatly influenced by her family's legacy in the Civil Rights Movement. Her aunt Carlotta was one of nine students to desegregate Central High School in Little Rock Arkansas and is a Congressional Medal of Honor recipient. She is a writer and actor for the HBO series* High Maintenance, *did branding and marketing for Gaia and Under Armour's Unlike Any campaign, has appeared on the BBC, featured at the Tribeca Film Festival NYC 2021, and curatorial director of The Dirty South choir and short film for the Museum of Contemporary Art in Denver, CO.*

Philip Brady

Excerpt from *To Banquet with the Ethiopians: A Memoir of Life Before the Alphabet*

...The alphabet. Awkward at first—
Stuttering so the stylus could keep up.
The process—'transcription' the manual called it—
Taxed but soothed too—nothing like
Entrancement when each utterance
Dervished through his rocking torso.
No rapture with the alphabet.
His loins remained cool, his mouth moist.
Triangles, rhomboids, circles and half-circles
Hardened into stanzas, passages.
At last, he stepped back from the workbench
And squinted at the scarred, translucent scroll.

Never before had he seen the *Iliad*.
Never realized its nuance and dimension.
Till now his version changed with every venue.
At palaces he trumpeted Agamemnon,
At sports events Achilles,
Weddings, Hector and Andromache,
At the tittie bars the Ares bondage scene.
He'd never made it through in a single go—
That would take weeks and leave the listeners dead.
He'd never paid heed to any blueprint.
Sure he eavesdropped on scholiastic gabble—
Great gas to hear the junior geezers fret
About interpolations and mixed dialects.
Did the *Iliad* portray a bronze age—or iron?

Did 'hearing voices' mean the primitive
Corpus callosum failed as of yet to knit
Hemispheres of the prelapsarian brain?
Did Achilles suffer PTSD?
Did rhapsodes remember the poem
Or forget everything else?
But the alphabet began to change his mind.
No improv, no entrancement.
It was hardly verse-making at all.
An encryption, a visual echo.

SL: Phil, you're amazing at recitation, you have whole verses of many poems embodied. I have so many questions, but before we get into that, tell us about this page? Why did you choose it?

PB: This is a cutting from the seventh chapter of a book-length poem, *To Banquet with the Ethiopians: A Memoir of Life Before the Alphabet.* I chose it because *Sign & Breath* highlights the dual nature of poetry: oral and written, and the memoir delves into that duality—set on the border between myth and time, which is a passage we all make from childhood to adulthood. It's a transition that Western culture made about 3000 years ago when the Phoenician alphabet spread throughout the Mediterranean world. The first texts of the *Iliad* and the *Odyssey* come from that period. We don't know exactly how or when these poems were first written down, but we know that they emerge from a long oral tradition.

The source of this cutting comes from that transition as experienced by Homer as I imagine him—an oral poet confronted—or gifted—with this new artistic modality—the alphabet. What a cataclysmic shift. Imagine living in a world with no writing. Yes, there were pictographs—arcane symbols reserved for an elite class of accountants and historians—but story and poetry were oral—as I have it in my memoir, "Lines were conceived and spoken in one breath." Then to discover this new technology—hieroglyphs 2.0—that records the spinning world by reducing it from three to two dimensions. When the scholar Milman Parry studied oral bards in the 1930's in Yugoslavia, he found that, by using meter and formula, they could compose and perform poems of great length and complexity. He inferred that this was Homer's method—one that predates recorded history. So, my book traces that transition from myth-time into our time, which is really conducted by our introduction to the alphabet. When we learn to write we start to see things in a linear way, rather than in the child's more holistic and dream-laden way.

SL: What comes to mind is *The Republic* by Plato. Within it, I believe that is where there is a debate about the fact that once things are in print, that's the beginning of the end. So, with this embodiment that you have of orality, what's your stance? Especially as we think about spoken word or the performance of poetry versus (and I don't like to really say versus) written poetry? Do you think we are getting back to orality? How do you see orality of the word and the written word as a publisher? How do you approach it in your work?

PB: A wonderful thing that I have seen during my lifetime is the movement toward embracing the oral source of poetry. When I was younger, the common question was "Does it work on the page?" But now, I think there's a much larger place for the oral element. We've given ourselves permission to enjoy poetry the way we enjoy music, dance, and theater, simply through the sounds coming through the physical body. Shanta, you're a performer, you know how this works. And I think at the same time, this movement has had political and cultural repercussions. Should we foreground the moment rather than the record? Can we more closely attend to work that is malleable, in progress, ephemeral—mere breath. Rap, hip-hop, folk and rock music lyrics approach the condition of poetry—and they allow us to lift poetry off the page, out of timelessness, back into its origins in breath and motion. Also, these arts entwine with other art forms: instrumentation, music, theater, rhetoric, and visual art, as represented, for instance, in your book, *Black Metamorphoses.*

SL: And speaking of, let's wrap up with this question, how are you defining voice? What are your reflections about voice? Especially given the range, you work on both ends as someone who's an author as someone who is an editor, how do you define voice? What is voice and your vision of it?

PB: As you and I have discussed as part of the impetus for this book, voice is a term that is difficult for us to really get our heads around. And yet we know that it is something every poet and writer wants to understand or at least be able to render. Is it mere inflection? Is it the genesis of the piece itself? Is it unique to each poet or is it the thrum that rises up from the chthonic power of language? One of the things I love about the idea of voice in poetry is that it is the prime connector between poet and listener or reader. When I listen to you recite, I'm drawn to follow your voice through enormous ranges of digressions and associations, regardless of theme or plot. Poetry has that freedom—It's unique in that way: it subverts time and narrative expectation. Even if I'm listening to something like scat or lilting or rock choruses that have no words at all, I still can follow in some basic human way, mammalian if you will. And I think that voice is what gives us permission to activate and follow our aural imagination.

Philip Brady's *newest book is* The Elsewhere: Poems & Poetics. *He is the author of two essay collections,* Phantom Signs *and* By Heart*; a book-length poem,* To Banquet with the Ethiopians: A Memoir of Life Before the Alphabet; *the memoir,* To Prove My Blood*; and three previous books of poetry. He has edited a critical book on James Joyce and an anthology of contemporary poetry.*

Rita Banerjee

"The Spirit Door"

To say that the artists in my family saved me is an understatement. My first encounter with art, at the age of five, was an accident. Salt Lake, a planned neighborhood for the bourgeoisie on the outskirts of Kolkata was a big deal. But I had no idea it was when I visited *Chōto Dādābhāi*, my great uncle Satyen Ghosal. He lived in a house ornamented by banana leaves and cactus plants. The cacti grew spiky and dense on the footpath cutting through the front gate. As a child, I was attracted to the terracotta dancing girl sculpted on the side of the house garlanded by cacti. She was in such motion. Such commotion. Her skirt shimmered in the air, her blouse seemed caught by the wind, her arms fluid, her eyes full of some mischief I had yet to know, yet to master. It felt like so many hours of the afternoon sped by as I studied her. While someone else pressed the front doorbell for me, while my great aunt opened the door with a worried scowl, while my great-uncle, the painter, peaked out from behind her, laughed, caught my hands and said, "Mistu, it's you!"

From my great uncle, I first learned about curiosity and what it meant to see the world through the eyes of an artist. His paintings were inspired by the idea of nature in meditation. He wanted to get to a realm in his art where human desire and the individual ego did not override everything. He wanted to bump up against the unfamiliar, dive into the unknown, and hang in the imagination of others.

As an artist, my great uncle was a collector of enigmas, and when I visited him that first time in Salt Lake, inside his minimalist home that summer afternoon, the objects on the television mantle spoke of imagination and adventure. One of my favorite *objets d'art* was a tableau in green glass and rosewood, of an ancient house and a village square in China, set in a time centuries past. The figures and the scene were carved by hand and rendered three-dimensional by layers upon layers of thin beige-gold cork.

The left side of the tableau featured the house—you could see into the house and out of it simultaneously. Inside, women wrung laundry, chased after cats and children, hung spices in the kitchen, dusted mirrors, and curled under the courtyard tree to read a book. Outside, a merchant stopped by the front door steps to sell rice and sweets and promises. An elderly woman peaked behind the spirit door to greet him.

Further beyond the merchant's baskets and mule and rickshaw, whose carriage had been tipped down to the earth, was the yard in which children played—boys and girls kicking balls and flying kites. Some of the girls drew their names in the sand. Some of the children studied chalkboards. They jumped and played and imagined. Their language was a language beyond English.

And beyond them still was the street in which wagons and passersby came and went. The wheels of their carriages kicking up dust. The gate to the main city almost visible in the distance. The rice paddies and river growing wild. The sun rising, then setting on the scene. The wind curling clouds until they waved across the sky. The herons standing still and quiet by the pond. The cranes taking flight, jeweling the rolling clouds as the day turned into night.

SL: It's exciting to talk about this essay excerpt, "The Spirit Door," that you shared. There are two things that struck me when you were talking about your great uncle Satyen Ghosal. The fact that he was someone who created work that "hung in the imagination of others," and you considered him "a collector of enigmas." As a writer and with this concept of *Sign & Breath* in mind, how do you think about yourself as a collector, interpreter, and translator of enigmas on the page?

RB: I think an enigma is one of the greatest attractions of good storytelling. Some of my favorite stories when I was a child involved puzzling through and trying to solve enigmas. When I first started reading adult fiction as a child around the age of ten, I would often read detective stories because I loved trying to figure out who the culprit was, what was at stake, and what was being purposefully concealed before we arrived at the story's final epiphany.

There is something beautiful about being a poet, an essayist, a filmmaker, and a novelist in that as a writer, you get to puzzle through enigmas or walk through labyrinths and figure out why things are happening the way they are, or you figure out how and why you arrived at a particular destination. This journey through enigmas helps to reveal a lot about your own personality and psychology as a writer on the page. It also helps to illuminate a journey that you didn't know you were on.

More than that, I think it allows you to see possibilities and to see outside of the frame of conventional thought in many ways. I love enigmas because they hold their mystery. They hold communication in a world whose container is slightly opaque. It's like a barrier that you can't completely walk through or penetrate. That realm of possibility, that realm of further conversation is still contained within an object of thought, which, in and of itself, can be very beautiful.

SL: That is beautifully said. In speaking of walking through and piecing together enigmas, let's talk about voice. This is really a two-part question. How do you define voice in your work? How do you think about the concept of voice?

RB: I remember being a very young MFA student in my early twenties and trying to write poetry as I started my graduate program in Seattle. One of the discussion topics of our first semester's poetry class was: *What is voice? How does the writer capture voice? How does a writer create a voice on the page that's uniquely their own?* I remember submitting some of my poetry, maybe ten pages to the Seattle Poetry Festival, and talking to one of the judges who had read my work for the festival and saying, "I'm not sure if I've fully developed my voice, and I don't know if I'm coming across on the page yet." The judge, who had selected my work for the Seattle Poetry Festival, was surprised by my worries because she thought my voice came across so clearly on the page. What that moment revealed to me was that while I was going through my MFA program, I didn't know if I was allowed to call myself a writer and have my words in print or out there in the world yet.

Voice is the confidence with which a writer expresses themselves on the page with a certain kind of critical authority. This writerly authority is related to the idea of owning your strengths, your weaknesses, your foibles, and your illuminations. This ownership of your own words and diction can convey a certain kind of style, a certain kind of rhythm, and a certain kind of personality on the page. For an author to truly express themselves, they have to take who they are and amplify it for the world. This can happen on the written page or in a performance. It can happen in a film, and it can happen in a podcast. But when you take away the fear of expressing yourself and make yourself vulnerable and open to critique, you allow yourself to groove, to riff in many ways, and thus, intensify your voice. I think when the voice is particularly strong, it takes the author by surprise as much as it does the reader. It's that embrace of style, artifice, and swagger that all contributes to voice.

SL: How does voice shift across all your genres?

RB: When I write poetry, especially in some of my earlier work, I can have a very meditative, lyrical, and thoughtful voice. Or I can have a more staccato, interrupted, rhythmic voice when I compose poems that have slightly shorter, more abbreviated lines and that aim to express the difficulty of cultivating tidy meanings or express the ineffectiveness of language in capturing experience, emotion, or the desires of the body. Sometimes I compose poems where the syntax is interrupted or filtered through other languages, such as Bengali, Hindi, Japanese, German, or French. I'm a very multilingual person, and when I think of a metaphor or an idiom, a poetic rhythm or form, or cultural iconography and folklore, sometimes I'm thinking of it in a different language, and that comes across in my poetry.

When I write prose, that multilingual, transnational element appears in my nonfiction and fiction. When I'm writing nonfiction, and especially as I'm writing this memoir on *female cool*, the artifice of the style and the artifice of this idea of *cool*, itself, appears strongly through the voice. In my book, I speak with maybe a little bit more panache or swagger on the page or sound like I'm Debbie Harry or PJ Harvey or Björk or Natasha Khan or Janelle Monáe and embrace that kind of lead-singer, glam-rock persona. It's spicy, it's fun, it's playful. It's what this book celebrating *female cool* calls for.

And if I'm working on a different type of project, such as my novel *Mélusine*, which follows a Tamil-Jewish family in crisis during a post-authoritarian regime, I cultivate and nurture a different kind of writerly voice. My novel *Mélusine* takes place in 2072 when American society is divided into the elites and everyone else. Mélusine Cassin is a biracial Tamil-Jewish American visual artist who navigates the hellish world of art, power, sex, and money in New Manhattan until her family finds themselves landing on the wrong side of the political divide. Daughter of Feroza Rao, a once famous pro-government, pro-corporate TV anchor, Mel thinks she can play it safe She's comfortable being the wallflower until her kid-brother, Louis, decides to stage a protest against the US government and its protectorate, the Avalon Corporation. Louis is rallying in Washington Square Park deep in the dredges of Old Manhattan, and demanding an inquiry into the disappearance of Feroza Rao, their mother, who vanished on-camera while illegally pregnant with her third child. Louie, jailed for his anti-government sentiment, disappears from his cell overnight. Mel, our artist, is left with a conundrum. She can either follow the trails of the abduction and possible execution of her non-elite family and become the political activist she fears to be. Or she can continue living as if nothing happened.

When I am writing this book, two distinctive registers of voice are accessed as we follow what Mélusine thinks versus her brother Louis. Her brother is a jazz musician, a performer, a political activist, and overall, very subversive. Mélusine is a wallflower, an art gallery attendant, who wants to be an artist but doesn't know how to express herself. Together the wallflower versus the performer, they create such a magnificent tension in the book. Through their inability to communicate, the book asks what happens when messages are sent out but not received? When will Mélusine finally accept her agency, her very complicated identity, and family dynamic? As she figures out where she stands and what she stands for, the voice of the novel illuminates all of her internal struggles. She is a wallflower trying to get out of that mold and the novel's voice follows her journey outward.

Across genres, a writer's voice can and does change. Even within genres, it can shift from work to work or from book to book. Voice does illuminate what's at stake for certain characters or personas and their individual journeys, but when voice is done well, it can make a character or a persona walk off the page.

SL: This brings me to my last question. You've written across genres, even your work with this latest book. What is your approach to the conventions and traditions to which verse or prose tend to be assigned? Are you more interested in staying tied to the traditions or breaking them?

RB: Genres are delightful and messy. There's a lot of fiction in nonfiction. There's a lot of truth in fiction. Poetry, itself, sometimes captures the lyrical and can go on an essayistic journey and arrive at the unexpected. But poetry can also be very animal, emotional, close to the bone, raw, and primal. What is significant in very good poetry is that the emotion that's felt within a poem can be felt by the audience. It feels incantatory in many ways. Each of these genres has its own strengths and elements that are entrancing. From a poem, you might be able to transfer that incantatory, lyrical feeling into a film or into a performance. I think you can borrow from every genre.

I would say that one of the ideas that has really mapped my writing life has come from a book by Friedrich Schiller called *On the Aesthetic Education of Man*. In the book and through his letters, Schiller argues that everything in the world declares itself to be true. Like a table declares itself to be a table and thus, an object of reality. It has a certain kind of function. A bed declares itself to be a bed, an object of reality. It has a certain kind of function. But art is the only thing in the world that declares itself to be false. When you're experiencing theater, performance, visual art, or when you're experiencing poetry or prose on the written page, what do you do? You know what you're encountering is a lie.

SL: I love that! People sometimes talk about beauty and truth within art. But where is the truth when you...

RB: Where is the truth in art? How can you find the truth in a lie?

SL: Yes!

RB: So, what can you do? In his letters *On the Aesthetic Education of Man*, Schiller argues that because we're encountering absolute artifice any time we encounter a work of art, and we're seeing something performed, and we're enraptured by it, we, as the audience, have to get to a state of knowledge that's beyond conventionally held truths or customs or understandings. We have to get to our own truth. We have to earn it. Basically, he's arguing that we get to our own very personal, very subjective enlightenment through art. We arrive at our own sense of meaning through art. As readers, writers, performers, and artists, you have to create your own meaning.

That's always been a guiding principle for me. Schiller's philosophy does inform the way that I think about craft elements like voice, where I know I'm engaging with artifice. When I'm revising multiple drafts, that's where I can ratchet up the voice. I can amplify the voice in a piece. Whether it's a persona or when I'm playing with a certain character's personality or their physical behaviors or their fears right on the page. Or if I'm working on my book on *female cool*, I can turn up the swagger to be more performative, or tone it down to be more vulnerable. Playing with voice and artifice on the page is like mixing a record in a certain way. It's fun. I love the mixing, remixing, and riffing because it surprises me. As an author, I feel like I'm often startled by the turns of a poem or a narrative. In many ways, this arrival at meaning through artifice is a learning process for me as an author. Writing holds that magic. It's a type of enigma.

Rita Banerjee *is an Assistant Professor of Creative Writing and Director of the MFA Program for Writers at Warren Wilson College. She is author of* Disobedient Futures *(University Press of Kentucky, Forthcoming),* CREDO: An Anthology of Manifestos and Sourcebook for Creative Writing *(C & R Press), Echo in Four Beats (Finishing Line Press), "A Night with Kali" in* Approaching Footsteps *(Spider Road Press), and* Cracklers at Night *(Finishing Line Press), and co-writer of the forthcoming documentary* Burning Down the Louvre. *Her work appears in* Academy of American Poets, Poets & Writers, PANK, Nat. Brut., Hunger Mountain, Tupelo Quarterly, Isele, Vermont Public Radio, *and elsewhere. She serves as Senior Editor of the South Asian Avant-Garde and Executive Creative Director of the Cambridge Writers' Workshop. She received a Vermont Arts Council Creation Grant for her new memoir and manifesto on female cool, and one of the book's opening chapters "Birth of Cool," was a Notable Essay in the 2020 Best American Essays, and another chapter, "The Female Gaze," was a Notable Essay in the 2023* The Best American Essays. ***"The Spirit Door" is an excerpt from a longer essay "Cool as Kin," which is forthcoming in*** **Tupelo Quarterly.** ***This essay is also part of Rita's new memoir and manifesto on how women have cultivated a culture of female cool against social, sexual, and economic pressure post-9/11.***

Bianca Stone

"A Suckling Pig's Prayer"

I have put aside all the blank meaningless words
and decided to go, totally naked
into the always luscious Elysian dump
of the hereafter. Say nothing at all.

May the wind take all this hair. Dissolve
these shallow scars, tear
whatever cloth is left hanging
between my legs and water, absorb me
into your passive liquid rush,

forget the marrow and calcium, the dust,
the single chaotic fluid—old pure
and muddy wind, leave me a shocked afterimage—
windblast even that still-quivering outline,
that empty silhouette the paper doll left behind—

to remember me
may my portrait be of an elderly nun
with a pitted face, rooting blindly
for the stone's breast of blood-black buttermilk—

Do not box me up like the ancient queens of Thebes
in gilded wood, alabaster, and obsidian.
Leave no trace of what sibling rivalry
occurred between us, the one who stood half
in shadow. Who made these words.

SL: Tell us about this page and how does it represent your practice? What was the inspiration behind it?

BS: This poem is towards the end of my book, *What Is Otherwise Infinite.* The poem is about wanting to come to the end of language altogether. There's a frustration that comes with writing poetry. Words fail you a lot of the time, and if anything, poetry comes closest to articulating the inarticulable, the ineffable experiences of being a conscious animal on this earth. At the same time, even in writing poetry, sometimes no words are the most poetic. Your interest in breath in this project, poetry, encapsulates that sort of wind, the absence of object, and the movement of air expressed through poetry. Language—which is dependent on the movement of air through the mouth, or the movement of the body—also includes that which is wordless.

"A Suckling Pig's Prayer," on one hand, is about that binary conflict between poetry being a word-based art, and it also about being something that is absent of words and very involved with breath. This poem deals with wanting to be outside of form altogether. This stanza,

> forget the marrow and calcium, the dust,
> the single chaotic fluid—old pure
> and muddy wind, leave me a shocked afterimage—
> windblast even that still-quivering outline,
> that empty silhouette the paper doll left behind—

It is saying, "I don't want to be bone. I don't want to be dust. I don't even want to be a silhouette. I don't even want to be a shed." What is beyond all of that?

I think human desire—or even the desire itself to be nothingness along with the anxiety about what that means—is involved with our feelings about death. All those things are unconsciously on our mind all the time. Part of my process as a writer is to investigate the unconscious material. This poem is a little nihilistic because even in desiring nothing, that sentiment co-exists with the desire to be done with the whole process in general, while at the same time, embracing this continuum of desire by writing a poem about it. I like that contradiction in writing poetry.

SL: I want to explore more of what you mentioned, walking between the tangible and intangible. How does the concept of voice play into your work? Especially the idea of saying the unsayable or the unsayable that can't be said, how does this enmesh with your practice alongside orality, and composition of the work?

BS: I think about this a lot because the words in our mind are not the same as when they are spoken. There's the added element of the psyche on the page, which is another kind of consciousness. We don't think about that when we do it. In a way, we just think it's all the same, but it's not.

What I think about more consciously nowadays—and what I think what poets do—is explore the craft element of: How do I listen to what's in my head? How do I access it before it's oral or before it's articulated? How can I listen for it and get into a state of receiving it, then letting it come forth, orally? Then there is speaking it, articulating it, putting it on the page, and then editing it to further deconstruct what the structures are there.

I think one issue between what's in our head and what's on the page lies within what we've learned about writing from other people in the past. I've been questioning that. How can I be more authentic to my words, to my mind, and to my breath? How do I avoid writing the same poem I've written before while listening to new ideas that my mind is putting forth?

Amid the narrative of writing a poem and creating a work of art is the work of investigating consciousness itself. It's nothing less than that.

SL: What I appreciate about your work and your conversations about the poetic is that you bring the poetic state into the space of the psyche in exploring how the internal becomes external. This next question is a multipart question: How do you define voice? What is voice for you? Especially in thinking about the internal landscape becoming external on the page or spoken, what is that alchemy like for you? And as you just mentioned, the words inside are different from what comes out, different from what is put onto the page, and of course different from what is edited. How do you define voice across all of that?

BS: I don't know if I can define voice, but I know that we all have a thing that we're doing. When I'm working with my students, I see their voices. They're all unique, even if they have major breakthroughs, it's still very much them. We all have an inherent voice, it's a matter of honing it.

I think, too, of the dreamer in the dream when we ask: Who is this dreamer dreaming the dream? I'm somehow involved and not exactly passive in the dream, but it's something beyond me as well. When I think of the voice in a poem, I think of coming to terms with speaking, embracing who you are, and somehow authentically speaking your truth. This also includes a voice you don't recognize and allowing *that* voice to come in, even though it's strange. So when I define voice, I think it's my unique musicality that is both learned and something beyond being learned, inborn and innate.

I think the voice is just that. I guess it's like an intentionality within me of great faith in what I have to say, the unknowable self, and the unconscious self, coming through. Voice is all of those things coming together, that's what makes a great voice. It's easy, folks! That's it, good luck!

It's a lifetime pursuit. We get very comfortable in our music and I think that's great because we get better at our voice. It's like that self in us that sings. It's the singing self, it's not quite the same as our talking self, but it's not NOT that self either.

SL: Did you want to add anything as we conclude?

BS: I really like the fact that we can never define what poetry is, and yet, it is so specifically something. I love that so much of poetry is about talking about what it is and what it isn't.

It's like meta conversation because I believe poetry truly is the original language that we spoke when we started speaking at all: fragmented, metaphors, and a deep relationship with the unknown elements of nature, mind, and self. So we honor that, and I love the fact that this project, *Sign & Breath,* is doing that.

Bianca Stone *is the author of the poetry collections* What is Otherwise Infinite *(Tin House Books, 2022) which won the 2023 Vermont Book Award in Poetry;* The Möbius Strip Club of Grief *(Tin House Books, 2018),* Someone Else's Wedding Vows *(Octopus Books and Tin House, 2014) and collaborated with Anne Carson on the illuminated version of* Antigonick *(New Directions, 2012). Bianca's work has appeared in many magazines, including* The New Yorker, The Atlantic *and* The Nation. *She teaches classes on poetry and poetic study at the* Ruth Stone House *(501c3) where she is editor-at-large for* ITERANT Magazine *and host of* Ode & Psyche Podcast. *In 2024, Bianca was chosen as the Poet Laureate of Vermont and will serve as the state's ambassador of poetry for the four-year term.* ***"A Suckling Pig's Prayer" is from the collection,*** **What Is Otherwise Infinite** ***(Tin House Books, 2022).***

II.

“A poet is a dancer, is a writer, is a novelist, is a painter. All of the arts have to be combined.

If a poet is not painterly, they cannot create images.
If a poet isn’t rhythmic, they cannot dance.

There’s this inextricable interrelationship between the arts.”

Rashidah Ismaili Abu-Bakr

Nell-Lynn Perera

Untitled

I didn't know how to love him
from a shallow place
treading on waters
when I could feel mud

I only knew how to dive deep
into the darkness
where the current was strong
and living things did not breathe

there, I loved him.
for there, was where he lived.

SL: Tell me more about this poem. I've seen so many different love poems, most of which have what could be characterized as the "shallow place," but yours (and what I have seen of your work) is different. Tell me why you chose it? How does it represent your practice?

NLP: Personally, I like reading prose that is thought provoking which makes me think in order to fully understand what the writer meant. I also like gripping pieces which might make me feel a bit uncomfortable as I relate it to my own experiences. I find there's depth and truthfulness in such writings. All these points I try to include in my practice.

SL: What are some of the themes that have made you uncomfortable? What kinds of themes do you engage with to have the same impact?

NLP: There aren't necessarily any themes that have made me uncomfortable but rather the depth of truthfulness. I think because writers write with readers in mind, there's some internal censorship that takes place. Also, not every writer wants or feels at ease sharing their experiences to the point that they feel exposed or vulnerable, even when they do want to write about something personal which they hope is relatable to the readers. I mostly write about life and relationships.

SL: How is your work received differently on the page and in performance? Do you compose with both in mind? You are a visual artist, so do your words you construct for prose or poetry ever speak to or engage with how you create your visual art?

NLP: My work hasn't been used in any performance to date, so I don't compose with both in mind. I have written knowing that I will be painting a piece to accompany it.
It is interesting to see how I translated words into shapes and colors.

SL: Does orality, or voice, play a role in composition? If so, in what ways?

NLP: Although I don't write with performance in mind, orality still does play a role in composition. It has to sound appropriate to what I am trying to convey in words regardless of whether it's spoken aloud or not. It is still *spoken* in the minds of those who read it.

SL: I know you are known as an HSP (a highly sensitive person) and you have chromesthesia (sound to color synesthesia), how do these engage with your sense of orality?

NLP: Being a HSP means I am careful with the words I use to communicate with. Be it spoken or written. Chromesthesia doesn't influence my sense of orality.

SL: What is your posture toward the conventions and traditions of the genre to which your work has been assigned?

NLP: I don't follow any traditions of the genre to which my work has been assigned. Thankfully, we live in such an age that one can invent pretty much anything, and so long as it has substance and speaks to a group of people. We can't be wronged for doing it our way.

SL: Your voice is a distinct one based on what I have seen across your work—your paintings, your prose, poetry—how do you define what voice is?

NLP: Voice is what lives in each one of us, which we either want or have a need to share.

***Nell-Lynn Perera** is a Malaysian self-taught artist, poet and writer. She has received many awards and honors for her creative work including the 2024 Best in Show Abstracts, Sapphire Artist of the Year 2023 and Crystal Artist of the Year of 2022. Her works have been featured in multiple magazines and journals including* Harper's Bazaar, New Straits Times, *and* Expat. *She currently resides in her hometown, Kuala Lumpur, working on her second solo exhibition.*

Rashidah Ismaili Abu-Bakr

"The Painter - 3"

He said he would
make of me
an image
immortal
etched
in African gem stone
and that I would be
colour come to draw
music stifled
in asphyxiated throats
stitched
lips longing to sing freely.

SL: When you're writing, do you write for the page or are you thinking about how it will be received when reading or performing the piece?

RIA: I hardly ever write for the response during a reading or a performance. I would like my work to stand on its own two feet within the need to respond, to push the buttons on certain words or phrases, or to evoke both an image and a response from the audience. I'd like to believe that I come to the work as honest and as free as I can at that time. Whatever I write is as free as possible for me, and that I've been germinating—whatever it is—for a while, and whatever I then put to the page is the closest to what I'm conjuring.

When I take the writing off my handwritten page and put it into the computer, it works as a first editing or redrafting process. It's that confrontation of what's on the page and what's on the screen. This process helps me galvanize my thoughts and select the best way to say what translates from my thinking.

SL: You mentioned you don't think about an audience in relation to your poetry, you seem to liberate yourself from that. Can you speak a bit more about that?

RIA: What I mean by not thinking about an audience is that I'm a writer. A writer, I think, at some point would want to be read, but I don't want to think about the audience in a sense that I'm trying to elicit a response from them, please them, placate them, or play to them.

I want to give them, the audience, whatever it is that I have in the purest and most honest way. The reader then reads my writing and hears it. Once the reader enters that agreement or arrangement with the writer or the speaker, there is an assignment for the reader to take some responsibility to hear me, read what I said, and try not to reinterpret what it is I've said.

Many of us have been in a position where people have asked us to defend what we have thought or wrote. Then we must proceed to rewrite what it is that we've written, from another's point of view. You don't have to agree with me, but I want you to try to understand what I'm saying. For me, understanding is what I mean when I say, "I'm not writing *for you*. I'm not writing to have your approval. I'm really writing to give you another way of hearing a word, a phrase, an idea that you can toss, augment, whatever." It demands, at least for me, a mutual respect for each other's intelligence.

SL: How do you think about voice in poetry, and your voice, especially woven into everything you're saying about this contract and agreement between the reader or listener? What's your definition of voice?

RIA: When I was younger and was teaching at Rutgers, every year I would teach an honors-level class. For the almost twenty years I was teaching there, almost every other year I chose Langston Hughes. I started with his essay about the Negro writer, and he says, "We independently declare our right to call ourselves writers. And that we declare at that time, that we are Negro. So, we are Negro writers, and he never equivocated about that. We assert our right to think, and to choose, and to pluck from wherever our experiences are. Whether *you* like it or not." This is a rephrasing of his words by me.

One of the few workshops that I was ever in was John Oliver Killens writer's workshop. He used to always tell us that a poet is never just a poet. A poet is a dancer, is a writer, is a novelist, is a painter. All of the arts have to be combined. If a poet is not painterly, they cannot create images. If a poet isn't rhythmic, they cannot dance. There's this inextricable interrelationship between the arts. As poets, we use architecture, we choreograph, we compose. All of the terminologies we think of for other kinds of artistic mediums. We also engineer because we put it all together. I thought that was brilliant.

I would often have this conversation with my dear late friend, Jayne Cortez. She would bemoan the fact that there were folks who were trying to clone her. Jayne would say, "Why can't they just take the time and talk to themselves, and find their own voice?" Of course she has a famous poem *Find Your Own Voice.*

To me, voice is self. Voice is purpose. Voice is individual. Voice is identity. Voice is intelligence, and integrity. If we do all these things without integrity, this is when we start to write for the audience. You have to believe and trust your voice, because you've spent a lot of time developing it. You have to believe in the integrity of your intention, and the integrity of your work, with all its limitations and its breadth.

Everything I write should not be inscribed in indelible ink. I'm not the last word. I'm not the greatest voice ever. I'm not the greatest poet. Speaking my words and having twenty people faint in response does not a poet make. You have to be humble and assertive. Voice is the encapsulation of all those things because it is the way in which we think philosophically. The voice comes through, and guides us when we choose whatever genre we're going to write in. To select even down to the last word—if there's anything I firmly and truly believe in—that is as close to any doctrine or theory.

I try to find the right clothing, the right house for whatever it is I'm thinking. For example, I wrote a play many years ago. There were things that I was writing about that I felt very strongly about, but maybe I hadn't chosen more accurate words to express those feelings. Again, some of the audience came with ideas about how they thought it should go. My play was about an interracial relationship, but the interracial part of it was the least of it. At the time I wrote the play, I was thinking about the way in which Africans, and in my case African Muslims, believe in serendipity or coincidence. We don't believe in it in the way way people think about it within the Western world. For example, we believe that maybe something horrific was going to happen to you Tuesday morning at eleven o'clock. However, because of divine intervention—which is not serendipity—which might've involved prayer, giving someone water, etc., the horrible thing that could have happened to you does not. Or if you're supposed to meet somebody, whatever constraints and stuff that might've placed you upon your path will not occur if that meeting or that person takes you off your path. Serendipity has to do with that concept. It's deeply embedded in me, and I was writing my play from that perspective.

As the play progressed, the male character, who's white, embarks upon a relationship with an African woman. She's a confident student, finished grad school, and so forth. Part of the workshop process was the fact that people were going to ask you things about your writing in ways that would help with your revision. One member of the audience during this process, a white woman, said the play seemed too facile, almost predictable. The whole "boy meets girl, girl meets boy, boy falls in love with girl, girl falls in love with boy." When this audience member said she thought that I hadn't succeeded in finding a way to not hit people over the head with my philosophy, I wondered: How do I handle this non-serendipity from my point of view? That's a charge the writer has to face. This audience member said she thought I smoothed over the racial aspect of the play with something else. I said, "If your family, or that family in the play, has a woman like this who appears in their lives—who's physically beautiful, intelligent, PhD, and caring, loving, and kind—why would that be an issue?" She didn't answer me.

Another audience member, a biracial man, said he thought that I had created a "Mary Poppins" character in the woman. Again, I was creating this character out of what African women think of "mothering" someone else's child. I realized that maybe I hadn't succeeded. I put that piece down for many years. I then rewrote it as a novel. The play at that moment was not the right vehicle at that point. I didn't know how to create the off-page subtleties that would not necessarily explain but expand a culture that people had already reduced to "She's this black woman, she should be grateful for marrying this white lawyer. Isn't he great?" Sometimes, we might think that we're writing a poem, or we may feel that we're writing a poem, but that "thing" that we want to express, the house of poetry, might not be the place to locate it. It might need another dress or home.

I think this is a lot about what finding your voice means. There's a huge emphasis right now on performative poetry, most of which I don't like because it's so dependent on hitting a button in an audience to spark a reaction. I think a poet has a greater responsibility than that. Words are biblical in a sense for me. Finding your voice also means finding your house, finding your dress, finding the right jewelry. You don't really need that kind of adornment. You need a piece of amber for that. You need to pull out all the stops. Sometimes, you just really need to say "Okay, I've said it to you subtly, I've said it to you like this, so BANG! Now do you hear me? Open up your head and I'll pour it in. Now, what do you think?"

There are times where you really have to be like that. If everything is on the same level all the time, where is the quiet? We need to have balance. Christians say there is a time for every season under heaven. Not everything is said with hands in your crotch. Even women, you just discovered that you had it? Think about what's above your neck. Our mind is this thing that separates us from other animal species, and yet the head is the last thing that we touch when we're performing. Have you ever seen a performer touch his head? How many times have you seen them touch their crotch? Where's the energy coming from?

Rashidah Ismaili Abu-Bakr, PhD *is the author of several books and plays including* Autobiography of the Lower East Side *(Northampton House Press, 2014) and* Rice Keepers *(Africa World Press, 2006). Her awards and honors from PEN America, Dramatist League, and the Kennedy Center. She has also contributed her work to the anthology* New Daughters of Africa *edited by Margaret Busby in 2019. She has worked as a professor, psychologist, and counselor for various universities throughout her career. She is a faculty member within the Wilkes University Creative Writing program. When Rashidah is not writing, she conducts a series of workshops, lectures, and writing seminars that are a part of Salon d'Afrique that has been ongoing for over 40 years.* ***"THE PAINTER – 3" is one of a small series from an unpublished manuscript and are placed at different points in the collection.***

D.M. Aderibigbe

"The Origin of Fear"

There is my favorite senior boy,
holding onto the evening's
garment; his girlfriend refused

to let him step his dirty feet
back into her life.
So he wet his flaming

intestine with a small bottle
of insecticide.
The matron is squeezing

those feet now. And the head nurse,
pouring all of her knowledge—syrups,
capsules—into his withering mouth.

Then, there is me, trying to close
my eyes. Because of him,
the night is scared to arrive.

PB: This is such a powerful poem in such a short lyrical space. What's your perception of the role of voice in poetry, and in this particular poem?

DA: I think of voice as something central to poetry. Voice encompasses language. It's almost as important for me as the structure of a poem. When I think of voice, I think of the question of power. This is because I write mostly from the view of a witness, as this poem shows. For instance, most of the poems I write come from experience: my mother's, grandmother's, my aunt's, and uncle's. People around me. This is because I haven't been through what they've been through. I understand there's a privilege I have in that dynamic, so when I write I always make sure I don't write like someone who already knows everything. I make sure the speaker is learning about this subject at the same time as my reader. Most times I write from the perspective of someone that's very young. I try to navigate that space. This way, voice takes me there. For instance, "Origin of Fear" takes place in a high school. I'm no longer in high school, but the fact the poem is about someone attempting suicide, which I had never done in my life, compelled me to write from not just the point of view of a witness, but also someone who's younger than this person who's attempting suicide. How do I get to the subject's true voice? I'm able to go into this space and try to show my reader: "This is what's going on, but I don't know much about it. Because I'm younger than the person the poem talks about." In African settings, age brings potential power. I say that because when you're younger than someone, they're automatically more powerful than you are. I think this is important because most of the people I write about are older, but they've gone through traumatic experiences I haven't been through. I always need to balance this, and voice helps me with that.

PB: I think of your sense of voice as having something to do with being a bridge between the people you are witnessing and yourself as witness—and now yourself as poet.

DA: Take my first book as an example. As a child, I witnessed women around me go through domestic abuse. I couldn't do anything then. I was just a child. But as an adult, I could go back into that space and write about it. And that's exactly what I did. However, when I step into these spaces, I don't present myself as someone who is all-knowing, who's looking back to say, "This is what should've happened or not." Instead, I approach the subject as that little child. I will admit that, because of the privilege of time, the privilege of age, the privilege of the position I'm in right now, I'm able to look at some things and present some of these views better (maybe) than a child would.

PB: How does the fact that you're writing and performing in the United States affect this voice and this relationship?

DA: Well, the fact that I'm in America now, working as a professor, complicates this question of power. Being in America now means that I'm even more powerful, at least materially. Before now, I only had imaginative power over those I write about, but with material power added, I have to be even more aware of my privileged position when inhabiting these voices.

***D.M. Aderibigbe** is from Nigeria. His book* In Praise of Our Absent Father *(Akashic, 2016) is an APBF New Generation African Poets Chapbook Series selection. He has received honors from Fine Arts Work Center Provincetown, James Merrill House, OMI International Arts Center and Boston University, where he received his MFA in Creative Writing. His poems have appeared in numerous journals including* Alaska Quarterly Review, Jubilat, Prairie Schooner, *and* River Styx. *He is currently an Assistant Professor for the USM Creative Writing program at The University of Southern Mississippi.*

William Heyen

"My High School Flame"

I found what seemed to be a human heart entangled in fish-
    line & beach grass,

or maybe something from nature had washed up, coconuts
    or brine-shaped

driftwood, or was it a rolled-up skirt or letter sweater
    or cerise blouse,

but, yes, it might have been a human heart, or should have been,
    but it was only—

I danced up to it & bent to it & kept listening—it was only
    an old song

I'd once sung, wouldn't you know it, not her heart, or mine,
    just our old song.

Form & Power

WH: In the end, beyond any other advice I give myself, this bottom line: Bill, see if you can get lucky enough to find/make something that you yourself truly care for. This ain't easy.

Luck & unconscious acquired craft will be involved. The poem will have to be rhythmic story listening to its own sound. It will make me forget, while I'm reading it, that I am experiencing art/artifact. It will be Emerson's "form," (the rational, empirical, understandable, ordered, expected, 1 + 1 = 2, adjudicated, grounded, controlled) that is, naturally thwarted (if I'm welcoming & chosen) by his "power" (the wild, unpredictable, primal, maybe zany, maybe nutso, inscrutable, surprising, upwelling, intrusive, maybe senseless, mad, breakaway, queer, maybe discordant, irresistible) that the Concord master fears even as he realizes his reason is weary of his muse's plans. Here's the way he puts it in an 1843 journal entry (I can see cursive light flashing from his brain & study as he writes):

> Form always stands in dread of power. What the devil will he do next?

And then, when this devil-muse claws its way into our creation, what then? If we're lucky, some kind of exponential Other we hadn't anticipated that may baffle us even as we know we've caught something deeper than we could have hoped for. What, for example, happened to me when, without forethought, I began writing this poem, "The Tooth"?

> After the beheading, they found
> the one gold tooth in Custer's mouth.
> They propped open his jaws,
>
> cut away his upper lip,
> & stared into the tooth in firelight.
> It was like a small television
>
> tuned to the news, & a white man
> in a white suit was already
> stepping down onto the moon.

All rational, & then that devil of a simile, the anachronistic TV, & the future (the technology that doomed the Indians) appearing at Little Big Horn. How did this profound lyric come to be? And "My High School Flame" the narrative so possible until my favorite word in all poetry, "but," appears at mid-poem, & then appears again, & that heart, in a leap of memory, becomes an old song that he & his teen flame had once sung, imagine that, a mysterious object becoming poignant music for him. Saying it, hearing it, I lose myself within this poem, & do not get tired of fathoming it even as it resists my rational intelligence. My poem is written in what I call my "single-line couplets." I'd like to create what German critic Max Rieser called a "rhythmical narcosis." Reader, hearer, let's sidle up to what should have been a human heart—his? hers? theirs?—but was only, yes, an oldie but goodie. I thought of making the "our" in the last line "my"—this would have revealed his own romantic folly to himself—but this is a love poem, & they were in it together, as you & I are, I hope, reader, listener, dancer.

A former Senior Fulbright Lecturer in American Literature in Germany, ***William Heyen*** *has received NEA, Guggenheim, American Academy of Arts and Letters, Pushcart and other awards. His two latest books are* Nature: Selected & New Poems 1970-2020 *(MAMMOTH Books, 2023) and* Diaspora: Poems: Fifteen Collections *(Cyberwit.net, 2024). His work has appeared in hundreds of anthologies, and in* The New Yorker, Poetry, American Poetry Review, Harper's, The Atlantic, The Southern Review, *and numerous other magazines. The author or editor of more than forty books, his* Shoah Train *(Etruscan Press, 2004) was a National Book Award Finalist.*

Diana Whitney

"Prom After-Party Revisited"

It doesn't get better than this, the Pittsfield Hilton in a sea of flounced taffeta, Stephanie Barlowe and Michelle West busting out of their strapless Jessica McClintocks as the soccer jocks loosen their ties and grind in a boy-girl-boy-girl sandwich—*joy and pain, sunshine and rain*. I'm there in the mix all glammed up in belladonna hair and jasmine kissing potion, twirling in layers of white chiffon, my halter dress like Marilyn's blowing up in a subway grate. Never mind my sympathy date two inches shorter, flat top and nothing to say. Never mind the couples fawning in the photo booth, the ecstatic crowning of the King and Queen. I spike the punch with my 100-proof desire. Kick off my pumps and dominate the floor. Dance in lace tights à la Madonna *Like a Virgin* stalking the rooms of her Venetian palace. No one leers or gropes me tonight. I'm unafraid to be single, potent, flawed and hungry, so bold I earn an invite to the afterparty at Steph's house where the parents are scarce and the bar is open, the spring night heavy with lilacs and ambition. I'm the unsung star of a new teen movie where the queer girl seeks her crush at the witching hour, obstacles mount but the plot keeps ticking and kids slough off their school-day selves. Some disappear, some pair off upstairs, but I spark a game of spin the bottle in the den, eyes lit with mischief and peach schnapps, lay a circle of petals from a wrist corsage, play the *Pretty in Pink* soundtrack like an anthem or a spell. *If you want me you can find me*, daring Michelle to crawl towards me on the rug. I meet her in the middle, laughing lips and feral hair, all eyes on us kneeling in flowers, remaking the world in an instant

SL: I know there were two choices for what you were going to read, but you suggested the prose piece, "Prom After-Party Revisited." Given that it's newer, what was it about this page that drew you to suggesting it as an option? And talk to me a little bit about how it represents your practice, voice, and overall work as a writer.

DW: This poem felt like the riskier choice, and I'm inclined to lean into that rather than playing it safe. The other poem I sent you was a near-sonnet contained in stanzas, a tight little nature poem (a familiar form for me). But "Prom After-Party Revisited" busts open without any line delineation, like it's so urgent it can't be contained on the page. In my writing and revision practice, I try to respect the shape the poem itself wants to take. This speaker is telling the story of prom night which is a completely made-up night that did not happen. It's part of a series where I'm rewriting my adolescence and my painful high school years, imagining what could have been, inspired in part by Stephanie Burt's marvelous book *Advice from the Lights*, where she reimagines her girlhood. It's a project of freedom and self-determination; I wanted long expansive lines and some of that breathless, narrative push we often get from prose.

SL: And I'm interested in this because it's a totally imaginative night. I think that sometimes we forget, even in poetry, the imagination. The fantastical. Tell me how that inspired you to go back and use your adolescence for exploring the imaginative on the page?

DW: This project began with a short poem called "My 7th Grade Self Sends Nudes to Nate Griffin." In it, I imagine what I would have done if I'd had the technology that today's middle schoolers do. Writing it broke something free in me. I love that instead of being chained to the facts of my adolescence—Junior High in the 80s, being in the closet as a queer person, filled with doubt and shame, etc.—I could range freely on the page with my imagination. And these are some of the funnest poems I've ever written. I don't know yet if anybody else likes them, but it's a liberating project. For "Prom After-Party Revisited," I had the idea jotted down as a title in my notebook for a long time. What if I hadn't had the most boring, terrible night at prom? What if I hadn't said yes to a sympathy date because the culture required I have a boy by my side, some guy I wasn't attracted to? What if I'd had the confidence to go alone, or go with my girlfriends, or even with a girl who I liked? What poetry gives us (and maybe any creative writing) is this place where we can build worlds. It's been healing for me to go back to a time when I felt trapped under these social burdens and expectations, and find that I can now, as my grown-up, middle-aged, poet-self, free myself from them.

SL: You know it's funny, I wrote a chapter in my memoir where I tried this approach. It was something like treating all the men that I've ever seen my mother with while

she was still married to my father as missed connections and interloping it with me pretending to be the boys I encountered during my adolescence. There was something about trying to inhabit and go back to the memory in that way on the page.

DW: Right?!

SL: I'm struck by how this piece takes the power back within the re-imagining. Can you talk more about how that felt of giving this piece its freedom on the page in that form? Do you feel you can do the same thing with performance? Is there a difference between your voice on the page, how you free it, and give it space versus the performance? Talk a little bit how you see the difference between the two or how they connect.

DW: I think you can't have one without the other. I don't just wait for the page, I read aloud to myself when I'm writing. With this particular piece, I composed a first draft in my writing group and wrote it really fast. Then I read it aloud in the witnessing of others, which is a very profound experience, and I got that voice reflected to me. In my subsequent revisions, it was always about the voice out loud, not just how the words appeared on the page. There's a rhythm I hear in the language even though the lines are in sentences. I noticed as I was reading it here that there's a lot of internal rhyme, that sort of musicality that poetry affords us. I find that I take a lot of pleasure in language, the sounds of words, and the rhythms of lines. And I think that's why, although I have the deepest respect and admiration for novelists, the forms of poetry that allow us to explore the orality of language are so compelling to me.

SL: Speaking of orality, what does voice mean to you? Given that you write across different genres, and you are now journeying into a new territory, what is voice across these different modalities?

DW: That's a huge question, one that poets and teachers of poetry have pondered for ages. Tony Hoagland wrote a great book called *The Art of Voice*, in which he says it's a mysterious element. He admits it's hard to pin down what we mean when we talk about "voice" in a poem, but we know it when we hear it. You might read a poem and not know who the author is, but you recognize it somehow. I often feel that way with Louise Gluck—I know her voice, though I can't always put my finger on its exact tonal qualities, how it's often mythic and distant. Is voice some aspect of personality? Is it how the personality expresses itself on the page?

As a reader, I recognize when a voice is inconsistent. I find that troubling, disorienting. I work as an editor with poets and essayists, and I'll say, "You know the voice changes here. It was first person and now all of a sudden, we're in second person. Was this intentional? Does it serve the poem?"

You make a pact with the reader from the very first line, that they're going to be able to follow and trust the voice wherever it goes. For the voice of "Prom After-Party," I wanted it to sound like the late 80s, early 90s so I filled it with pop culture references. There's Madonna, Bonne Belle kissing potion, *Pretty in Pink*. There are these anchor points from the culture, and the speaker has deep knowledge of that culture. Maybe one way the reader will trust the voice is that it gives us rich details. But craft choices matter even more than content. You can sense a distinctive voice from a poem that is written with no punctuation and a lot of white space, which is the opposite of this expansive prose poem.

SL: Last question, is there anything I didn't ask you or something you want to add as we wrap?

DW: I haven't done a deep study in prose poetry and how it differs from traditional poetry with lineation. I've read other people's prose poetry, and it feels, in some ways, more freeing. But sometimes I also ask: how is this prose poem different from a flash fiction piece?

SL: It is interesting because there are some people who would say there is a hard division between genres. However, I think that there's a way I've seen poetry within the prose, where it really feels like it could be flash fiction, flash nonfiction, and go into that line of hybridity. Flash fiction and flash nonfiction seems to give writers a sense of permission.

DW: I like that sense of not being locked in. More and more, I'm finding ways to inhabit queerness in my writing. Which feels risky. It's like, "F-you, who's going to tell me what genre this is?"

It exists as a piece of creative work. Maybe it wears the mantle of a prose poem. Maybe it's flash fiction, or it's both, it's everything. Don't label me. It's not the binary. That sort of queering of the genre is calling me right now.

***Diana Whitney** writes across genres with a focus on feminism, motherhood, and sexuality. She is the editor of the bestselling anthology* You Don't Have to Be Everything: Poems for Girls Becoming Themselves *(Workman Publishing Company, 2021), winner of the 2022 Claudia Lewis Award, and the author of two full-length poetry collections. Her first book,* Wanting It *(Harbor Mountain Press, 2014), won the Rubery Book Award. Her second,* Dark Beds *(June Road Press, 2023), was a finalist for the Poetry Society of Virginia's 2024 North American Book Award. Diana's writing has appeared in the* New York Times, Glamour, the Kenyon Review, Ms. Magazine, *and many more. She was the longtime poetry critic for the* San Francisco Chronicle, *where she featured women and LGBTQ+ voices in her column. An advocate for survivors of sexual violence, she lives in Vermont with her family and works as an editor and writing instructor.*

Kristina Marie Darling

"Sad Film (with Subtitles)"

The first scene was nearly untranslatable. Velocity and the little ache at the very back of the throat. Were we seeing a design in the narrative when all that was *really* there was the hand on the waist, the movement of a white dress in the middle distance:

And for once they traveled to a country that spoke another language entirely, without so much as a miniature dictionary to lessen the shock. To lose that thread the moment the wind picks up, to no longer be able to trace the progress of an idea, or the line that reason makes in the hot white sand, was to somehow always be on holiday. Still, they both had to wonder what the gatekeeper thought of them, their mouths that empty, not even a cough to break the silence.

PB: What a mysterious little koan of a poem. Tell me about how voice plays a role in your composition of that poem, Kristina.

KMD: I've been really intrigued by this legacy among poets that frames voice as an alterity that speaks through the writer. For Homer, this was the Muses. For H.D., the great modernist poet, this was the unconscious mind speaking through the writer. And for Jack Spicer, it was radio waves from outer space. More recently, in contemporary experimental texts, we see collaboration as a kind of alterity, or otherness that speaks through the poet.

With me, writing this poem, it's my reading life, and my life as a scholar that speaks through the poem. When I was working on this text, I was steeped in Lyn Hejinian, Joshua Clover, and all of those other great postmodern writers. I think of the poem as a synthesis of these influences. Every poem is really a deconstruction of, and kind of scholarly take on, everything that came before.

PB: With so many modes, is there a unifying theme or motif? Or does every poem demand its own form for you? Tell us about the proliferation of forms and scholarship that you engage in.

KMD: In general, my work traverses a wide range of forms and genres. But the one common thread that ties everything together is this impulse to defamiliarize. Where that comes from is my undeniable love of travel. When I was doing my PhD at SUNY Buffalo, I passed my qualifying exam and went long distance for my PhD thesis. I used that time to go to residencies, to write grants, travel the world, and meet other writers, scholars, and artists. The poet Eva Heisler says it best, "that to travel is to experience oneself as foreign." This defamiliarization of the self comes through in all of the ways that my poetry and my writing makes things strange, even the most ordinary things. I love to render commonplace experience as suddenly and startlingly unfamiliar in my poetry.

PB: I'm wondering how the poem is, in a sense, a foreign object composed in this technology we call the alphabet. When that poem then re-enters your body and is expressed orally, how does that mode differ for you from the way it looks on the page and the way you experience it alphabetically?

KMD: The question of the visual presentation of the work is an excellent one. Poems are visual even when we don't realize it. And what really intrigues me is the many preconceived notions that readers bring to prose. And with this prose poem, I really enjoyed capitalizing on those preconceived expectations, being aware of them and using them as writerly material. So in general, most readers will see a prose paragraph, and they will expect the language to unfold in a particular way. They'll expect it to be linear, logical; they'll expect a certain consistency in terms of the textures of language that they're presented with. And those preconceived ideas are just an opportunity to give the reader something that they really don't expect. A moment of beauty and emotional truth where they never expected to find it. That experience of giving the reader the unexpected, subverting their expectations, is also a powerful way to get at certain emotional truths that you couldn't get at otherwise.

PB: You've already spoken about the way tradition is the muse for you. What about your other experiences of art forms which also play a large role in your opus and your work?

KMD: Well, thank you so much for the opportunity to speak about film and its relationship to poetry because that is something that I never really get to talk about. I'm excited by this question. With my work as an editor, the first thing I did when I became Editor-in-Chief at Tupelo Quarterly was start a special section of the magazine which was dedicated to collaborative and cross-disciplinary texts: poetry films, cinepoetry, video poems, collaborations between writers and visual artists, sound poems. We had some incredible sound poems by Kate Greenstreet in a past issue, so I hope you will check them out.

But in general, what intrigues me so much about film and its relationship to poetry is that poets tend to envision pacing in a very boring way, I hate to say. But filmmakers use time in the most intriguing ways, and they use silence to give the audience an experience of time, to create suspense, and that is something that I wanted to steal for my own work as a poet. To use silence, to use white space, and time as units of composition in my poem. And when you see the poem in the anthology, there's a big gap right in the middle. That's part of what I'm talking about. This use of silence to make the reader wait a second, to keep them in suspense, to generate anticipation and hopefully heighten the effects of the narrative that I'm crafting.

Kristina Marie Darling *is the author of over thirty books. In addition to winning a Fulbright Scholar award, Dr. Darling's work has also been recognized with three residencies at Yaddo, a 2024 Civita Institute Fellowship, and ten juried residencies at the American Academy in Rome. A permanent faculty member at several art centers in Greece, Dr. Darling leads cross-disciplinary workshops at the Ionian Center for the Arts and Culture. Dr. Darling serves as Editor-in-Chief of Tupelo Press* & Tupelo Quarterly. *Born and raised in the American Midwest, she now divides her time between Greece, Rome, and the Amalfi Coast.*

Cynthia Hogue

"The Loire Valley (Solstice 2015)"

The uncoursed sun, a vulnerable
                    evening's chords
                    of fallow field,
the mounded rows you think at first are graves,
which we traverse to reach
                    the one-thousand-year-old
                    fortified grange.

Somehow it missed the war though everything
                    near the railroad's
                    gone to bits.
Nothing in this place to fix or modernize.
No one to claim it. Someone's vision
                    was to fill
                    the vaulting barn

once a year with music around now.
                    Silence opens wooden gates
                    made from the primeval forest
cleared to farm. The pock-marked limestone walls
enclose a cluttered courtyard
                    in the middle of which
                    humans mill, perusing

cd's, having drinks among the cattle stalls.
Inside is Bach,
and tonight an owl
whose contrapuntal hoots
you hear before you see him
land high in the rafters just
like your dream of flying.

At midnight, sun dipped down at last,
the full moon
floodlights the watch tower.
The gates closing, we're cast out
to the carless field, nor other farmstead near
to dim the sense of
not belonging here.

PB: Cynthia, tell me about why you chose this particular poem for *Sign & Breath*.

CH: This poem is in a more lyrical voice than I often adopt. The poem came to me as a vision, in classic lyric tradition, although it began as a personal experience. As I was having the experience, I was getting the visual images that I realized at the time were going to become a poem. That kind of direct reception of a poem doesn't always happen, but it happened with this poem particularly. I had the image to start with, the rows in the fallow fields that looked like graves, but I had no idea at the time where the poem was going to go. Where it went turned into a discovery that surprised me. I'm always excited about poems that discover something. We'd like to think that we always discover something when we write, but in truth, I don't always. Sometimes I just end the poem. But this poem ends with a vision of the post-human or beyond human—the couple being expelled, as it were, from the Garden (the language alluding to the closing of Milton's *Paradise Lost*). Specifically, the vision at the end is of a space, permeated by history, having transcended human impact and presence.

PB: I'm so glad that you talk about this being a vision song. When I look at the poem, I'm also noting the lines and I'm just curious if you want to talk about making those lines.

CH: The poem has an architecture that was also discovered as I wrote it. What you see, looking at the poem in front of you, are five mirroring stanzas, each with two short couplets separated by a longer couplet. The shorter couplets are indented and often contain images isolated on the lines. That form isn't a traditional form, obviously, but it's a form that emerged as I wrote the poem, as I tried to tighten it, trying to intensify the effects. There's a kind of columnar element to the architecture of the poem; of course, the poem is about a literal building that has survived 1000 years. It's about the space enclosed by the constructed form and about traversing that space. The poem isn't narrative per se—it's more visually and sonically driven—but the narrator does recount a chronology of moving through the space into the vaulting barn to listen to a concert. Thus, the space represents the confluence of human culture and nature, symbolized by the owl that gets into the barn and adds its contrapuntal hoot to Bach.

PB: Having made or discovered this architecture and this vision, could you talk about how those two things have left you looking at the poem now in whatever way you see it?

CH: Actually, as you're talking, I'm realizing something about the poem that was probably undergirding its writing, unconsciously more than consciously. It's a fortified grange, and fortification comes from the fact that there were so many threats. One tribe or people would rise to threaten another, steal the grain or steal the cattle. Mid-poem we encounter the ruin of the railroad, which was destroyed during World War II. We are in a region of France that was occupied by the Germans. The poem contains a real historical context, evidence of the tension between trying to cultivate the land to sustain oneself and one's people and to guard against forces trying to colonize the place and its inhabitants. That sense of history undergirds both the poem and the place.

The poem asks what transcends the historical threat and the ravages over time of humans attacking humans. Someone's vision was to fill that space of struggle with music. Attending the annual music festival was the occasion for the narrator to be in that space at all. And then the place, the architecture, the building, being repurposed to house human culture and beauty. It seems highly ironic to me that humans take the place of the cattle in cattle stalls as they wait to hear the concert being played in the middle of an almost primordial space.

One of the things that seems most evident to me as I read the poem is its internal music, the sonic elements that are really driving the poem, even determining some of the word choices and line breaks. An example would be the near-rhyme of *graves* and *grange*, which might have been an internal and perhaps more subtle rhyme with longer lines, but becomes highlighted because both words occur at the end of end-stopped lines.

I found that the inner ear was listening and discovering the sounds to determine the word choice, the key or chords to strike in the poem. I could play on the word *chord*, C-H-O-R-D, in the second line, already anticipating music that the speaker is going to hear. However, the word echoes *cords,* the long cord-like rows in the fallow fields, from which the speaker gets the impression of mounds of graves. Throughout the poem, I followed the sounds and discovered the meaning, something that really characterizes the creative process of writing this poem.

Cynthia Hogue *is the author of ten poetry collections, including* Contain *(Tram Editions, 2022),* In June the Labyrinth *(Red Hen Press, 2017), and* Revenance *(Red Hen Press, 2014) which was listed as one of the 2014 "Standout" books by the Academy of American Poets. Her honors include two NEA Fellowships, a MacDowell Colony residency, and the H.D. Fellowship at Yale University. Hogue is an Emerita Professor of English and lives in Tucson, Arizona where she teaches workshops at the University of Arizona Poetry Center.*

Arthur Sze

"Swimming Laps"

Swimming backstroke toward the far end of a pool in sunlight—

yellow flares in the nearby aspens—

in the predawn sky, Mars and Venus glimmered—

how is it a glimmering moment coalesces, and the rest slides like flour through a sieve?—

how is it these glimmerings become constellations in a predawn sky?—

reaching the wall, I turn and push off swimming freestyle—

how is it we bobbed in water beyond the breaking surf, and I taste that salt in
my mouth now?—

how is it, disheveled, breathless, we drew each other up into flame?—

how is it that flame burns steadily within?—

reaching the wall, I turn and push off swimming sidestroke—

with each scissors kick, I know time's shears—

this is not predawn to a battle when the air dips to a windless calm—

let each day be lived risking feeling loving alive to ivy reddening along the fence—

reaching the wall, I turn and push off swimming breaststroke—

how is it I see below then above a horizon line?—

how is it I didn't sputter, slosh, end up staring at a Geiger-counter clock mounted on a barroom wall?—

I who have no answers find glimmering shards—

reaching the wall, I pause, climb out of the pool, start a new day—

PB: Arthur, tell us why you chose this poem for *Sign & Breath.*

AS: I chose it because you were thinking about song and lyric. I felt that this was a particularly lyrical poem. The poem is in one-line stanzas with silences. There's repetition, but there's variation to the repetition. This kind of structure follows a very song-like quality.

PB: How does silence work in your poems?

AS: I think I've always been interested in silence. In the last six or seven years, I've been using this form of monostich because each line has its own integrity, and this form harnesses white spaces between the lines. It shows the reader that one shouldn't read from one line to the next without pausing. There's a visual cue that there are silences with duration. These are breathing spaces in between the motion of language. They're not mere empty spaces. They're really a form of charged silences which help clarify and create tension with the language that's there.

As a side note, I was just thinking about musicality before we started this interview, and I remember Isaac Stern in a famous interview.

He was asked, "How do you know a violin concert is going really well?"

The interviewer expected him to say, "Oh you know, by this incredible riff of gorgeous notes."

Instead, Isaac Stern said "I know the music's going really well by the quality of silences."

PB: One of the lines I think silence makes even more stark is the line with the barroom Geiger counter. It's like a reality check. I was curious about that because in the poem it feels as if we're swimming; it feels as if we're in this very sublime space...

AS: I'm glad you asked about that. In a poem like this where there are gorgeous images, I don't want to let a reader be lulled into some kind of tranquility where everything is beautiful and serene. I think it's really important to occasionally disrupt that smooth motion and destabilize it. That Geiger counter and that image of a speaker who might spend his days drinking in a bar staring at that Geiger counter disrupt the flow.

PB: I am thinking about the musicality of using the different strokes, and the disruption that happens there.

AS: In using the four different strokes (backstroke, freestyle or crawl, sidestroke, breaststroke) I was also thinking consciously of the rhythm in language. With backstroke there's the sense of being able to look up to see aspens, Mars, Venus, to be opening up while looking up at the sky.

When it switches to freestyle, I felt that, rhythmically, I was trying to heighten alliteration in those lines to show a quickening, and in terms of voice, there was also a shift that corresponded to the shift in physical movement.

PB: So many different sources and traditions are evoked in this poem, and in so much of your work. What is your relationship to the poets that you were read on and brought up with?

AS: I like to draw on many different sources and traditions in my poetry. I draw inspiration from them, but I am not limited or bound by them. In many ways, I am writing and finding my way through them. In this poem there are several classical references. The phrase, *time's shears* is actually a reference to Dante in the *Paradiso.* He is told if he doesn't keep creating, trying to create something that endures, time will go around his fabric, around his work, and shear it off.

There are other subtle allusions to the classical tradition, but I don't necessarily expect a reader to get them, or even want a reader to get them. Instead, I hope that a reader recognizes or senses that the language looks very simple but that there's also a lot of depth there. What are the enactments of refrain, repetition, and variation? Those are all classic song-like strategies that there's a long tradition of.

PB: Tell me about the orality of your work which is so pronounced and refined.

AS: When I'm writing, I am speaking words out loud to myself to hear the texture. It's very physical. I need to hear the texture of the language as I'm creating. The sound is primordial and right there from the beginning. It's an essential part of the fabric or the weave of the poem.

Arthur Sze *has published eleven books of poetry, including* The Glass Constellation: New and Collected Poems *(Copper Canyon Press, 2021), selected for a 2024 National Book Foundation Science + Literature Award, and* Sight Lines *(2019), which received the National Book Award for Poetry. His latest book is* The Silk Dragon II: Translations of Chinese Poetry *(Copper Canyon Press, 2024).*

Christine Gelineau

"Poem for my Brother on the Occasion of his Daughter's Wedding"

Our daughters have become orchards,
petalled and fragrant as light.

In the agile branches brash song
and incandescent orioles.

It is their turn to be divine now
while we grow more mortal

every day. We wake to the ash
of dreams upon our tongues, and catch

the intermittent scent of accidents
and inevitable calamities we have yet

to suffer, yes, our throats swell
with the vibrato of everything we've

been compelled to know, but today
beneath the red-nippled trees, long-haired

meadow grasses shiver and daffodils
gesture the lithe hands of their fronds.

Let the heart twist like a flower breaking
into blossom, lasting is not all.

SL: What I love about this piece is that it juxtaposes the question of mortality and living. Here we are, on a wedding day within the poem and we see someone has their life ahead while it simultaneously invites thoughts thinking about a life lived. Can you say more about the inner workings of your piece?

CG: My niece was getting married in Provence, a small wedding to which only my brother, sister-in-law, the bride's sister, and a couple of her friends were invited. My niece and my own daughter had both been born the same summer, the first babies of that generation in our family. Though I was not present for the wedding, the babies of that summer, my own brother, our childhoods, and time's passage, were all very much in my thoughts that day. As I started the poem, I thought it would be a poem to the bride and groom but found the poem addressing itself more to my brother, to that sense of a generational transfer, and I suspect that would be how mortality came into a poem that began with the idea of being an epithalamium. That juxtaposition, I think, is what turns thoughts of mortality insistently back to living in, appreciating, the moment.

SL: What motivated you to choose this piece for the anthology?

CG: I had difficulty deciding which piece to choose. I was looking for a piece that, you know how we say "Oh, that's poetry," whether it's poetry or not in the way that it's laid on the page. I wanted something that irrespective of how it will be laid on the page, that it would have enough of those musical elements that people would feel that way about that piece. And so we have all of those open vowels—daughters, orchard, agile, incandescent, orioles, brash—those open vowels have that feeling of lushness and plenty that gives us the musical elements in the piece. Rhythmically, building complexity of the syntax in the lines,

> ...We wake to the ash
> of dreams upon our tongues and catch
>
> the intermittent scent of accidents
> and inevitable calamities we have yet
>
> to suffer, yes, our throats swell
> with the vibrato of everything we've
>
> been compelled to know...

And then at the word but, "but today/beneath the red-nippled trees, long-haired/meadow, grasses shiver and daffodils/gesture the lithe hands of their fronds," this sort of untangles the syntax and slows the rhythm in that way. And then finally, the even simpler, more direct—so that it almost feels the syntax is this feeling of sureness, of what little sureness is there. This is what we're sure about, is this moment. In this moment of celebration and wedding and springtime, the fullness of that moment is what matters. I felt that the music of the language helped to enact the meaning of the poem. That's why I chose this piece.

SL: How does this page represent your practice in terms of how you think about syntax and the overall movement of all that you just described?

CG: I would put that with one of the questions you had about how does orality, or how does voice play a role in the composition? I would say I have a two-part response. My mother's parents were both born in Ireland. My grandmother was born in the Gaeltacht, meaning Irish was her first language. Though she spent most of her life in Massachusetts, for all of her life, she spoke with a soft brogue. You know the word "brogue" actually means a rude shoe. And the OED—the Oxford English Dictionary—is a little dissembling—they say, well, you know, maybe it meant they were insulting them. Yes, they were insulting them. To me, it was such beautiful music, the way my grandmother spoke.

My father's first language was Québécois French. He didn't learn English first; he was French Canadian, though he was born in the United States, as were his parents. But my mémère and pépère always spoke English to us, the grandchildren. But to their friends they'd speak French or this mix that they called Franglais, with emphasis on the French part of it. In addition to that, I was raised to be Catholic and was sent to Catholic school. Every Sunday at Mass—it was still said every Sunday morning in Latin—I sang in the choir, Gregorian chant in Latin. I lived in a landscape marked by the Algonquian language: Meshanticut, Misquamicut, Narragansett, Apponaug, Sockanosset, Mashpee, and Popponesset. My childhood was filled with the sounds of languages that I could repeat but that I would not be able to write down. There are a couple of words I still can't even find on Google. From my earliest times, I thought language was both communication and music. It had meaning, and it was aural or oral delight. It was practical and ritual. It was a tool, but it's also magic. So that'd be the first sense in which I'd say orality, for me, is at the center of composition.

And then to speak more directly to what you asked about syntax. The second sense would be to do with incarnation, with embodying the word. That tradition that I was raised in has a Godhead that speaks the world into being and that talks about at least one aspect of the Godhead as being the word made flesh. Orality is when words bring the body, the mind, the heart—it's all seamlessly enmeshed, that to me is orality.

My other passion besides poetry is horses, and in riding horses, I find a real apt parallel to composition. Riding is this language that you speak with your whole body to another species. It's a kind of cross-species sign language, you could say, in which the most significant of the signs is touch: the weight of your body, the feel of your leg, the touch of your hand. It's the opposite of cerebral language. It is so bodily, and it's full of subtlety, rhythm, attention, a kind of simpatico for this other being that is not of the same species as you. What I have learned about the fluency in this language of riding, I do my best to try to put it into the language of my poems and essays in ways that seek to incarnate orality, even to writing that's intended to be there on the page.

I'm not sure if you were going to ask about how one can bring aspects of orality to the page, I wanted to talk a bit about that.

SL: I was actually going to adjust the question given that you grew up with Catholicism, with liturgical language, and hearing Latin. You also talked about writing, the body, and movement of the body. I am curious about how these different elements, in addition to orality on the page, come together for you? The other part of that question is your definition of voice and how they take on these different levels of meaning within these elements within your life?

CG: One of the early influences for me in my early twenties was reading William Carlos Williams' *Spring and All*, a genre-blending early book that would mix poetry and prose and diary entries and letters, that sort of collaging of different materials that could spark off of one another, and that were not necessarily linear. When I was an undergraduate at the University of Connecticut, Charles Olson was technically employed by them. He was sick at the time, and I did not work with him but with George Butterick, who was an Olson acolyte who had followed him there to UConn. From that point on I had a sense of the page as it being whitespace and words, that we have choreography of the page, that there was a way to bring bodiliness to the page. In that way—just as in choreography—you can suggest movement and change and relationship by specific placement. I started writing before there were computers to do it on. I never composed on the typewriter, but once there were computers, there was something sort of liquid and deep about the computer screen to me that felt like a place where that kind of movement could bring embodiment. To me, I would think of that as voice. Performance is great. It's a great opportunity. You get to bring your personality, your voice, your inflection to the work. Voice would be when you can bring enough of that to the page that even when you aren't there, the reader can access a good portion of what they would get if you were there. To me, that would be voice.

SL: As we close, is there anything else you want to add? A question I didn't ask that you would like to address?

CG: There was a question about genre, and I was interested in that. I'm not sure that I am totally at ease with my own response to that. I need to think that through more. In a way as the writer, there's a way in which you can just ignore genre. To me, in a sense, genre has to do with publishing. Whether it's performances that are your publication or the page in a book is your publication, that's the point at which you have to figure out what does this look like? And how is that going to translate over to the audience? Whether the audience is a reader or someone there? That's form, genre's form, right? It's how you're going to shape it so that you can transmit it to someone else. Sometimes people see form as limiting, but I think of it more as skeletal. Where the skeleton enables and articulates and makes something possible. And yes, I mean, the skeleton of a rabbit can't graze the top of an acacia tree, and the skeleton of a giraffe can't shoot into a hole to get away from predators. That does not necessarily mean I wouldn't focus on that limit; I would focus rather on that articulation, that ability, that motion, and liveliness that the skeleton can enable. Genre doesn't matter when I'm writing, necessarily, but it does matter when you want to bring it to the world.

Christine Gelineau *is the author of three books of poetry:* Crave *(NYQ Books),* Appetite for the Divine *(Ashland Poetry Press) winner of the Robert McGovern Publication Prize, and* Remorseless Loyalty *(Ashland Poetry Press) which received the Richard Snyder Memorial Prize. Her latest book,* Almanac: A Murmuration, *a work of creative nonfiction, was published in 2025 by Excelsior Editions (SUNY Press). Her poems have been featured in several journals including* Verse Daily *and* Rattle. *She is a recipient of the Pushcart Prize and has had three essays cited as Notable Essays in* Best American Essays. *She teaches poetry and creative nonfiction in the Maslow Family Graduate Program in Creative Writing at Wilkes University.*

H. L. Hix

"They find their way by these stories?"

In my family the matriarch gets
to tell about the patriarch one nearly-
fell story. In my mother's mother's, it's
a spring day, Oklahoma, rainy.
My grandfather, a postal carrier
(old days, small town, leather shoulder bag, on foot),
slips on wet grass, slides down a hill (longer
each telling) on his butt, but bounces upright
at the bottom, not a letter lost or wet.
In my mother's, it's winter, south Texas,
freak storm, metal fire-escape steps slicked, a coat
of ice, my father slips on each, misses
none, dances down without losing his feet.
We laugh, like we laughed last summer, last Christmas.

PB: Harvey, as you know, the anthology is based upon "one page that sings," which comes from a tagline of yours, "Nothing attested, everything sung." Tell us why you chose this poem for this anthology.

HH: I hoped it would fit the anthology because of its double relationship to singing: the sonnet form sets this poem to singing in one way, and the two stories it recounts supplement that way with another.

The sonnet has proven itself a capacious and durable form. It has a rich tradition in English, never mind in other languages, but as poetic traditions go the English-language sonnet tradition is still young. The sonnet did not originate in English, and even in its home language, Italian, it developed in writing rather than in speech. The sonnet originated as, and still feels to me, a page-bound form. Its musical structure has the complex architecture of compositions that were first written down. The music of a sonnet resembles the music of classical composers who think up pieces in their heads and write them down on the page before the symphony performs them. As compared to folk music, say, that somebody sang first and passed down to others before anybody thought to write it down.

But that tag-teams the other relationship to singing I hope this poem performs. The sonnet didn't originate orally, but the stories this poem recounts *did*. I know these stories, not because anybody has written them down, but because I've heard them both a thousand times if I've heard them once. My grandparents have both been gone for some time now, but the story of his sliding down the hill and "landing" upright still gets told. And when I recall the story, I still hear it in my grandmother's voice.

This poem, then, aims to be equally inkbottle and voice box. It is written, but the stories it recounts originated and were conveyed orally for decades before the poem came along.

PB: You have a long history with sonnets. How does the sonnet form speak to the longer, more complicated, and sometimes original forms that you have made? Is the sonnet a major impulse? Are there multiple impulses?

HH: Multiple impulses, certainly, but the sonnet is an especially strong one. For me it has been originary and remains generative. The sonnet vividly exemplifies how not only musicality, but also structure, generates meaning. Structure links loose Legos into buildings and boats, and it makes words "huge and particular as hope." Even a structure as simple as the relative proportion of the sonnet, eight lines followed by six, still fits one portion preparation and another completion, still demands that evidence outsize conclusion.

That ratio, of preparation to completion, is the basis of timing. In any narrative form, timing is important. It's true of "high art" such as a fugue, but it's just as true of jokes: there's always some form of build-up followed by some culmination. We can describe it variously: going in one direction, then turning to another; rising action, falling action; and so on. However, it occurs, as return to the 1 chord after the 4 and the 5 or as the punch line after the shaggy dog, we respond to this sense of preparation and completion. The sonnet is visibly, audibly, and beautifully representative of that. You can see the sonnet on the page, but you can hear it, too. If someone reads it to you, and you can't see the page, you still hear the preparation and the completion the way you hear it in a story.

The sonnet has been provocative for me as something to work with and as something to work against. Over the years I've tried to write sonnets that *are* sonnets, and sonnets that *aren't*. I've tried to push back against the sonnet. I've tried to hide sonnets where you only hear them and don't see them, to create sonnets that are visibly sonnets, but not audibly. I've wanted to think about sonnets per se, but also to think through them about proportion. Does the sonnet alert me to something that I can then replicate in a form that's not the sonnet? Something that may not have the *same* proportions, the *same* way of preparing and completing, but that still gives a way of preparing and completing? The sonnet has been inspiring in that way.

***H. L. Hix** is the author of numerous books, including the recent poetry collections* Moral Tales *(Broadstone, 2024),* Constellation *(Cloudbank, 2023), and* Bored In Arcane Cursive Under Lodgepole Bark *(Middle Creek, 2023). He has co-translated the work of Estonian poets Jüri Talvet and Juhan Liiv, and Lithuanian poets Eugenijus Ališanka and Tautvyda Marcinkevičiūtė. He has been awarded the Vern Rutsala Book Prize, been Fulbright Distinguished Lecturer at Yonsei University, and been a finalist for the National Book Award. He teaches philosophy at a state university in the Mountain West.*

Colum McCann

Excerpt from the novel *Apeirogon*

Once upon a time, and not so long ago, and not so far away, Rami Elhanan, an Israeli, a Jew, a graphic artist, husband of Nurit, father of Elik and Guy and Yigal, father too of the late Smadar, travelled on his motorbike from the suburbs of Jerusalem toward the Cremisan monastery in the mainly-Christian town of Beit Jala, near Bethlehem, in the Judean hills, to meet with Bassam Aramin, a Palestinian, a Muslim, a former prisoner, an activist, born near Hebron, husband of Salwa, father of Arab and Areen and Mohammed and Ahmed and Hiba, father too of the late Abir, ten years old, shot dead by an unnamed Israeli border guard in East Jerusalem, almost a decade after Rami's daughter, Smadar, two weeks away from fourteen, was killed in the western part of the city by three Palestinian suicide bombers, Bashar Sawallha, Youssef Shouli, and Khalil al-Sharif, from the village of Assira al-Shamiya near Nablus in the West Bank, a place of intrigue to the listeners gathered in the red-bricked monastery perched on the hillside, in the Mountains of the Beloved, by the terraced vineyard, in the shadow of the Wall, having come from as far apart as Belfast and Kyushu, Paris and North Carolina, Santiago and Brooklyn, Copenhagen and Terezin, on an ordinary day, at the end of October, foggy, tinged with cold, to listen to the stories of Bassam and Rami, and to find within their stories another story, a song of songs, discovering themselves—you and me—in the stone-tiled chapel where we sit for hours, eager, hopeless, buoyed, confused, cynical, complicit, our memories imploding, our synapses skipping, our hearts brooked, silent, in the gathering dark, remembering, while listening, all of those stories that are yet to be told.

CM: My reading is from the middle pages of my novel *Apeirogon*, a novel about two fathers in the Middle East, one Palestinian, one Israeli. The book is written in one thousand and one sections, or cantos. The book builds from canto one up to five hundred, and then from five hundred down to one, so that it can be read both backwards and forwards. The page that "sings" (or is supposed to sing) is the exact middle section. This whole idea borrows from Scheherazade of course and *One Thousand and One Nights*: the grand cathedral of storytelling in the face of death.

PB: You mention Scheherazade and the idea of storytelling as a ruse against death, and I'm just wondering, as you create your novel, what is the role of orality in that work and in all your work?

CM: Orality. Strange and wonderful word. If we're talking about making the work sing, if we're talking about sounding it out, there is little that is more important. I would always, always, always take music over meaning. I'm not as interested in what the work actually *says*, as what it allows you to *feel*. And so, the rhythm must be right, and the tone must be right, and the mystery must be right too. Whether it's orchestral, or chamber, or rock, or rap, the most important thing that a writer must do is access the musical in his/her/their work. Nothing beyond music, as Heaney might have said.

For this page I was going for something orchestral, I suppose. It begins with a suggestion of myth ("once upon a time and not so long ago"), and then becomes a series of almost journalistic facts ("a Palestinian, a Muslim, a former prisoner"), then moves into a sort of everyman phase ("Belfast and Kyushu"), and then becomes very specific ("on an ordinary day at the end of October"), mentioning a "song of songs," and then it implicates the reader in the passage ("you and me"), moving through to the final swell ("all of those stories that are yet to be told.") I wanted it to be local and universal at the same time. And I wanted a lot of sounds in there. I was conducting the orchestra and trying to get out of the way at the same time.

This page arrives in the exact middle of the novel. It gives the whole of the plot away, but the real discovery for me was the "you and me" line. To be honest, Phil, I had worked on this book for almost two years and still did not know who the narrator of it was. It confounded me. I was racking my brain. I didn't want the narrator to be me, or at least not *just* me—that would be boring. And I contemplated all sorts of things. At one stage I thought it was a Welsh peace activist of all things. And then—a didn't know if it was one of the smartest things I ever did as a writer, or the plain dumbest—I discovered that the reader was the narrator. That liberated me—the idea that you, the reader, are telling the story. But then it struck me that maybe all readers are narrators of the novels we engage in? Maybe we all sing along? Still, I was making—or at least I hoped I was making—the reader consciously complicit in the story.

It's all one sentence, obviously. I got most of it in one single day, but then I spent a lot of time crafting it and re-crafting it. The final twenty words or so were technically very difficult. We tend to forget that all this stuff takes a lot of work, but you have to give the appearance of ease. One of my favorite pieces of writing advice comes from my friend Aleksandar Hemon: "It's all shit...until it isn't." I like that. It deserves an exclamation mark, but I'm not going to give it one, which makes it even more of an exclamation.

PB: One of the things that's come up is the idea that somehow voice is not necessarily a singular thing. It's not owned or directed. And I think of your book as this righteous testimony woven in dream language. And I'm wondering about how that technique relates to voice or sound. Tell us about your idea of voice.

CM: My idea of voice first of all, is that we get our voice from the voices of others. It comes in off the wind, and out of the water, and up from the ground, and from all the songs that surround us. A Song of Ourselves. And you know, one of the things that we do as younger writers is we read, and we develop, and we mimic, and we sing, and we hear that music, and it gets into our heads. It's important in this sense to be a promiscuous reader, especially in the beginning. So, I would say to the younger writers out there, read as broadly and widely as you can. Start listening across all sorts of genres to find the notes that will create your own composition. And for me, it's about poetry. To be honest, I couldn't write a poem to save my life. But poetry and sound and rhythm are all incredibly important to me. I try to find a poem in each sentence—it's just that the end of the line defeats me. And so, I just keep going. Trudging on. Yet I try to make sure that every sentence has a rhythm that will get into the reader's head. As a writer you don't *impose* rhythm upon the reader, you don't make them hear it, but you allow it to happen. You want your reader to find the music because the most interesting thing about being a writer is not telling anybody what to think, because that's pedestrian. We're told all the time what to think, but allowing somebody into a new space, and finding a music in that space, is absolutely what voice is all about for me.

And once you have the voice in a story, everything follows. The real difficult thing is finding the voice, achieving it, and then maintaining it. Every now and then, you will lose it. You will lose the music of it. And this is where the hard work of sitting and waiting and fighting comes in. You must take on the terror of the blank page.

We are essentially musicians and the original voice, the original song was surely that of the person who wanted to make you happy, or make you sad, or tell you that they love you through the sound of the words, the way they touch against one another.

PB: You've founded an organization, Narrative 4, dedicated to storytelling as empathic. How do the voices that you hear from these storytellers influence your voice?

CM: Every story I ever hear, every piece of music, becomes part of the overall score. I'm pretty sure that in heaven there's a giant jukebox and you have access to it all. In Narrative 4, we bring young people together to tell one another's stories. They step into someone else's world. They extend the music.

Colum McCann's *most recent books are* Twist *(Random House, 2025) and* American Mother *(with Diane Foley, Etruscan Press, 2024). Previous books include* Apeirogon *(Random House, 2020),* Thirteen Ways of Looking *(Random House, 2015) and* TransAtlantic *(Random House, 2013). He is the recipient of multiple awards and honors including the U.S. National Book Award, the International Dublin Prize Literary Prize, and an Oscar nomination. His fiction has appeared in* The New Yorker, Esquire, *and* The Paris Review *among other publications. He is the President and cofounder of the non-profit global story exchange organization Narrative 4.* ***The piece included in this anthology is an excerpt from*** **Apeirogon** ***(Random House, 2020).***

Haleh Liza Gafori

"Lets Love Each Other" is a poem by Rumi, translated by Haleh Liza Gafori

"Let's Love Each Other"

Let's love each other,
let's cherish each other, my friend,
before we lose each other.

You'll long for me when I'm gone.
You'll make a truce with me.
So why put me on trial while I'm alive?

Why adore the dead but battle the living?

You'll kiss the headstone of my grave.
Look, I'm lying here still as a corpse,
dead as a stone. Kiss my face instead!

SL: I would love to know more about this poem and how it represents your practice?

HLG: I enjoy the shifts in tone and the leaps between stanzas in this poem and in much of Rumi's work. Here, he begins with an invitation, "Let's love each other,/let's cherish each other." The warm tone of this opening invitation morphs into a graver one when he reminds us of our mortality and lands on a piercing question, "Why adore the dead, but battle the living?"

In few words, he both highlights the tragic absurdity of our ways and encourages self-inquiry, then shifts to the image of the gravestone, reminding us again that life is finite. In the final stanza, he lightens the mood with a comic and playful invitation that has made me, and others laugh aloud. The variety of tones in this poem and the swift movement between them thrills me.

On three occasions so far, I've been told this poem has catalyzed the mending of relationships, opening the way for conversations between estranged family members. I was happy to hear this, and it didn't surprise me. There is a utilitarian aspect to many of Rumi's poems. He is a wise guide and worked as a preacher before he became a poet. Many of his poems retain the didactic quality of sermons, and because he is such a master of imagery and meter, unafraid to confess his own struggles, to poke fun at himself at times, and to do it all with tremendous skill and humor, the preacherly aspect of his voice is palatable, even delightful.

This poem is a ghazal, a string of couplets, and each couplet, like a bead on a necklace, is independent, extractable, and connected by a refrain or a rhyming word that appears at the end of each couplet. I do not attempt to mimic the rhyme scheme in my translations, nor do I always preserve the end position of the refrain. Following a common tradition among singers, translators, and even Iranian editors publishing Rumi's poems in Farsi, I have strung together selected couplets in this poem.

SL: Speaking of movement on the page, I've had the pleasure of being a part of something that I co-curated this summer and I got a chance to see you perform! How do you think of the intersections between your translating and you as a vocalist and composer? Do you compose with performance in mind? Is it stage versus page? How do you think of all these dimensions in your work as you're bringing it to an audience?

HLG: I generally know a poem is done when I can recite it by heart, when it moves through my body and out my mouth without a glitch. When I'm working on a poem, I'll run down the page over and over again like a sculptor with a chisel and other tools, carving, honing, buffing the piece again and again. Then I'll take a rest, lay down on a couch or bed, and recite. If I know it by heart, if it comes naturally without a glitch, if it rings, sings, resonates, then I know it's done. Rumi's poetry is rooted in an oral tradition. He often composed spontaneously and aloud, free styling while friends transcribed the poem. While my translation process is obviously very different, my reliance on recitation as I get close to finishing the translation honors the process that created the poem. When I recite the finished pieces to an audience, I hope the poems emerge like revelations—alive, pulsing, and fresh.

SL: Let's talk about the question of voice. In terms of translation, are there distinctions for you among these different factors of your voice versus or alongside the original voice of the poem (like in the case of Rumi)? How does your voice work with Rumi's voice? In what ways do you approach voice across these different dimensions in your work as poet, as translator?

HLG: Translation is a collaborative process. On occasion, a literal translation is best. On other occasions, the line may be elusive, the wordplay not replicable, so the translator has to interpret and call on their own creative skill.

Someone asked me about the process of translation around the time that images from the James Webb telescope were released online, and it seemed to me the telescope was an apt metaphor for a translator. Like the telescope traversing the mysterious terrain of outer space, translating infrared wavelengths into visible wavelengths to produce those shimmering images, the translator traverses the mysterious terrain of a language unknown to readers, and brings back images in the wavelength of a new language, while hopefully maintaining the infrared heat—or let's say, spirit—of the original poem.

How does one make a poem in the new language? Does one prioritize the music, meter, and form of the source language and try to emulate it? Does this leave the reader with forced rhymes and forced meter that compromise meaning? Does one prioritize the images and messages of the poem, shedding the music and form of the original language in order to honor the musical and metrical conventions of the target language, achieving what Wsilawa Szymborska called "that rare miracle when a translation becomes a second original"?

SL: What is your posture towards working within the tradition of translation? Obviously translation has gone through different periods in terms of belief systems about how to treat the original voices that one is engaging with. How do you stay within or break from the tradition of translation? There is also a cultural layer as well; how do you work within these dimensions? Or do you find yourself creating new conventions within the work that you're doing?

HLG: In this case, understanding the philosophy of Sufism, having an awareness of the "sama" practices of deep listening and whirling dance which Rumi cherished so deeply, of the 99 names of God he chanted in devotional ceremonies, and of the backstories of certain figures like the saint Mansur al Hallaj who was persecuted for declaring that the divine dwells within, for instance, is essential.

Some words have different meanings now than they did 800 years ago. During the process of translation, I referred to dictionaries that list contemporary and ancient meanings as well as define obscure or extinct words. For instance, the commonly known definition for the word "edrar" is "urine." An older and lesser-known definition is "wages," which is what Rumi meant when he used the word in Ghazal 2144.

When faced with a very elusive line that requires interpretation, it's helpful to be familiar with the poet's full body of work. There may be a similar phrase, image, or reference in another poem that offers clues towards an informed interpretation.

Out of the thousands and thousands of poems Rumi wrote, I chose to translate those which delight or challenge me, poems that speak to me and to our times. Sometimes within these poems, I focused on my favorite couplets. This tradition of picking and choosing couplets is common practice among translators and others. An Iranian vocalist may sing 4 out of 16 couplets in a poem. The contemporary Iranian poet Kadkani published excerpts of his favorite ghazals in Farsi, leaving aside couplets he wished to exclude. And those reciting Rumi's original text at public events often pare down to favorite couplets. What the vocalist, poet, editor, or translator chooses reflects their leanings, inclinations, concerns, and taste. For the translator, this is where the process of collaboration begins. And of course this is a major source of variation between translations.

SL: One of the main things I do know about Sufism is that it involves physically spinning, so it makes sense that you talked about the embodiment of Rumi's poem. It also speaks so well to the specificity of this project and why it makes sense that you would need to ensure that you write what you know, ensuring that the poem is within your body because it was created through movement and through embodiment.

HLG: Rumi was a master of rhythm and meter. His poems dance and are often composed to the beat of the drum. In whirling, the dancers return to the same point in a room over and over again. Similarly, a ghazal takes a couplet-length spin and then returns to the refrain or rhyme. It's a whirling poetic form.

It's a pleasure to recite these poems in the original Farsi. To feel the different rhythms. To walk through a park while the poems sing in my ear. To sleep with them. To let them coarse through my blood before transmitting them into English, and specifically into contemporary American free verse which has its own demands, its own poetic and musical conventions. Hearing the music of the source language, the translator makes new music in the target language, sometimes echoing the original.

SL: How do you define voice as a translator? As a vocalist? As a composer and as a poet? Is it the same or different depending on what dimension you're entering?

HLG: Deep listening is central to composition, translation, recitation, to the process of "finding" one's voice or another's. There is a voice within us and beyond us which perhaps we access when our minds are silent. Rumi often calls himself and his listeners to silence in the final couplet of his ghazals. Poet Marilyn Nelson said, "Poetry emerges from silence and leaves us in silence." Perhaps Rumi agreed and would call for silence to allow for reflection and for the emergence of the next poem. He says, "Take the cotton of the mind's doom-ridden chatter out of your ears/ Hear the booming voice of the heavens,/ hear the roar of fate,/ hear the ruckus the muse makes."

The spinning mind, the monkey brain chatter, the doom-ridden narratives are all options for our attention. But what voice emerges when the mind is silent? When we train the mind to quiet down and successfully experience moments or longer stretches of silence, what words, if any, emerge? This was one of Rumi's concerns and one of mine. What voice speaks when we are frantic, what voice speaks when we are calm and at ease, what voice speaks when we are in a state of surrender? And how do you trick the muse into emerging? When Rumi engaged in the practice of whirling dance, he often composed poetry. This practice, which demanded motor coordination and deep focus, brought him to a heightened state of creative freedom where he felt himself a conduit for a voice that was beyond his own and very much his own. Creative people often say they get their best ideas while engaged in a repetitive task. This was a repetitive, and spiritual dance, replicating the whirling of micro and macro entities—electrons, planets, etc.—in our whirling galaxy.

When I present Rumi's poetry in English and sing his words in Persian, I usually don't go on stage with a clear plan about what I will say or a clear order of poems or songs. I know many of the translations by heart, so I rely on the present moment to direct, and then I recite what comes to mind, or circumvents the mind, whatever travels straight to the tongue.

Regarding this multi-dimensional entity called the voice, what is the wind saying? What is the toad saying? What is the water saying? Everything is speaking. Everything is in conversation. As a translator, I am in conversation with my 800-year-old poetic ancestor.

As a poet, I'm in conversation with this sensual world.

Haleh Liza Gafori** is a translator, performance artist, musician, and poet born in New York City of Iranian descent. Her book,* GOLD, *translations of poems by Rumi was released in 2022 by New York Review Books/ NYRB Classics. A 2024 MacDowell fellow and the recipient of a 2023 grant from the New York State Council of the Arts, Gafori has woven a cross-media performance piece weaving translations from* GOLD *with original text, anecdotes, and musical compositions she sings in Persian. The piece debuted at New York Public Library for World Heritage Month. Her work has been published by* Columbia University Press, Harvard Review, The Brooklyn Rail, Literary Hub, *and elsewhere. Gafori performs, lectures, and leads workshops at universities and festivals across the United States and abroad, including Stanford University, Sarah Lawrence College, Lincoln Center, LPR, Swarthmore College, the Women's Library and Information Center Foundation in Istanbul, and the Bradford Literary Fest.* ***"LET'S LOVE EACH OTHER" is a Rumi poem translated by Haleh Liza Gafori from the full collection **GOLD** ***(NYRB Classics/Penguin Random House, 2022).***

Kaylynn Sullivan TwoTrees

"I to i"

small clues of mysterious and illusive memory
come when I am still
it touches me
I shrinks and expands
my individuality
  falls away
so what is uniquely, essentially my self
becomes *i*.

Individuation remains in the letter—
a mark—retaining shape and distinction.
The dot—the infinite relationship from which
this individuation springs.

To experience these moments at will
I need rigorous and consistent assistance—
protocols for the integrity of the soul.

As gentle rocking sometimes stills the cries of a child
the rhythm of breath nudges the mind
first to curiosity
then on to stillness and focus

Breath opens
in the space between inhale and exhale
i am

The mark that defines the substance of me
fills and stretches to the dot above
where *i* am whole

Memory comes full in me
not creeping from my peripheral vision
but filling me
with an experience beyond the sensory

My being extends beyond that mark of *i* to
        the grasses and insects
        the stars and planets
        the birds and fishes
        the wind and clouds
        the angry and joyful
        the blessed and invisible
        the grieving and celebrated

There is no end to the naming of myself
i am becoming *we.*

SL: Your piece reminds me of your latest work and recent exhibition *Falling into Language*. Your exhibition is where I was first introduced to Ursula K. Le Guin's, *She Unnames Them*. What stuck with me is the way that Eve unnamed everything in that story and in doing so, became more connected through the act of unnaming. Can you talk to me a bit about why this selection that you shared, and what it means for you? What are your thoughts around language and voice?

KS: Well, I have to admit that these words came to me twenty years ago and they came through a practice I had. I lived off the grid on a ranch out west, and I would walk the perimeter of the ranch every day as my reconnection practice. In the course of doing that, this flood of words would come, I would go home, and I would write them down. Over the course of twenty years, the context has changed so drastically as I age, in this country, in this culture, in the way that I move in the world, in the way that we're all moving in the world, in terms of the pandemic and everything. And I go back and look at the words and they still feel connected. They feel connected to breath, to the land, to beingness. I feel like there's something that I was trying to do with "Falling into Language" and what I feel like these words do, which is always trying to catalyze or initiate or evoke, provoke the connection we have to the Whole in the Holy—to the Great Mystery, to the Source from which all things come. Whatever you call that, the unknowable, the ineffable as it exists in our lives today, as it exists in the moment that we're having, not in some abstract way. There's nothing abstract about it for me.

SL: I've often heard you talk about your practice of invoke, evoke, and provoke, how does that relate to this piece? How do you think of or define voice? How does the concept of voice relate to this piece?

KS: I'm gonna dance around that a little bit. Because I use the word *invoke*, but actually the thing I really mean or how it applies to me is surrender. I surrender. I try to surrender myself so that something can come through me. That's my invocation. My invocation is surrender. Following what comes through me and not trying to will something, or not trying to create a good idea. I'm much more interested in the calling that comes through me than a good idea. In that process, I'm doing that so that I feel that I am connecting to that which connects all of us...the life force that is connecting all of us to *evoke* a memory in other people so that we remember that we're connected and that nature is our greatest reminder. We are nature. I know when I say that, it *provokes* some resistance, some deep memory some remembering and not wanting to remember. Some "Oh, but no." Some "Yeah, but...," lots of "Yeah, buts...."

That feels like generative tension to me. Generative tension for me is what breaks open seed coats of consciousness. When I say tension, I mean simultaneous attraction and repulsion that destabilizes the status quo.

SL: That's so cool. It's funny because I know you have also performed, you've danced, and you work across a range of mediums. You composed this piece you shared twenty years ago. As you revisit it for this anthology and in thinking about how you composed it, did you ever have performance in mind versus the page, especially because you work across mediums? When you think about *Sign & Breath*, is there ever a moment where your modes of work are in tension with each other? Are you thinking about how It's performed for the audience versus how you might see it on a page?

KS: This writing came out whole. I did not craft anything. I would come back from those walks, and—this is a terrible image—but it was like I kind of vomited it out. It was like a hairball, you know, and I coughed it up on the page. I have written in the past for performances, and sometimes for choral voices. I did performance work years ago for orchestrated voices using text. I worked then with language as music creating vocal parts with specific text—a baseline, melody and harmony and directed the voices like a choir. I do the same kind of orchestration with images now and add voices for texture.

I think that it depends on what's coming through me at the moment. I realize "Oh, this needs to be like this." For example, when making "Falling into Language," the paintings were never only paintings. I knew that they were going to be a score to be sung. I knew that they were also going to be a libretto for moving images. I still make them the way I'm going to make them, but I know that I'm going to change and they're going to change because when I change the medium, I also get changed. I learn things when I expand from one medium to another. I learned a lot in "Falling into Language," continuing to reshape the pieces and the whole for each iteration. When the context changes, I'm always learning from it, as it moves through its iterations or changes or transformations.

SL: Would you say that's true of your voice over time? Where it's instructing you, or where somehow, you're opening yourself up as a conduit such that you're learning from it, through whatever is going on through different modalities?

KS: Absolutely over time and as I get older. Just aging and what you can do, what's physically possible for you to do at one age, but not another. I learn in that way. I also learn how much of me needs to be present in the actual work. In the beginning there was a lot of me when I was performing in it. Then I had the thought that I could actually do more if I wasn't in it. That I could be a bigger conduit if my presence wasn't in it, so I stopped being in it. I'm not sure what comes next, but I always love the process of discovering. I'm loving film and music, I really love those mediums. I think it's a constant...shifting and growing and learning.

I also think that it's about the fact that I'm close to leaving. When I started making work, I was not far from coming in. Sixty years later, I'm close to leaving and that's a different perspective. I stand in a different place. The context is really different. We don't talk about that very much.

SL: No, we don't.

KS: No, but I think it's really a big deal. For me at least, for my work.

SL: We're so focused on the emerging artist, or the concept of youth within creating, that we don't think about creating across lifespan, how that impacts one's work. It has me thinking what does *Sign & Breath* mean within all those iterations of life? Is there anything else you want to add as we close?

KS: I think that one of the things that I really appreciate about this process, as opposed to other writing that I've done in the past, is that it feels like it has more breath. I always think about things I've written in the past as frozen. I keep moving and they're frozen in that particular moment. There's something about this process that includes both the text and the conversation that feels like it has more breath and that it will feel less frozen.

***Kaylynn Sullivan TwoTrees** is an artist, catalyst, guide, and writer. She is the author of* Somebody Always Signing You *(University Press of Mississippi, 1997). She is a past recipient of the Lila Wallace International Artist Award, and her work has been exhibited in collections in the US, Europe, and New Zealand. She was the first Artist in Residence in the Masters of Leadership for Sustainability Program for the University of Vermont. Through A Practice for Living, A Living Practice, she offers coaching and lessons that focus on life purpose, creativity, and awareness.*

Shin Yu Pai

"Heyday"

"Heyday" was Shin Yu Pai's last creative project as the fourth Poet Laureate of The City of Redmond in Seattle. She composed a poem reflecting on the city's efforts to extend its tree canopy. Courtesy of the poet.

SL: One of the things that everyone will notice in the anthology is how visual this piece is. What inspired you to choose this page? What was your process in terms of how your piece came into being?

SP: For this anthology, I was thinking about this notion of sign, and it felt like a visual format could be something interesting to do with a page. My excerpt is screenshots and stills of an animated video poem that I created in 2017 with Michael Barakat, the designer, and filmmaker for the piece. We took a poem that I had written for the page. I had this idea of how I wanted it designed and executed. I had worked a bit in the past with concrete poetry. When I went to Michael, I talked to him about how we could push that, make the poem animated and dynamic. I gave him examples of visual poems by writers like Ian Hamilton Finlay and Guillaume Apollinaire. And we talked about the ways that I wanted to apply those concepts to animating this piece that I'd written about an environmental initiative that was happening in the City of Redmond.

I think that this particular piece represents some of the ways I like to work visually or work with text that disrupts, or plays with the reading experience. This video poem does not have any voiceover, so the ways in which the phrases are broken up visually give some sense of how the work might be read, or where the breath might fall.

SL: As we think about voice and orality, this also raises the question or the idea of the animated voice, the voice that becomes translated into the visual thing. Can you speak to that? When did you know that you first wanted to play with language or voice or orality in that way?

SP: My sensibility around the notion of voice has certainly evolved since I made *Heyday.* At the time that I made it, I was the Poet Laureate of Redmond, a city on the Eastside of Seattle that's home to Microsoft. I was in this civic poet role where I was being asked by the city to present my work to thousands of people and find the right format to engage popular audiences. After doing a couple of large civic events, I really felt that the right move wasn't being on a stage and using the voice to read a poem. It didn't seem effective, because when folding poetry into a large civic festival around holidays, or whatever the theme is, people aren't necessarily there to listen to poetry. It's not the right occasion for it or the right format to necessarily present that.

I thought about what it would mean to take my voice and body out of the reading experience. Making a visual concrete poem that could exist as an animation projected on city hall at night could invite the reader to play around with reading or encountering poetry in a very visual way. I was also curious about the idea of removing my voice and my body from the work. Who I am as a BIPOC person in the world? I wanted to know if people would respond to that work differently if they didn't know that it was written by a woman, or that it was created by a BIPOC poet. I wondered if there would be differences in how it would be perceived if there was anonymity of the author.

So, that interested me, but I think what I realize now was that there was a level of erasure that I was enacting on myself. Making myself invisible and literally not giving myself a voice. I wanted to see what were the different ways in which voice could show up or be removed. How could I represent voice in different ways, and give the reader or the viewer some cues about how something might be experienced? To give them more autonomy over their reading. Or, a deep listening type of experience in silence. For that moment of when I made the piece, it was an effective strategy for the thing that I was trying to do, but it isn't how I think about the voice now.

SL: I would love to hear how your definition of voice has changed over time. What is your definition of voice? What have you noticed that has surprised you about how the definition of voice has shifted for you?

SP: Voice for me now is very much about agency, visibility, and the claiming of voice. There have been a lot of things that have happened in the world since 2017. Beginning with the start of the pandemic, there were anti-Asian sentiments that arose during the Trump administration, which were very impactful. Those were followed in March 2021, by the massacre of six Asian women in the Atlanta spa shootings. Those particular occasions and this climate of anti-Asian bias and discrimination really touched me in a very deep way. It forced me to reconsider and reimagine what it means to have a voice and to be able to use it. As an Asian woman, I had perhaps chosen certain cultural ways of being in the past that had been deeply socialized within me. I realized that my silence and reticence to speak out was not sustainable or healthy for me. Especially as somebody who is now a mother to a young, mixed-race child. I've come to feel and know that one must absolutely use their voice to make space for others. There's that layer of using my voice as a privilege.

For much of my life, I was always interested in the voice as an instrument to the extent that when I was a young person, I participated in vocal jazz ensembles and classical choirs through high school and college. I took voice lessons, and auditioned for music school and that path didn't work out for me. I took a long break from singing. But when there were opportunities to sing and use the voice as an instrument, as a vehicle, those opportunities were interesting to me. I take voice lessons occasionally with a wonderful teacher who was based here in Seattle for a long time, Jessika Kenny, she is now based in Los Angeles. In working with her, I have thought about what it means to decolonize the voice and decondition it from the ways in which we may be trained in Western traditions to think about voice, or to sing in certain ways. The voice now for me—and as I think of it when I write or perform—is very much about an expression of spirit and that connecting to something that is beyond words. That the voice can be incorporated into performance in a way that isn't simply about the reading or the performing of language, but it can also be about inviting the body, embodiment, and inviting listeners to be present in a different way when the voice is animated as an instrument of spirit.

SL: I'm curious about something you said earlier. What does it mean to decolonize the voice? It's something I've not thought about. I have observed conversations about the decolonization of language, as it were, but decolonizing the voice? What does that look like or sound like, in your opinion?

SP: There are a couple dimensions of that. In my late teens, when I was preparing for music auditions, the music that was assigned to me by my classically trained opera singer voice teacher was Schumann. It was straight out of the Western operatic art song tradition. And even though I had no interest in singing in that way, this is the thing that I was made to present to my audition panel. Because it's canon. There's that layer of privileging the European.

Currently, I do a lot of writing for voice for public radio. That involves script writing and the reading of the text. Some of the feedback I've gotten during the taping sessions have been very interesting. It was suggested that I should calibrate my reading to a "neutral voice." So, then I had a long conversation with my voice teacher about what is this thing called neutral voice? What *is* neutral voice? And is what we really mean white, male, public radio voice? That isn't actually neutral. Is that the voice I want to perform and deploy a version of the girl next door who becomes more approachable to an audience? I wanted to find a neutral voice that could tell the stories of Asian Americans. So, I'm being the neutral girl next door, performing a certain kind of voice but we're in a very different neighborhood.

These are just some of the ways in which I think about voice these days because I am able to write into the voice and many different kinds of mediums which then make me really consider what relationship do I have to my voice right now? Is it representative of who I am or who I feel myself to be? How do I want to relate to voice?

SL: That's a very interesting thought too because I'm also doing a lot with radio right now, so listening to myself and saying, "Is my voice even or am I getting too excited for the listener?" Or am I being this kind of Shanta instead of being able to say, "Oooooh gurrrrl," I feel like I can't express things in that way in my radio segment. Why can't I say this in my radio segment? So, I love this idea of decolonizing the voice. Is there anything you want to add as we wrap up? Is there a question I did not ask or anything you would like to add about some of the concepts or thoughts that you've had around this piece, or in general?

SP: I want to give a brief context about the *Heydey* piece. The city was developing an environmental initiative for which they were trying to gather some support from the community. Specifically, they were wanting to become better environmental stewards by extending their tree canopy, which affects their water, and their watershed. I didn't want to write a propaganda piece, but I was really interested in the city's history of environmental stewardship and moments when there had been extraction and trauma.

So, really bringing that into the story of the narrative. In order to understand the present, you have to understand the past. That was very important to me in creating a thoughtful piece. The images themselves derive from shaping the words in the poem into these images of trees, the environment. That was kind of the thought or the different strategies that went into making that piece.

Shin Yu Pai *is the author of several books including* No Neutral *(Empty Bowl, 2023) and* Less Desolate *(Blue Cactus Press, 2023).* Ensō *(Entre Ríos Books, 2020) is a 20-year survey of her work across creative disciplines. She is the former Civic Poet of The City of Seattle (2023-2024) and served as the fourth Poet Laureate of the City of Redmond. She is host and creator of the chart-topping, award-winning podcast* Ten Thousand Things *which she made for three seasons with KUOW/NPR. Currently, she produces the show independently with Wonder Media Network. The show has received awards from the Asian American Podcasters Association and The Signal Awards, and received a regional Edward R. Murrow Award.*

III.

"You could say that I was waiting for the voice to haunt me."

Mihaela Moscaliuc

Ru Freeman

"Write in imitation of KL, my friend PL says."

I write:

I do not want to write to you, husband. I wanted to write a lie. I did not want to write honestly about immigrants like me. About brown bodies, and black hair, and brown superstitions, and black eyes, and brown aversions, and black ink, and brown curries, and black tea, and brown earth, and black tar. I did not want to write about green trees. I did not want to write about eighteen varieties of mangoes, fourteen of which are only found on my island. I did not want to write about how the land is owned by brown women and how the laws of the land favor brown women and how brown women get to pick which brown man they'd keep to cultivate those lands.

I did not want to write about where we come from. I wanted to write an American memoir.

I wanted to write a lie.

I wanted to do that old brown work of sucking up to you who pay us to suck up to you every day. I wanted to write about our families' relationships to saris, and arranged marriages. I wanted to write about our dependency on rice, and spices, and coconuts, and chutneys, and sweets made with sugar *and* condensed milk. I wanted the book to begin with me weighing nothing and end with me turning curvy, my belly flowing over my jeans. I wanted to flavor the book with the salty warnings of my grandmother to avoid white men who don't wash their arses, so unlike us back home. I did not want you to laugh.

I wanted to write a lie.

SL: I would like to start with this business of wanting to write a lie, what a concept? Why did you choose this piece? What does it speak to in the broader sense for you about your writing?

RF: I think as an immigrant, which is how I always place myself, there's a question people often ask me, "Where am I from *originally*?" And I say, "I'm *always* from Sri Lanka." I'm not originally from somewhere and now from somewhere else. I'm always the place that raised me, the culture that raised me. So, that means you're kind of carrying two things with you when you're in the US. As an immigrant and as a writer in the United States, it's a whole other thing where there's an expectation of people like me and what we write about. There's an expectation of the things we are expected to write about, so if we write against that, then there's the salutation of, "Wow, she's breaking the mold and writing this other thing."

There is this kind of odd negotiation that you're always making when you write in the United States as an immigrant. What are you faithful to? What is the story you're telling? Why are you telling that story? Are you telling it because it's the most popular story? Are you telling it because you want to actually tell the true story? It's this blurry place. I also always say that all fiction is nonfiction, and so this is also a book that is in-between those spaces. Like I said, I just finished it, and someone was asking me, what is it? I said it's prose. I'm not calling it fiction or nonfiction. It's prose. And what it's going to be is an exploration of memory in some ways and how memory is also never authentic. It's not ever true. It's always this kind of mess. So that's why I chose this piece, because I think it speaks to the heart of some of those issues that I'm trying to think about in the book.

SL: I love that, and I do believe that's very true, that memory is a falsehood. We're always adding different pieces that were never there, right?! And you speak of place, can you tell me how place might impact voice? How do you define voice and orality?

RF: If I think about the things that I write, there is a very strong sense of where I came from, no matter what. Even if I am writing the lie, even if I'm writing the American memoir, whatever it is that I'm doing, there is a very strong sense that this is not someone who grew up in the United States and did an MFA program and learned how to write. It's not that kind of writing. It is a very messy kind of writing that comes from a culture that is also messy but also acknowledges and embraces its mess. But there is an order to that mess as well. The prose that I write is very long. It's these rambling sentences. There's lots of characters in it. There's lots of references to things outside the small, contained piece of the thing that you're writing about. I think it's very easy to place myself inside my work. It is not different in some sense than how I live or talk or do the things that I do. And if you're an immigrant, I think there is a space that is a creation of a world in which you fit, that is possible to do when you're far from the place where you actually fit, which is your home, from the place that you feel most at home. So that, I think, is my way of thinking about place in writing, in how I write.

SL: And how do you define voice within that?

RF: I read a really interesting quote the other day. I want to say it's Francine Prose—I like Francine Prose very much—however, I think it was a quote by someone else. And sadly, it was on Instagram, and I think I may have even taken a screenshot of it and reposted it in my story. I often repost things because of my students, and I want them to be paying attention. It was something about how to teach voice. The thing is, you can't *teach* voice. You can't teach any of it. It's what it is that you come with. It's your own personal alphabet. And we can teach as professors or teachers, we can teach how to string that alphabet together to make certain words.

You start with ABCD, and now you can say "bat" and "dog" and "see Jane Run," or whatever Jane is doing, but you have to come with that alphabet. I think of voice in that way. I think my own voice is developing over the course of practicing new languages, new phrasings, new ways of putting things together and new things that I want to talk about.

The book that I just finished has a very different feel to it than the other books that I wrote. But I couldn't write that book without those other books, that accumulation of things. So that is how I think about voice. It's something that you create constantly, and you create it from something that's very internal to you, that you bring into the space and then you use it to make the thing that you're trying to make.

SL: It's the ever-shifting sculpture or a shapeshifter.

RF: Right. If you said there was some particular thing called a particular voice, then that means that everything that you ever want to write fits into that voice. But that would mean that we are also immutable, unchangeable static things, but we are not. Cadence might be a better way to describe it. There is a cadence we recognize in a particular writer. George Saunders, Jamaica Kincaid, José Saramago, but the voice is the one they create anew for each work.

SL: Last question is in terms of your writing, you've talked about the perspective of the immigrant, and also existing within another culture or within other cultures. How do you see your writing as it might be positioned or assigned within the tradition of a genre?

RF: I think if there was a genre that I would want as a label over everything that I ever write is as a social justice activist. That's the genre under which all these other things fit. If people were shelving books by people's lives rather than the thing that they created, then that's where it would fit. That's where any book that I wrote—poetry, fiction, nonfiction—would fit. Anybody who reads the various things that I write can see those. That's what's moving all of it, at some level. And it comes from where I was born and how I was raised, the family I was born into. The way we look at the world is always this sense of what is it that we are doing for that world? How do we exist with the people around us? How are we moving all of ourselves forward somehow or uplifting each other? That is the primary focus. Even the things that are very personal that I'm writing, they're still written with consciousness of something outside, something bigger than my little life.

***Ru Freeman** is a Sri Lankan and American writer, poet, and activist whose work appears internationally. She is the author of* Bon Courage: Essays on Inheritance, Citizenship & A Creative Life *(2023), the short-story collection,* Sleeping Alone *(2022), and the widely translated novels* A Disobedient Girl *(2009) and* On Sal Mal Lane *(2013), a* New York Times *Editor's Choice Book. She is the editor of the anthology,* Extraordinary Rendition: American Writers on Palestine *(2015) and co-editor of* Indivisible: Global Leaders on Shared Security *(2018). She is a winner of the Mariella Gable Award for Fiction, and the JH Kafka Prize for Fiction by an American Woman. She teaches creative writing in the US and abroad.*

Felice Belle

"the following does not depict any actual person or event"

when the detectives come to question you
keep gardening, lifting boxes, cleaning the gills off the fish

new yorkers can't stop moving
you need to pick up your kids

you wish you could be of more help
but you're late for the airport, class

if there's cash on the body, it's not a robbery
every suspect has means, motive, and opportunity

the evidence speaks

the president of the abstinence club could be the rapist
they recycle storylines

it's not the first time the killer is an adult,
pretending to be a high-school student

trust your gut

a patriot can be turned
we can't all be good

it's the third law of physics
equal and opposite
can't have the high without the low

if it feels personal,
you're too close to the case

PB: Tell us about the origin of this poem, Felice.

FB: I'm a huge fan of *Law & Order*, the franchise in general, but specifically *Special Victims Unit*. And I have watched so many episodes that I literally think of myself as a detective. What's funny is my best friend, in addition to being a writer, is also a licensed private investigator. So, she finds it offensive that I think I'm a detective. A few years ago, we wrote a two-woman show called *Other Women*, and this poem began as a monologue where I was making my case for my crime solving abilities. A lot of the lines reference plot points from *Law & Order* and other procedurals. But I think what's interesting is when you string them all together, it becomes this whole other narrative of its own, which I appreciate about poetry in general, but this poem specifically.

PB: In this poem, that's such an interesting source. But of course, you bring so much more to it. You bring not only New York, but a whole dynamic, a whole system of personal perspective about *Law & Order*. Tell us about how your poem speaks to the social world, that this poem lives in and speaks for.

FB: When it comes to storytelling, specifically how we tell stories in American culture, there's a good guy and a bad guy. There's very little nuance. The truth is, we've all got a spectrum within us, and we make choices every day to pick good over evil or whatever. This poem is aiming to get at those nuances. The idea that "the president of the abstinence club could be the rapist," right? Whichever identity I present, there are a bunch of other identities that are not coming to the forefront. How those contradictions play in the world, internally and externally, is something this poem is moving through. Same with a line like "a patriot can be turned." The fact is belief systems can change. I find myself challenged by the world constantly, reevaluating things I hold as unassailable truths. What do I do when my belief system is destroyed by the realities of the world? How do I create a new one out of the rubble?

PB: I know that orality is very much a part of what you present and I'm wondering how that plays into your composition. How does the oral recitation of your poems become an aspect of your composition?

FB: For me there's never been a separation between the composed poem on the page and the orality of it. Those things are very much intertwined. My parents are from the Caribbean, specifically Guyana, South America. To this day they can recite poems they memorized in their youth. The idea of the poem being alive when it's recited is something that's in my DNA.

I also use the orality of the poem as an editing tool. If I'm reading the poem to myself out loud, I can hear things that are not working within the meter of the poem, but also sentiments that ring false or untrue. I want it to feel like the poem has its own rhythm. I want there to be a musicality to it. I want there to be moments of slowing down and speeding up and I think orality can do that, but I also think the text on the page can do that. And so those two things combined help me to create a mood and music to the poem itself.

PB: It's interesting that you bring up the orality of your parents and the traditions from the Caribbean, but you also come from a tradition of science and engineering. Tell us how your background—so eclectic—influences your sense of composition and your sense of tradition.

FB: I love science as a field because it's all about discovery, right? Having an idea, thinking it's true, and then going into the process of whether it holds up under different circumstances over time. I used to be the type of writer who had to write things as is, and I think that might have been the science influence. Like if the chair was orange in real life it's going to be orange in the poem because that is what was "true".

Poetry has softened me a bit, so it's less about the literal truth and more about the emotional truth. How do I get to the truest expression of the thing? Another overlap between science and poetry is an idea that comes up in my poem "ne me quitte pas", that words have a place value, in the same way numbers do. If I can construct a poem with each word in its proper place, then the cumulative effect of the poem will have the greatest value. There's a precision when it comes to the editing and revision process that is informed by my science background.

PB: You've talked a little bit about the use of orality, maybe tell us a little bit about the use of typography in your poems.

FB: Early on, I was taught that the poem on the page is your notation for the reader. So in an ideal world, anyone can pick up this poem and have the reading experience that I might deliver if I was reading it in front of the audience. And that's true to some extent. But definitely when it comes to the construction of the line, the number of words, the breath, where the breaks are, those are very much conscious in a musical notation kind of way. Hold this for half a beat, this one's going to be a full whole note. That kind of thing is always at play when I think about the poem on the page.

PB: Who are the poets that you hearkened to that first brought you into this journey?

FB: Two of my earliest influences were E.E. Cummings and Ntozake Shange. It's because of them that almost all my poems are written in lowercase. That just felt right to me. There's something about all the words and letters being the same size that feels like, this is how you do poetry. One of the things I loved about E.E. Cummings was his playfulness and wit. And Ntozake expanded my idea of what's possible in poetry, in terms of form and content. My introduction to her work was the play *For Colored Girls*, which she calls a "choreopoem", a word she invented. I love that if the word doesn't exist for whatever it is you are doing, you can create it. If there's no genre to hold the leaps and risks you want to take, you can make your own, which is what she did. I also love discovering new art and artists through a writer's work, and *For Colored Girls* is filled with so many references to songs, musicians, historical events and figures, that it becomes a map to the worlds that influenced her own.

Felice Belle *is the author of* Viscera *(Etruscan Press, 2023). Her writing has been published in journals including* Oral Tradition, Bum Rush the Page, *and* UnCommon Bonds: Women Reflect on Race and Friendship. *Her playwriting credits include* Other Women, Joy in Repetition, *and* It Is Reasonable to Expect. *She has performed at the Apollo Theater, Joe's Pub, and TEDWomen. She received a BKLYN Incubator grant to develop the documentary-style theater performance* We Hold These Truths. *She is a lecturer in the low-residency MFA Program at St. Francis College in Brooklyn and Artists Network Director for the global nonprofit Narrative 4.*

Alycia D. Jenkins

"Girl in the Yellow Dress"

I stand
with gun in hand
my eyes are blazing
The wind is hollow
The spirits sing
They telling me to take souls
to kill
to protect
the time is here
for many to walk
on water
and become the Jesus
we've always been
with guns in hand
we be too militant
for the weak ones
wearing white symbolizing
power
death
spirit
as we cast
the Devil back to hell
with the spell
'Moi c'est femme en le jeune
Robe danse avec les ancêtres
Et nuit, et nuit, et nuit,
Ils sont blues, ils sont blues
Le jeu lasser le jeu danse, lasser le jeu
Danse dans tes yeux
Dans tes yeux et nuit, et nuit.'

SL: I've had the pleasure of sharing a stage with you a couple of times! Before we get to that, why don't you tell us about this page? Why did you choose this page and how does it represent your practice?

ADJ: This piece is at the end of my book, *The Laughing Elephant In The Room*. It's the very last stanza in the prose, and it's my favorite part of the book. The end of the book is where I focus on my African American feminist ideology and practice in regard to taking care of Black women, all our voices from the young to the elders to the ancestors. "The Girl in the Yellow Dress," talks about how Black women can and have come together in a way that honors the feminine. Yellow is a symbol of the goddess Oshun from the ancient African religion in the Yoruba tradition. I was thinking about you, the audience, when I wrote this. I was told by my ancestors, all the women on my mother's and my father's side, to write about the girl in the yellow dress. I was sitting at a cafe in New Haven, Connecticut at Yale's bookstore, Attica. There were these portraits of Black women, who were multiple skin shades, each wearing a yellow dress. I forgot the name of the artist, but seeing their work inspired me to write that piece, but I already received the message. I just needed more information in order for me to write because I can be a bit stubborn.

SL: You work across many mediums; I am curious about how you compose your words. Do you compose with performance in mind? I'm asking that because you also have studied dance, theater, you're a playwright, you've also done spoken word, and slam poetry. What is the difference for you between what comes out of your body onto the page or what you do on the stage?

ADJ: When I'm doing something, like when I do my playwriting, I think of the stage as I think of everything. On this day, I must think about the lighting, costuming, makeup, hair, sound, and spacing. When I wrote this book, I was not thinking about performance. The book is written in prose, but the structure of it is biblical, meaning it looks like it's the "Book of Psalms," or the "Book of Matthew." It's written in that stanza space. It was automatic, so I wrote my book in that regard. Once I started reading it out loud, I was like, "Oh, this can be sung. This can be spoken." So, I guess I'm an automatic spoken-word writer. I was not thinking about having it be spoken out loud when I was writing it. In the space of me writing my book, because I've been writing it since 2012, in 2016, the idea of this being a book was strong because of the support from my friends and family who were with me at the beginning stages of this process. At first, it started as a long poem and then became a book.

Once I started dancing with it, then I was like, "Okay, this can be performed through dance." I was in the creative mind of being like, "We can do a dance theater thing like Alvin Ailey." I could put music to it, and I can find themes and music that match the theme in my book. I've been a spoken word poet since I was 16, but I am more of a poet.

SL: This brings me to another question, how do you define voice? Does that change depending on what medium you're working in? Does voice, for example, mean something different through dance than it does through your written and spoken word?

ADJ: It does change. When I'm writing for spoken word, I make sure to read it out loud to myself, and I make sure to listen to the message I'm conveying in between the lines, and that helps me breathe in between how I tell my story. I make sure my story is told and can be reached by the audience. When I do spoken word poetry, I'm very concise and precise. I'm calm, constantly scratching stuff out. I'm constantly making my journal ugly or making the poem look ugly, just so that I can fix everything. I grew up in the church. The church was the first place that I was able to perform and speak to an audience.

In crafting the book, I utilized the experience of growing up in the church and being in the choir. This also included memories of hearing the pastor to preach, his breathing tones, and all of that as ingredients in my spoken word. This is why when a lot of people hear me do my spoken word, they hear that I sound almost country, kind of southern. I also sound a little bit Caribbean, because I'm half Haitian. I grew up with my mother singing to me and listening to Haitian Creole Music, Cuban music, and listening to gospel. So, I utilize all the things in my cultural background, from the Evangelical Church, which has Baptist roots, to listening to a mix of Haitian Creole Music. I mixed all of that into my book.

For my written word that's not necessarily spoken all the time, I make sure my story is told. I ensure that people can experience what I'm saying. I want you to feel the words coming off the page. I want you to see the words coming off the page. I think of my writing in regards to the laughing elephant in the room as somewhat cartoonish, so that the words can fly off the page and become its own thing. Kind of like a spell working. When I am writing a play, I want the story to be told in a concise way, but I get real deep with it.

Within my spoken word, I'm a little more lighthearted. I go far, but not deep or far enough within spoken word. My plays go far enough. My written words go far enough.

SL: What I gather is that voice, for you, across all your mediums, is visceral, it's the unsaid. The voice includes the ingredients of your culture and identity. It's an incantation. It's ethereal but also very rooted. Would you say that is true for how you see and experience voice in your work? Also, is there anything else you want to add as we wrap?

ADJ: Yes, and I want to go back to being rooted. It's a rooted tree that moves. African Americans in America, those of us who descend from the enslaved, which I am heavily rooted in in my work as a girl of Mississippi heritage from the westside of Chicago, I've noticed that Black folk in this country have always been forced to flee. As a child, we were always on the move; we never had stable housing. We've always been forced to move.

We, as a diaspora, have been forced to forget about where we came from. We were forced to forget that, but we never forgot it though. So, like when Black folk migrated from the South to the North, they were forced to forget being southern. They had to assimilate to the northern way and had to get rid of their country accent so they could switch their language and their voice to access work. They were still rooted because Black folks still went to Mississippi and still went to Alabama for family reunions. You feel me?

As far as the Haitian side of me, my mother's mother allegedly immigrated to America in the 1950's. I am not a Black immigrant; my grandmother was. As far as I know, my grandmother's life is a complete mystery, but I do have some inkling that she is of Haitian descent. She was possibly forced to speak English not just assimilate into the American way, but blend into the African American way, in order for her to fit into the box that America labeled as black and white. It was in that restriction that you would think that we within the Black diaspora would suffocate, and sometimes we do. When we go back to who we are, we're rooted into who we are, and we dance with that tree. Listen to the trees. Some trees aren't your friend, but some trees are. I have 10-11 plants in my house, and my house plants are like trees, in my opinion. They move with me so I will never forget where I come from, no matter where I'm at. And I'm constantly going to remember where I come from.

The rootedness is multifaceted because the tree roots always find a way to water, and Black folks always find a way to water. It doesn't matter where we come from. Whether we come from the Caribbean, Mississippi, Alabama, or Chicago. This is what I find fascinating, that I keep a constant thread in all my work that white folk can't figure out how it is that we're still alive. We're still alive because the tree lives a long life. We're still alive because our memory is that of the elephant. The elephant has a long memory, so do Black people. And no, we are not lost.

Alycia D. Jenkins *is an emerging scholar, a freelance teaching/performing artist, poet, writer, and environmentalist. Ms. Jenkins is a Trinity College graduate. She is a proud African American feminist who believes in the power of liberation of Black and American Descendants of slavery families. Ms. Jenkins advocates to change the world one city at a time. Ms. Jenkins currently resides in Connecticut.* ***"Girl in the Yellow Dress" is an excerpt from the book,*** **The Laughing Elephant In The Room** ***(Renewing Your Mind Ink, 2022).***

Jerome Rothenberg

"That Dada Strain"

the zig zag mothers of the gods
of science   the lunatic fixed stars
& pharmacies
fathers who left the tents of anarchism
unguarded
the arctic bones
strung out on saint germain
like tom toms
living light bulbs
aphrodisia
"art is junk" the urinal
says "dig a hole
"& swim in it"
a message from the grim computer
"ye are hamburgers"

PB: Jerry, hearing you perform, I realize you don't do readings, you do experiences. You managed to bring in so many different elements—physical presence, the communication between you and your audience. How has that developed in your work under so many different rubrics and genres?

JR: Yeah, well some of it has developed in collaboration with other artists, particularly musicians. Straight poetry reading would be a different tone, but I started working with the musicians, particularly percussionists and contrabassists. So long time collaboration with Virtual Turetsky, a contrabassist, and other musicians, changed my way of reading because it reinforced the rhythm, got me into the rhythm of what I had already written. The "zigzag mothers of the gods of science, the lunatic fixed stock," and I can beat it out that way.

It was a process, and we were—I and many others—getting into performance and the first time I did a serious performance of poems from *That Dada Strain*, a student had made me a Hugo Ball costume. So, I was also playing Hugo Ball. *That Dada Strain* was transformed into a theater piece by Luke Morrison into what he called the Center for Theater Science and Research. And I was the leading actor in that. I don't know if I played myself or Hugo Ball or both, but it became a theatrical event first here in San Diego, and then in upstate New York, and with a cast. There are a number of people involved in the performance. But it was to emphasize the musical side of what could be seen anyway in the writing, but I learned to do it that way. I hadn't done it that way before. And that has stayed with me. Where appropriate, sometimes one wants to tone that down, just keep on a more level field.

PB: Maybe tell us about how your exploration of prime cultures has enriched your sense of the orality and physicality of poetry.

JR: It was done in celebration of my own discovery of the roots and sources of poetry and the universality of the poetry experience and how developed it is throughout the world. Civilized and pre-civilized and hunter and gatherer and all stages, all possibilities. And in the same way that we were creating new forms of our own under that impulse of the avant-garde experimental, I was finding other forms of poetry so often tied up with performance in oral cultures.

PB: I'm curious about your sense of the nature of identity as is expressed in poetry because it seems as if you've brought so many kinds of identity, whether it's costumed as Hugo Ball, or being with the Seneca people, or your explorations into the Holocaust with *Poland/1931* and *Khurbn*. Tell us about how that multiplicity of identities has worked its way into your work.

JR: Well, particularly from the mid-60s till the end of the '70s there was a series of works. *Poland,* and well *Technicians of the Sacred* came in 1968, which tried to bring all these things together in the form of an anthology or assemblage covering with a particular emphasis on orature as it is sometimes called—oral poetry. You know, performance in a multiplicity of cultures. And then to explore ancestral sources of my own in the world of Jewish mystics, thieves, and madmen, in a book pulled in 1931 in the early '70s. And by then we were spending time at the Seneca Indian Reservation in western New York State and a book came out of that called *A Seneca Journal*. And one would have to look into that and see how, as not a Seneca, but you know, being there, impact that it was having on me, which the book expresses, but it doesn't end there.

Other things keep coming into it. Curiously too, *Poland/1931* was completed when I was living on the Seneca Indian Reservation. So, a Jew among the Indians, "What am I doing in this strange place that these people with strange eyes—could be trouble, he says could be, could be." There was that, and then later in the '70s, I tried to bring some of that together with the early experimental modernists from before our time, you know, with the dadas. In a little book called *THAT DADA STRAIN*. So there Jews and Indians came together in what David Nelson was calling my Jewish surrealist vaudeville.

A noted poet and anthologist, ***Jerome Rothenberg (1931-2024)*** *authored or edited more than 70 books of poetry. Rothenberg received grants from the Guggenheim Foundation and the National Endowment for the Arts. His awards include two PEN Oakland Josephine Miles Literary Awards, two PEN Center USA West Translation Awards, and the San Diego Public Library Local Author Lifetime Achievement Award.*

Fred D'Aguiar

"M-C Mami Wata Channels C.J. 'Fiery' Obasi" (i.m. Gboyega Odubango)

Mami Wata say   all must stand an' be counted
    We stand   you count for us

Mami Wata say   all a-you   balance on one leg
    We balance   children on our backs goods on/in our heads

Mami Wata say   everybody hop, skip an' jump
    We move our best foot forward for you

Mami Wata say   plant your feet, grip land, even as you leap for sky
    We harvest, pour libations, sing-drum-dance, birth, an' bury our dead

Mami Wata say   people dey be people, different *and* one an' de same
    We see ourselves in each other   in de mirror o' de sea

Mami Wata say   flesh an' blood come from womb o' de sea
    We dive into sea folds, sea rolls   for memory

Mami Wata say   current waves, rip an' sew, tear an' mend, fabric o' de sea
    We study salt wata   sea-geography see history

Mami Wata say   I spot my many selves in all a-you
    We see ourselves in Mami Wata

Note: Based on a children's game that we played in the village of Airy Hall, on the East Coast of the Demerara River, in Guyana, a game in which one child issues reasonable commands and everyone obeys. Those who are too slow to respond to the call, drop out of the game, until one person is left. That last person wins, and in the next round of the game, earns the chance to issue commands to the group.

SL: What inspired you to choose this page? Did you talk a little bit about the call and response and the musicality of it?

FD: In the 70's and 80's, in the UK—I left in 1992 for a job in the States—poetry as a form was largely page-centered. Rap was happening, Calypso too, and reggae DJs (speaking over the B-side of a track, and 'toasting' at live events, that is, a DJ talking to basslines). There was also Linton Kwesi Johnson's "Dread Beat An' Blood," an electrifying collection of his voiceprint poetry put to music and presented in book form.

Those of us who were trained in English Poetry, which is a British poetry tradition embedded in the Romantics of the eighteenth and nineteenth centuries poetry (think Wordsworth, Keats, Shelley, Coleridge and Lord Byron!), we were caught up, nay, trapped like flies in an ointment, in the English idea of the page which herded us away from orality.

As I've aged, I've gone back to a coalition of the page and stage in my work, to finding ways to represent voice in print and remain obedient to the rigors of sight and line and stanza revisions in my work and in my teaching as much as humanly (and humanely) possible. Even though I don't do the cafe performances, the standup and throw-down, in your face, embodied dance and delivery of poetry, there's still a part of me that sometimes feels like I want to grab a mic and deliver what I can only phrase in a borrowed term, an echolocation of spirit. I understand from that impulse to connect to an audience, what Kamau Brathwaite calls the crucial audience dimension of poetry, that love of community is central to my art, not least because I love listening to rap, reggae, calypso, and so on.

My poem, "Mami Wata," showcases call and response and is my homage to my Caribbean upbringing. I spent ages 2 to 12 in Guyana, before returning to London where I was born of Guyanese parents. The poem is a commission for the film, titled, *Mami Wata*, by Nigerian filmmaker, C.J. Obasi. Shot in spectacular 16 millimeter black and white, the tones of black skin and night and day are nothing short of sumptuous. The time of the film is slow, deliberate, and lyric in its declared love of comprehension of a story. Nigeria's Nollywood is renowned for its action flicks. *Mami Wata* is an outlier.

Mami Wata got me thinking about my Caribbean heritage and its continuity with Africa. Not divided by an ocean, but united by one, if we see the Middle Passage as a library of sorts for contemplation of the ancestors buried in the Atlantic. An underwater road of bones, a reliquary not for lost souls, but for recoverable bodies and 'throwaway' lives waiting for our attention. The Middle Passage, then, from Charles Johnson's novel to now, presents a miracle of continuity. How, with all the destruction of the trans-Atlantic slave trade going on, did our ancestors succeed in carrying in their spines, hearts, and minds, the culture for our present survival, despite the assaults on their bodies? How did we reproduce it when we were transplanted and have these amazing oral creations that testify to that heritage?

And so my poem sides with oral remembrance over forgetting and neglect. I replay a childhood game from my years in Guyana as a form for the poem.

SL: What about your work being received on the page versus performance? You talked a bit about that just now, can you speak more to how this plays out across the different genres that you write? Also, is it different when you are thinking about orality versus the page? Does it depend on what genre you are working within—like prose versus poetry versus a play? I recall you once said that you like to switch lanes as a writer, is it all the same for your approach to your work?

FD: That's a great and complicated question, Shanta! In the course of my day, if I see an image that's arresting, and it's a clear image, it may be put into prose or it could be a poem (though these divisions mean very little really). If I hear a line, it might be dialogue from a story, but it could easily be the line that is spoken by a character. I do find that a lot of pieces of language come along, cross dressing, as it were, as one thing or/and another. You put it into a poem, but it could easily be that this person's speech hits the margins and therefore results in paragraphs. Or it could be a scene in a play because so much of what we do is dialogic.

We have a presumed listener—could be the self, could be a loved one, it could be family or community or a ghost(s)—but there's definitely a sense of call and response in our thinking when we talk, we have somebody (or bodies) talking back or pushing back to make us qualify our speech and move down the page and build on the exchange and interchange. That I-speaker, who may be plural as well, that is, splintered, makes sense of a complex set of feelings.

The Socratic dialogue—a buildup of meaning or at least an exploration of it, through questions and answers—between one person and an 'other' or a communal "we" where different people take the microphone and take turns, may be one person channeling a collective. The writer is multiple in that sense. So, I do see pieces of speech and language dropping into these areas that are artificially demarcated as poetry, fiction or drama, while being more accurately, intersectional, moving across and between forms and indebted to multiplicity.

What form the writing or speech act takes may be a function of the pressure of speech versus the length of an idea and its depth. I find I'm more suited as a writer to longer contemplative acts, that is, serial poems that explore a theme or themes from several angles. Or the longer chapters of a novel that delve into an idea's many invitations. I prefer the long take. Some of my poems are short, though, sonnet-like in length and form, if not entirely loyal to the tradition of the sonnet (since I'm interested in bucking tradition!). Longer poems appear to be deeper dives. Or, if the idea and feeling is a building, then the longer work tries out various exits and entrances to that building.

I'm interested in Black being as well. That is, the outside and inside of people designated belonging to the Black race. In other words, I accept that race is a social construct and embrace the fact that Black being is something, some quality of consciousness, that's not shaped by whiteness even if influenced by mixing with it. I am suspicious of Blackness defined by the surround sound of whiteness as a negative reinforcer of color.

When I think of Thelma Goldberg's term of 'post-race,' I think of this imaginary that does a Tracy Smith and heads straight into space for the freedom of contemplation not defined by negative social and economic forces. It's jazz, say, the improvisatory spaces made by Cecil Taylor's free compositions. It's dance too, say, Jawole Willa Jo Zolla—Urban Bush Women, bodily (and bodacious) displays. It's *da* blues (Ma Rainey, Bessie Smith, Robert Johnson!) because it comes from deep inside as some pressure, desire, hunger, ambition, and necessary dream. So I am interested in black being outside of the space of the white/black binary of race.

Black being, as an interior gaze, is for me beautiful and bountiful.

SL: Your answer flows into the question about voice. Does the definition of voice change for you? How do you define voice? Is the voice dictated based on place? What do you think about voice especially within the different modalities of your expression?

FD: My voice is plural, partly because I am plural (Whitman's, I contain multitudes!). I see the change in my sound, the sound of my voice when I move from poetry to fiction. And also, when I hear something that I try to sing, (I can't sing!), I sound different, so I do see a single voice. It might be singing atonally, but it's definitely a voice sounding like many different voices, especially when I do different things. So, I think it's plural and the sound is in part dictated by the sense of lines and of sentences, stanzas and paragraphs, their many rhythms. I tend to like something at the end that will be an upsurge of thinking and insight rather than something that declines into doom and gloom. When I think of Guyana, I idealize that space of my childhood before the interference and growing up awareness of the politics of space. Colonization messed up a lot of indigenous spaces!

I have these habits of a childhood experience in a place before it was spoiled by the ravages of colonial (and post-!) awareness. I embody both of William Blake's songs, that is, both innocence and experience simultaneously. I see the landscape, the flora and fauna, and the person together in a shared space as defined by indigenous philosophies and ways of life in the Amazon region for thousands of years and informed by African ways of being that survived in the bodies of the enslaved transplanted to those places. Those habits are tied to my voice, hence my claim of plural voices, of communal dimensions to utterance rather than a singular capitalized or commodified and insular voice.

SL: Did you want to add anything as we wrap up?

FD: Two ideas. One is a QR code for the book that brings us to a website or something. The other one is a fun one, it is to build a playlist. Get a song suggestion from each of us who contributed to the anthology.

SL: I recall you always talked about building a playlist for your students and encouraging your students to have a writing playlist! I'd have a hard time doing this myself. Like writing something while the music is playing. That's interesting asking people and then actually almost having that as another dimension for the anthology!

FD: Yes! For my track I want the great Nina Simone's, "Feeling Good"!

SL: Wow, I like that. And thank you for your time.

Fred D'Aguiar *is a celebrated British-Guyanese poet, prose writer, playwright, Professor of English at UCLA, whose career has spanned 35 years. D'Aguiar's many accolades include: Guyana Prizes for poetry and fiction and the UK's Society of Author's Cholmondeley Award. As a writer, D'Aguiar engages in what he describes as the writer's "inevitable contract" to contend with both the present and past. His most recent nonfiction book,* Year of Plagues: a Memoir of 2020, *published by HarperCollins in 2021, recounts experiences battling the plagues of cancer and anti-Black racism during the COVID19 pandemic. His latest poetry collection is* Naming the Dead *(2023).*

Diane Raptosh

"Fourteen"

I know when it begins to stink, you've got to do something.... You have to go round, making suitable noises.
–Mary Midgley

Fourteen
Words,
14 or
14/88
refers
to
these
14-word
slogans
penned
by white
supremacist
David
Lane:

We
must
secure
the
existence
of
our
people
and
a
future
for
white
children. earth.

Because
the
beauty
of
the
White
Aryan
Woman
must
not
perish
from
the

Because the white speaks the white
Secure the white future Because the white *For*
Because the white *Because*
Not the earth because white perish Earth
Perish beauty the woman Earth speaks the *White Must*
because white speaks Because White speaks *Perish*
Because White Existence Earth speaks *perish*
Because White
speaks white
Because the white *Because*

Speak because Earth because woman
Because speak of the *from* of beauty
        Speak of *because the not perish*
          Speak from the *of* of the earth

PB: When you first submitted this poem, you said that you thought you had a poem that would speak to the project. Please tell us about why you chose this poem and how it speaks to *Sign & Breath.*

DR: Sure, this double sonnet seemed like it might be especially appropriate for this anthology. The second half of the poem feels especially oral. It came to me in a kind of earth-voice, as a disruption and remix of the words from the white supremacists. For this collection of American sonnets, I had been thinking about and researching the number 14—all it stands for. Turns out this otherwise magical number has disturbing significance for white supremacists.

I wanted the second 14 lines of the double sonnet to sing in a voice that contrasted that of the white supremacists. Again, I wanted to disrupt and remix the words from the hateful slogans. What emerged was that Ur-voice fighting for the dignity of Earth, using the very words of the white supremacists against their original purposes. I couldn't help but notice that some of the words within those awful slogans were among our most urgent and necessary words; I wanted them to be repurposed: *beauty, woman,* and *earth.* Again, the source from which the second 14 lines of this piece is spoken felt like the very voice of the Earth, or perhaps Earth's representative—a ringing both in and beyond me. That voice felt supremely powerful. So, I thought that in a discussion about voice and orality, this would be a good one to choose.

PB: I'm curious, as this poem emerged, about 14. I didn't know that that was an element of the white supremacist, but of course it's also 14 lines. What about the line here, Diane, the way you've constructed it on the page, and the way you hear it.

DR: The first three rows of 14 lines in the initial half of the double sonnet are one- or two-word lines—including the actual white supremacist slogans: three stacks of minimalist lines posed in very stark terms surrounded by whitespace. The voice of the Earth occurs in the second set of 14 lines; they did not want to be linear. Those lines wanted to come out in a more organic way. So, I forged and turned these lines in less predictable places. And in that process, adjectives became nouns, prepositions became nouns. It was as if the Earth was saying, *I don't care about the parts of speech as you have categorized them. What I want to focus on is preservation, the cherishing. Preserve the earth,* not *perish.* I felt that I was receiving these signals from Earth itself, uttered across the page in the ways, more or less that they appear now. The Earth speaks in non-linear terms.

PB: What is your feeling about the tradition of the sonnet?

DR: I am obsessed with the sonnet and all it can do. I've been experimenting with double, triple, and even quintuple sonnets. It is a pleasure to find and reconceive what one can do with sets of 14 lines. For starters, they provide an opportunity to pose an argument and employ a volta or turn. In this double sonnet, the turn happens after the first 14 lines, when the words are repurposed. The second set of 14 lines itself turns at "Speak because Earth because woman / Because speak of the *from* of beauty / Speak of *because the not perish* / Speak from the *of* of the earth."

I've been writing almost exclusively sonnets for the past decade because I needed the limitations of form to help set me free. The sonnet's 14 lines provide a perfect small space in which to begin to turn things around. Big enough for the voice of Earth to come through.

PB: You're bringing a new perspective altogether, which is that the voice is neither personal nor typographical, but possessed of this third quality from beneath.

DR: When I thought about the questions posed for this anthology, I found myself in a paradox. I believe what Baudelaire said about the poet: "The poet rejoices in the privilege that he can at will be both himself and another, like a lost soul searching for a body he enters when he wishes into any character, for him all is vacancy." The voice of the poet is multivalent. I don't quite trust myself when I try to describe what constitutes *voice*. The poet's voice should entail both self and something larger than the self to reach all selves that poetry longs to sing to. Whatever roars from the human depths must inhere in the individual self and expand far beyond the throat of the poet.

***Diane Raptosh** is the author of several books including* American Amnesiac *(Etruscan, 2013), which was Longlisted for the 2013 National Book Award. Her other titles from Etruscan include* Trio, Human Directional, Dear Z, *and* I Eric America. *She is the recipient of three fellowships in literature from the Idaho Commission of the Arts, and holds the Eyck-Berringer Endowed Chair in English at The College of Idaho. She teaches creative writing and literature as well as directs the program in criminal justice/prison studies.*

Shanta Lee

Everything doesn't make it to swallow

Everything doesn't rise to chew

They taught me about here

bout the ways some bodies require, demand to be sucked in

Taken...whole

Some bodies stay untasted,

unwafered

No body, no kill

No blood

"Hallowed Hunted Body"

Sucking whole bodies started with nuns ended with his body began in a church
Her body, his body, that body turned the wafer I could never have
He made women writhe. He made foam surface from mouths,
telling us we were his sea, he our Poseidon with how chests heaved
higher than waves with how legs were never stilled
Then came time to take him, in mouths, the worthy mouths.
That wafer, his body that wine turned them all vampiric
He IS our maker training tongues to hunger.

Who has a to give a fuck about original sin with this?

This is the garden where we learned how the mouth works
with eyes, with tongue and through learning us real good through ache
He whose body was wafer was my first, You can't have
Mama never let'em have my body. On Sundays, I sat on hard pew
Maybe if I tasted him like they do, drink his blood like they do,
eyes wet with want like they do, then I woulda known how the tongue
got wildly tamed. A wild thing tasting original hunger taught by pimps
at the pulpit

Mama never gave 'em, but they still took, took my body whole

Trained in how to want to devour a man
Trained in how to become like him

A body, my body the body the wafer they crave to put the fire out in their throat

PB: Shanta, why did you choose this piece for our anthology and how does it represent your practice?

SL: Thinking about a practice is a strange thing for me maybe because I write across different genres, and I also work in the medium of photography. If I really think about it, my only practice is to try to pay close attention. And across all my creative work, try to go beneath the surface and face the work outward so that people are encapsulated or forced to sit with themselves and ask the hard questions that the work is inviting them to ask. Other times, my practice involves encouraging a viewer or audience member's intellectual tango with their own questions.

This piece is included in my chapbook, *This Is How They Teach You How to Want It...The Slaughter: A Field Guide for the Hunted & the Hunter, The Dead-Alive, The Live-Dead Ones, The...* (Harbor Editions, 2024). The work explores the very old and mythic idea of the wild hunt. The wild hunt is a story about ghost riders who are essentially hunting something. There are also the tapestries at The MET Cloisters that illustrate the stages of a hunt (and the eventual catching of) a unicorn.

I was fascinated with exploring what this kind of hunt—predator and prey—relationship looks like between humans alongside our relationship to/within the natural world. I was also contemplating the widening gap between what is out in the world, in a field versus how it may end up on our plates or nourishing our lives in some other way.

PB: I love that phrase "intellectual tango." It's interesting that you bring up so many different points of entry. I'm thinking about the fact that you are not only a poet (although we shouldn't use only and poet in the same sentence). You do many other things, and you are a multifaceted artist. How does orality or voice play a role in the various modalities of art that you have been exploring?

SL: Lately, I've been saying to a few people off and on, I've been interested in wanting to know about vows of silence. What that would feel like and be like—as someone who enjoys engaging in my voice and no, I don't want to take it away from me—to be silent?

I like using my voice, and I appreciate thinking about the concept of voice in different ways: on the page, through movement, photography, film, etc. I feel like language creates realities, but it also breaks them. Voice plays the same role. Voice is also complicated because it exists on so many different levels. It is not necessarily just what comes out of our throats and into the air. There are also the levels of language or voice that are internal that no one can hear. There is the voice where it feels like something is speaking to you or through you if you are paying attention. This level of voice and one's exchange with it can't always be articulated. Even as we talk about voice, I also keep thinking of the levels of noise that voice or voices all together can become. Right now, I've been confronted with noise or sound within a school. When I was doing radio, I thought about how I must recognize the certain things that needed to be said or edited in a certain way for the ear based on a reliance on the voice versus seeing it on the page.

I don't have a definition for what voice is. The more I think about it, it keeps coming back to listening. I am also finding the concept of voice elusive, difficult, challenging...especially because I find that voice is used in so many harmful ways. I often ask myself questions about when, where, how, or if to use voice? All these different things along with how can it be juxtaposed against or with silence? How is silence its own communication? The power of silence.

So, I don't think I have an answer, but I will wrap my answer to your question with this.

I've always thought it was maybe too confining for artists to be told, "You've found their voice," or to be asked, "What is your voice?" because what if you decide that this concept of your voice needs to change? Shouldn't one's voice change across their work? If we say that someone has a specific voice, then we box them in based on who, what, and how they need to be within their work.

PB: Of course, if we had a final answer, we wouldn't need this anthology. But when you talk about silence over air, and its relationship to voice and language, I think of something that John Cage wrote, "What we require is silence. But what the silence requires is that we go on talking." In your last book, *Black Metamophoses,* there's a real attention to bring the page into a dynamic and kinetic place. Your use of space on the page is quite original, and stunning, frankly. I'd like to ask, how is your work received differently on the page like that, knowing how much intention is made to create those spaces? And how does that feature differently in performance?

SL: That's an interesting question. I'd like to think that they both bring their own amounts of power. There's also another dimension, maybe with a performance, it becomes ephemeral. It becomes something that you can't quite categorize. However, my hope is that they—my words on the page and the performance of them—have their own different lives.

With performance, there is more room for improvisation and permission to present a different kind of edit in the way that it doesn't appear in print to the audience. I also find that there is feedback and response or engagement with the audience during a performance. When I received my Abel Meeropol Social Justice Award for writing in April and did that keynote, it felt like an invitation for me to do something different. I went out of my comfort zone to have a certain kind of exchange with the audience that would have been very different had each of those individuals read my keynote and had their own experience with it on the page.

I think there's a story about Keith Jarrett during one of his performances in the 1970's. As the story goes, he was invited to perform, but there were so many details to the backstory of the performance like the fact that he was in some physical discomfort. There was a certain kind of piano Jarrett wanted to play, but when he got there, the piano he was presented with was a mess! It was ragged, he couldn't play it. During Jarrett's actual performance, he had to do all sorts of things physically to make the instrument commit to sound. This performance I reference turned out to be one of his most memorable and greatest performances.

But there was only one performance like that because of all those factors that came together and culminated in *that* experience. What I hope, with each performance, just like my curations for art, I hope that they're each different. I hope that each of my performances are all in some kind of communication and exchange with only the set of circumstances that brought them to that moment in time that could never happen in that same way again in ways that never happened before.

A page does not do that. It stays that way, and we try to make it stay that way because of preservation, right? That is what makes performances so special.

PB: Right. And that vortex, that place where, as you say, everything is changeable, winds up depending as much upon the listener as it does upon the poet. A poem isn't complete until it's found itself in the heart of someone else. And that happens most often in performance. When you talk about voice, you are, in a sense, blending and recalling echoes of so many other voices. In *Black Metamorphoses*, there are many voices which offer different perspectives all the way back to Ovid. What is your thought about the traditions and the conventions of the genre that your work has been assigned to, in this case, poetry?

SL: I am not reeeeaallllly a traditionalist which may apply to many things. I'd like to think that even if all of my arts or creations are not yet consciously aware of what they are rooted to in terms of lineage, that they are, on some level, self-aware and in conversation with everything that came before.

And so, even if I am not directly engaged with the lineage, the lineage is engaged with me. I also have an opportunity to blur lines because genres are very problematic for me, though from a business perspective, I get it. They need to know how to categorize a thing in order to sell it.

I'm also a disrupter. What's that axiom...you have to know where we've been in order to know where you are going? But even if we're not aware of where we've been, we must listen. We must listen because even if we're not aware of it, it's very aware of us. We must be open of mind, body, spirit, heart...soul to it, and engage in that conversation and be surprised by it. At the same time, do not be bound by it, the lineage, because creating is also an invitation for you to become the very thing that something or someone may be paying attention to so that they may have a sense of permission, a way forward, in ways that you cannot yet see..

PB: You and I have been on panels together and one of the questions that people tend to ask is what are you working on? And I think your answer today is much more about what is working on you?

SL: Yes

PB: For example, what would be the voice of photography?

SL: Great question, especially for a medium where it's been about power dynamics and staging history. I will have to sit with your question Phil!

Shanta Lee *is an award-winning visual artist, writer across genres, author, and public intellectual who often says she is a "...practitioner of entanglement" due to all of her interests. Winner of the New England Poetry Club's Grant for Poetic Achievement, Abel Meeropol Social Justice Writing Award, and a 2024 National Arts Strategies Creative Community Fellow (New England), her work has been widely featured in* Harper's Magazine, The Massachusetts Review, ITERANT Literary Magazine, Palette Poetry, BLAVITY, Prism, Ms. Magazine, and DAME Magazine, *alongside of her former radio segment she created, produced, and reported for Vermont Public. Shanta Lee's previous books include: A double volume of two chapbooks,* Close is... *and* Hopscotch Between the Living and the Dead *(Diode Editions, 2024);* This Is How They Teach You How to Want It...The Slaughter: A Field Guide for the Hunted & the Hunter, The Dead-Alive, The Live-Dead Ones, The... *(Harbor Editions, 2024);* Black Metamorphoses*—named a finalist in the 2021 Hudson Prize, shortlisted for the 2021 Cowles Poetry Book Prize and longlisted for the 2021 Idaho Poetry Prize—illustrated by Alan Blackwell (Etruscan Press, 2023); and* GHETTOCLAUSTROPHOBIA: Dreamin of Mama While Trying to Speak Woman in Woke Tongues *(Diode Editions, 2021), winner of the Vermont Book Award. Shanta Lee has an MFA in Creative Non-Fiction and Poetry at the Vermont College of Fine Arts, an MBA from the University of Hartford, and an undergraduate degree in Women, Gender and Sexuality from Trinity College.* ***"Hallowed Hunted Body" is included in her work,*** **This Is How They Teach You How to Want It...The Slaughter: A Field Guide for the Hunted & the Hunter, The Dead-Alive, The Live-Dead Ones, The...*****(Harbor Editions, 2024).***

Sheryl St. Germain

"To Drink A Glacier"

I filled several water jugs last week with water from the glacial falls near Skagway. I reach for one of the jugs as soon as I unload the car with the supplies I picked up in town. I've developed a real thirst for this water, not unlike my thirst for wine. As I bring the jug to my lips and drink I'm aware that this water is possibly over a thousand years old. It's the sweetest, purest water I've ever tasted, which says something for old age. It looks like liquid silver and feels, as it moves through me, like a kind of healing potion, some gris-gris drink from that Witch of all witches, Nature. I feel heady with the pureness of it, almost intoxicated. This is the mother of all wines, wine before we knew wine. It is mouth and nipple to all waters, east or west, even that river I know as so tainted, the Mississippi where it wraps around New Orleans. If I close my eyes I can feel myself back to the falls, kneeling, cupping my hands and dipping them into the water that rushes like arterial blood from the wound in its ice white skin. I bring the water to my lips and drink. That drink is like a kiss, a kiss that takes in the entire body of the other. To drink is the most physical of acts, to feel the body of that other touching our lips then entering our mouths like some wondrous omnipotent liquid tongue, touching our own tongue all over, the roofs and sides of our mouths, then moving in us and through us to where it knows, in its wisdom, it must, to touch every cell of the body. I hold the water in my mouth as if it were a fine wine, or the blood of a god before I swallow, trying to make the spiritual, sexual sweetness of it last. It doesn't have the tingle of wine, but it warms me nonetheless. Robinson Jeffers would write some years ago that we had become "a little too abstract, a little too wise"; I might add, a little too untrusting, a little too cynical, a little too paranoid. To drink this water is to submit to the earth instead of manipulating it, to trust the nonhuman other in the way, before AIDS, we could trust the body of the human other. I kneel to gather and drink water from a river of glacial melt, believing that water to be pure. This kneeling and drinking is a form of prayer, which is also a form of trust. To drink is to pray, to have faith in this water to heal us, to ask for the water's blessing and wisdom, to trust that it will nourish, not poison us.

SL: There's something in that piece that is so sensual. There have been so many conversations over the years about the environment and our impact, even saying "the environment," as if we're separate from it. What I really like about this page, in addition to being very sensual in the description, but this piece is also about communing with nature. Why did you choose this page?

SSG: It's what I would call a lyric essay, I write both poems and essays. I wanted, because of the description of the anthology, to offer something other than poetry. I think of the lyric essay as like a poem dressed in old clothes. Some people would never pick up a poetry book, but they would pick up an essay collection. I write my essays as if they were poems without line breaks. So that was one reason I chose this piece.

It's also a piece about stopping and reflecting, and I think that's what poetry does. That's what voice can make us do. It's a piece that has a lot of the craft elements you find in poetry. There's simile, there's metaphor. There's repetition of words and sounds. There's a highly iambic rhythm that runs through it. But I think one thing that I do in all of my work is that there's something "real," and it's often nature because I love nature, but what I love is what's underneath that real thing. So, here's a small piece about literally drinking water, but it's also about trusting. It's about thinking about the Earth in a different way and water in a different way. That complexity is important to me.

SL: As the listener and as someone who's read the piece, it feels like it brings the holy together with what we would think of as the profane or the everyday.

SSG: I want it to feel both sexual and spiritual at the same time. I want the reader to feel what I was feeling, the feeling of having sex; someone or something enters you, like the water enters me in this piece. Drinking the water—I think about Whitman sometimes and just how I think he was pansexual, everything was erotic to him—was an erotic experience. And the longer piece is interesting. Because I was middle aged when I wrote it, I felt this kind of overflowing energy that a woman sometimes feels in middle age. The power of the melting glacier reflected that for me, everything was pouring out of it, and it felt both holy and profane at the same time. I'm glad you picked that up.

SL: Your piece makes me think of Audre Lorde and her concept of living the erotic within everything we do. In other words, bringing the concept of the erotic out of the bedroom into the world which makes this piece so interesting. I also think of the

implications of orality and voice paired with Audre Lorde's concept within your piece. For you, what is voice? What else would you want to say in terms of thinking about your voice as it relates to this piece or other work that you've done?

SSG: I'm glad you mentioned Audre Lorde because she was so important to me early on in the way that she approached the erotic and some of her writings about that I've never ever forgotten. I think when you talk about what voice is on a very literal level, your voice comes from your family. From your mother, your father, your genes. For me, the first thing that I remember as a child is my mother reading to me and I remember her voice and the rhythms, that's inside of me. When I speak now, I can hear my mother's voice. I can hear my father when I'm angry. My father used to scream and yell, and I can still hear and feel that. The arguments we had at the table growing up in New Orleans, the kind of sloppy, slow, languorous, sexy rhythms of Dr. John and Professor Longhair, and the Second Line music during Mardi Gras. I'm getting chills thinking about it. I could never be a certain kind of writer, like a very formal poetic writer, because of that wild background I have. That's a kind of family too.

I think voice comes from, of course, actual family, but it also comes from the people you read. They live in you in some way. It comes from your community. Over the years as I've written, I feel like I've not found my voice so much as I've allowed it to *be,* have acknowledged it. Sometimes I think we want to deny where we come from and thus where our voice has its origins. My family members have a heavy New Orleans accent, and for a long time, that felt like a sign of ignorance for me. I tried to lose that accent, but then I began to find this beauty in just letting it be. Letting the voice be what it wanted to be, slow, languorous, and sometimes sexy, like New Orleans, like my family. Accepting that I was from this place. Much of the color, the energy, the music of my voice comes from this place that gave birth to me, comes from New Orleans. It comes from my family and their fighting. This glacier piece is not a piece that's about that place, but I think that I brought my voice into a place that was unknown to me, Alaska. I was able to make it sing, I hope, and make it feel as seductive as the place where I came from.

SL: You and I have that in common. For years, I avoided the use of African American vernacular, especially because I was not raised to speak that way. I rejected using it in my work for many years. Now I've embraced it as a kind of linguistic play on the page. What you have said about the voice, family and the relation sparks so much for me. As we wrap, is there anything else you would want to add? Do you want to speak to a question I did not ask?

SSG: The only thing I'd say is I do think it's important to learn the tradition of whatever you're writing in. I move back and forth between poetry and lyric prose. I think it's important to learn how to write formal poetry, how to write a traditional essay, and take off from there. I love classical music, but if jazz and improvisational music didn't exist, I don't know how I would live. I think that there's a place for both of them. There's a place for tradition. There's a place for innovation. As I was training my voice, I worked in both traditional and improvisational ways, and I benefited from both.

Sheryl St. Germain *has published six poetry books, three essay collections, and co-edited two anthologies, for which she has received numerous awards, including two National Endowment for the Arts Fellowships. Sheryl's son, Gray, died in 2014 of a drug overdose. Her last book of poetry,* The Small Door of Your Death *(Autumn House Press), and her latest collection of essays,* Fifty Miles *(Etruscan Press), both take as their subject the life and death of her son, and offer a look at the toll addiction takes on family and country. Recently retired as Director of the MFA Program in Creative Writing at Chatham University, she now resides in Savannah, Georgia, where in addition to writing, she makes art quilts.* ***The piece included in this anthology is an excerpt from "To Drink A Glacier" in*** **Fifty Miles** ***(Etruscan Press, 2020).***

Bruce Smith

Untitled

Utopia's sirens annul the contract I had with dream.

The individual wandered off, the assembly adjourned, 4:44 AM

in the ink of it, the body/mind accusing, reminding me of sirens

flexing in the prison yard at noon, *to test the system*, by the coiled,

electrified voice of Emmett Till's mama, a call to prayer for inmates,

a call to dominion for officers. Night's neck, night's rib

cage, night's wrecked sentence, night's lupine, night's a boy

in a boat in storm wound in his sheet. I'm coming to understand

the asymmetrical nature of art, no target, no trigger, no collateral

damage, no one dies from it, one lives with it like a murmur.

PB: So complex and intense, Bruce. We were just talking before the recording about an idea that you wanted to share with us.

BS: Poet and critic Fred Moten, citing Amiri Baraka, made a distinction between voice and sound. "I always thought that 'the voice' was meant to indicate a kind of genuine, authentic, absolute individuation, which struck me as (a) undesirable and (b) impossible," he said. "Whereas a 'sound' was really within the midst of this intense engagement with everything: with all the noise that you've ever heard, you struggle somehow to make a difference, so to speak, within that noise. And that difference isn't necessarily about you as an individual, it's much more simply about trying to augment and to differentiate what's around you. And that's what a sound is for me."

PB: That quote is very interesting because it speaks right to what we're talking about when we've used this word "voice," and this is casting a different perspective on that idea. What do you make of that, Bruce?

BS: I think I've always been kind of paralyzed by the idea of voice or I felt that voice was something that I couldn't define, something that I never had, that I was working towards. But this quotation which distinguishes voice from sound is more in tune with what I think happens, at least in my work. You know sound connects for me various cultures. In this case, waking up in the middle of the night from a dream in which I'm hearing sirens, and that sound of the siren call which you can expound on Phil, I know with your knowledge of the classics, you know it's a different siren call.

And it reminds me of the Federal Penitentiary in Lewisburg, which we both know, and I taught at Lewisburg for four years after I finished at Bucknell and before I went to New York. So every day at noon, at the Penitentiary the sirens would go off. They would "test the system" which I say in italics in the poem. For me that's like testing a larger system of who gets incarcerated and who gets to go free. Kind of a reductive way to think, but that's what I hear. So that sound of course, that siren sound, not luring me to the rocks as in Homer, but it has incited me to make those other connections, and sound has been so important to me in my work. To improvise within the traditions that we have. I think that defines for me both what jazz is and what poetry is: a way to improvise within the traditions, so the sound becomes a way to engage in that process for me, "this intense engagement with everything."

PB: When I get to the electrified voice of Emmett Till's mama, I realize that I'm in some half-mythic, half-hyper real world. Even though the poem is small, I somehow don't know what's coming next. Is that part of your intention? The idea of kind of disrupting scale?

BS: Yes. I like your idea of the scale, and the changes in that scale that I think are amplified or diminished by the sound. I like to take the big stuff: utopia and sound and Emmett Till and the racial history of America and put it in a small space. It is one of the things we've learned from both singers, and in my mind a poet like Emily Dickinson, who takes immortality, her flood subject, and puts it in a form, like the hymn form. So, singing, but having this huge subject, small space. Whitman did the opposite. He unscrewed "the locks from the doors and the doors themselves for the jams." He blew it all out, and there's power in that. And there's power also in taking big subjects and putting them in 10 lines.

PB: Could you speak about your engagement with the tradition?

BS: This kind of coincides with what we were saying earlier, which is the tradition for me, was first as a young boy overhearing the songs on the radio and wondering what was that? What was the power of that? How were they so memorable? How did they cross invisibly through different neighborhoods in Philadelphia, where I grew up. How did I explain that? And leaving that as a question, I get to college and there it became a kind of more academic exercise where you would study the traditions, and these were mostly American and European traditions. Then right after that I worked for four years at the Federal Penitentiary of Lewisburg and that again blew apart the tradition, the academic tradition and invited other traditions which were song traditions, oral traditions, the blues, jazz. The stuff that was played on the radio stations inside the federal penitentiary. So, my early conception and then my middle conception, that was academic and then the conception that made me reevaluate, was what happened at the jail.

PB: So, those traditions all emerge in this poem, where "sirens" has many different meanings, the call of the past, the call of myth, and the call of man. And tell us about this new book that you have coming up, *Hungry Ghost*.

BS: A lot of the work is like the one I just read, untitled 10-line poems. And in between those, I have a sort of a long meditation about when I was in Rome when Prince died. There's a longer poem that meditates on trying to understand Prince in a European setting, trying to explain or understand his genius. It was a great moment, by the way, just because I walked into a café near the Vatican. I was staying at the American Academy in Rome, and the nuns and the police were both pointing upwards. I didn't understand what they were pointing to. They were pointing to the speakers in the ceiling at the café that were playing Prince songs in honor of him. And so to see the nuns saying "Prince" with the police pointing to the speakers was the moment of provocation for the poem.

***Bruce Smith** is the author of several books of poems including* Spill *(University of Chicago Press, 2018),* Devotions *(2011), and* The Other Lover *(2000) which was a finalist for both the National Book Award and the Pulitzer Prize. He is a "Discovery"/The Nation Award winner and has received a Guggenheim Fellowship as well as grants from the National Endowment for the Arts. His work has appeared in* Best American Poetry *and the 2009* Pushcart Prize Anthology. *He has been co-editor of the* Graham House Review *and a contributing editor of* Born Magazine.

Jeff Talarigo

Excerpt from *In the Cemetery of the Orange Trees*

The American continues to wander, to gather stories: to Egypt and Sudan; Japan and North Korea and China; to many cities in his own country.

Sometimes, when alone on a secluded beach or on a mountain before dawn or in bed at night, he thinks of his bundle of stories, the need to tell them, and how they have become enmeshed with his, to where now there is no border dividing them.

*

But there is this one, a moment he will carry with him to the grave.

He is sitting in the chaos of Gaza City, not far from the place he first arrived ten weeks before. It is an April day and he wishes it would rain, but knows he will have left Gaza long before it ever does again. This thought, leaving, both excites and saddens him. It is a rare person in Gaza who can even dream of this. And maybe this is not even possible; can one dream of something that they cannot even fathom? And here he sits, pining about a few months.

He is taking a break from many hours of walking. A soldier on patrol looks at him, he at the soldier, both framed by the vendor's stall. The shutters of shops rattle, unraveling to the ground as merchants close for the afternoon general strike. He has another hour to go to Jabaliya and he tries coaxing himself up off his backpack on which he sits.

Looking up, and through the madness of the city, the American sees a young girl, wearing a white headscarf, walking over to him. Shyly she smiles and hands him a bottle of Gaza 7-UP. He thanks her, holding up his hand for her to wait. Digging into his backpack, he finds a small doll, which he gives to the girl. Many times over the years, he thinks of this moment and knows that the young girl, now a woman, still has with her, the doll, and he, the story.

PB: Jeff, tell us about how you make these sentences, and how you think about them in terms of their lyric power.

JT: This was an interesting book. This was my third novel, and I'd never written anything about myself. I had a couple of friends who suggested that I write something about Jeff Talarigo in Gaza, which I was fairly resistant to, but I did go home, and I started playing around with voice. I used first person voice and that was just very heavy for me. It was difficult for me to use the word "I" and so I stepped back, and I played around with a third person voice, which the book *In the Cemetery of the Orange Trees*, a lot of it's in third person. I felt very comfortable using myself, the American in the book, and that really gave me a lot of freedom, opened a lot of doors that I really didn't have in mind. And it allowed me some separation between the word "I" and third person. I felt that it worked. And this scene that I just read here, this really encapsulates much of what I try to do as a writer, as far as traveling, writing stories about these people and trying my best to use a poetic voice.

PB: There's a sense of fable going on too. Tell us about how that approach–the fabulist, nonlinear way of moving.

JT: This fable-like quality has come into pretty much all my books. What I do before I write my books, this Gaza book in particular, I steep myself in the mythology of Gaza, the folktales. I went back and read a lot of that, just to get the voice, once again, the voice of how these stories are told. And it sort of happened by mistake that I found the voice of animals talking.

One morning I went to this coffee shop in Boston, and I wrote a four-thousand-word story with a talking goat, and I had no idea where that came from. And I think a lot of that came from being steeped in mythology, in the folktales of the countries that I traveled to and write about. I'm very intrigued by them. I've always loved those; I think because of the animals. And it just gave me distance once again to tell the story and tell this story about the Palestinians in a different way. Tell it in a way it hasn't been told. And I began to feel confident with the fable-like stories when a Palestinian who was living in Kuwait read this story about the talking goat, and he wrote back to me and said, these animals are telling our stories better than we could tell our story. And I thought, okay, maybe this is it. And it turned out to be that way.

Again, the fables, folktale type of stories, they lend themselves to poetry. The language, the voice is huge. That's the main thing for me when I'm writing a book. To me, voice in a book is comparable to what I do in photography, playing with the light. The way I manipulate light in my camera and take photos. I think voice is the same way, where you manipulate the language to tell the story.

PB: Of course, when we talk about fables, we have to say that your book is a deeply serious story. How much does your sense of orality play a role in your composition?

JT: I think it's huge. There are different times, Phil, when I'm writing, sitting here at my computer, or using my yellow legal pads, where, as I'm writing the sentence, I'm saying them aloud as well. And the idea of writing by hand as well is another thing, just the whole idea of connecting. Before I write, almost every morning I read a page of poetry to get me into language and voice, and it's just the beauty of language, the beauty of words. And I read my stuff aloud a lot. I read my favorite books aloud, I sit in my chair and read the pages aloud. And I think that's really helped me to read publicly as well, with the tone and everything like that.

And I always admired how so many poets read so well, and poetry is meant to be heard. It's great to read, but when I read poetry, I read it aloud. I lived in Japan many years and the idea of Haiku poetry, you know, seventeen syllables exactly. You have to choose the right word to fit in the number of syllables, and I just love the brevity of language. I think that's magical, and the simplicity of it, but it's, of course, very hard to do.

My Grandma Talarigo was the storyteller in my family. She was the person that told stories that began with X here, and then an hour and a half later, she connected X. In the middle, she was going in every direction, but also that's the way I like to write as well, in fragments, almost, and little scenes. And that comes I'm sure from my Grandma Talarigo. We have no other writers in my family. And just hearing the way she would tell us stories, you know, and it was great, and she's Italian, her hands are flailing everywhere. So I really think that's where I got the sense of storytelling, I really do.

***Jeff Talarigo** is the author of several books including* The Pearl Diver *(Anchor, 2005) and* The Ginseng Hunter *(Anchor, 2009) and* In the Cemetery of the Orange Trees *(Etruscan, 2018). He was a fellow at the New York Public Library's Dorothy and Lewis B. Cullman Center for Scholars and Writers in 2006-07. He has lived in both Gaza and Japan and currently resides in Oakland, California. He teaches in the Maslow Family Graduate Program in Creative Writing at Wilkes University.*

Mihaela Moscaliuc

"Giovana speaks: He will not remember my face"

—west to east to west Romania, July 2021

1. Departure

I did not come from anger or with anger.
My older sister saw my mother's face through birth
and said she did not curse me as she did the others,
wrapped me in her only petticoat, kept me
the longest, a month and three days.
It would have been longer even, had the men
not minded my cries as they did
and poured palincă in the milk bottle.
I met this sister only last year.
I did not envy she got to stay and know
our mother. When the door opened she recognized me
and looked pleased, and fed me borscht,
but she struggles too hard to see me again.
Her boys prowl streets for fights, her insides ache
with cuts. My son did not come from anger.
I cried like a sky when I felt him ready,
cried through and through, a solid day and night.
I did not want him out. Stay a bit longer, I prayed,
for I knew that's all the time we'd have together.

5. Return

When both front tires came loose between villages,
riders bonded in the ditch bushy with mousetail,
spat in their palms to smear off the day's work
and shared slană with chunks of bread, a bottle

of palincă someone meant to sell at market.
The woman heading to town to fix the tooth abscess
that had erased her features summoned me,
swaying her sagging jowl in kind jest.
I was sitting by myself inside the mini-bus,
in no hurry to get to any town.
It won't move any faster if you sit there,
the woman yelled and signaled me to step out.
She looked like someone I could trust,
but I was too weak to answer about my whereabouts
or why I smelled so powerfully of heated railroad tar.

MM: These are the first and last stanzas of a poem in five short sections that follow a character named Giovana from the Western to the Eastern part of Romania and back. Her small son whose name is a version of hers, Giovanel, lives in the East, in a state institution for children with severe disabilities. Giovana spends 36 hours on train rides, four hours on buses, and the night on a train station bench, hoping to see her son. It's July 2021, toward the end of the pandemic. He's seven, and she hasn't seen him in almost three years. Giovana grew up in a state institution herself, and she's someone I know well.

The poem willed itself out of rage, at both injustices that the character suffers and at larger systemic ones. In initial drafts, that's all it was, a poorly veiled rant. I realized that that was not what I wanted, ultimately. I wanted Giovana to tell her own story, the best as one can through a voice that was and wasn't hers. And I wanted to attempt and restore some of the dignity that had been stripped away from her life again and again. Giovana appears as a 'character' in other poems, including some in my most recent collection, *Cemetery Ink* (2021).

Capturing the particulars of her speech was crucial to me. It was the main challenge. I remembered the novel *Zoli* by Colum McCann, one of the most beautifully crafted novels I've ever read, written primarily in the voice of an Eastern European Romani singer named Zoli. McCann mentioned in an essay that sometimes he would wait for days, weeks, for the voice to come. He had to be patient. He had to wait for the voice to emerge, speak to him, and then inhabit it. After a while he would close his eyes, and she would be right there. That's what I aspired to do. You could say that I was waiting for the voice to haunt me. I wanted to write from Giovana's perspective and animate the innocence and directness with which she speaks. Like McCann, in my work I'm always interested in compassion and clarity and making new worlds available.

PB: These kinds of cross-fertilizations of language, how do they affect your writing? You are also of course a translator. How do those different language elements enter and feed your sensibility about voice?

MM: That's a great question. I believe I'm often categorized as an immigrant poet, and that doesn't bother me at all. It did at first, when I desperately wanted to feel kind of unproblematically and pleasantly at home in the English language and in the American culture, but I came to embrace that label and my accented English. Even when I'm not writing about subjects related to immigration, even when I'm writing about a fig, I'm still doing it with the awareness and sensibility of someone who is not just irrevocably of two worlds but someone who writes out of the personal as much as she writes out of the collective.

"We get our voices from the voices of others," writes McCann, and I'm with him on that. Some poets write in their own voices. There's something, an accruement of distinct features, that makes their voice immediately recognizable. Even when ineffable, certain qualities help us recognize poems as belonging to certain writers. I think my voice is a cacophony of voices, and that suits me just fine. It's who I am as a person and a writer. My own writing, my own voice is very much informed and fueled also by the poems I translate—that is, by the work I do as a translator, but also by other 'translated' voices like Giovana's; she insists on becoming visible, insists on entering my own voice and merging and conflating with it to some extent. I'm ok with not having a voice that is undeniably mine, with having a personal voice that is more of a collage of other voices.

Mihaela Moscaliuc*'s most recent poetry collections are* Heartmoor *(forthcoming, Alice James Books),* Cemetery Ink. *(University of Pittsburgh Press, 2021). She has translated poetry by Romanian writers Carmelia Leonte and Liliana Ursu, co-edited* Border Lines: Poems of Migration *(Knopf, 2020), and edited* Insane Devotion: On the Writing of Gerald Stern *(Trinity University Press, 2016). She is the translation editor for* Plume *and Professor of English at Monmouth University, NJ.*

Kazim Ali

"Golden Boy"

Almost afraid I am in the annals of history to speak
And by speaking be seen by man or god
Such then debt in light be paid

Atop the Manitoban parliament building in Winnipeg
What beacon to dollars food or god
I hallow starvation

This nation beneath the body hollowing
Its stomach to emptiness and in breadth
The river empties

Who sew spoke the craft born along
Long echo and echelon grains of light
And space we width one and other weight

The soul not the spirit breathe through
Spirited went or wend why true
Weave woe we've woven

A dozen attempts these tents pitched
On the depth be made biped by pen may
Perch atop the temple pool

Proven the prove these richness wheat and
Cherries and prunes what washes
Over woven ocean

Frayed I am most sir desired
Sired in wind seared and warned
Once in wild umiyak sworn

We parley to mend be conned be bent
Come now called to document your
Meant intent your indented mind

Haul oh star your weight in aeons
There in prayer money morrow more
You owe and over time god spends

The spent river melt into
Summer sound out the window
Sound out the spender

Where does the river road end
In what language can prayer or
Commerce be offered

Ender of senses pensive atop
Plural spires be spoken or mended
Broken and meant for splendor my mentor

SL: Tell me more about this page, why did you choose it? What does it represent, especially within your practice?

KA: I just lose myself in sound in this piece. I feel like I'm in one of those echo rooms where the sound just keeps resounding in your ear. I was in the South of India once, and there are these ancient temples from the Chola Empire, around 600 CE. They had these little, kind of small little stone niches that you could go into and sit on this bench, and if you hummed an OM, if you started chanting, it was precisely built to amplify and echo the sound. It was tremendous. You could feel it in your bones almost.

I loved filling all the cavities of my body with sound in this little poem. Of course, you can't really tell solely by listening to it, but there were a lot of puns. Like when I say what sounds like "Hollow star your weight in eons," the text on the page is "Haul oh star your weight in aeons," and address to the star and not what it sounds like, a description of the star as "hollow." So, there was a lot of that. And then of course, there are a lot of riffs off of things. So, a dozen attempts, "these tents pitched on the depth be made biped" like a person, biped and so on, you know. I found my way through sound into deeper layers of meaning, or more primitive, primeval meaning.

SL: That's what I felt too! There's also hearing it versus reading it, both great experiences. Like the cascade right? I'm curious, how does orality and voice play a role across your work and within this piece?

KA: I grew up listening to multiple languages in my earliest childhood, and I do think that affected my ear, but I didn't start learning to speak other languages until adulthood. When I began to learn how to speak other languages, that brought me into even more of a strong connection between sound and words. The English word for *rock*, for example, has such a connection to that object. The solidity of the word and the solidity of the object. Of course, in other languages, it's not that word. You start to have different relationships to a word based on the sound that it's given. A different relationship to what the word represents based on its sound. I think of the word *rain* in English, and in Urdu, that word is *barish*. The word for rain: barish, and I think of barish as like the sound rain might make in the pools on the ground as it falls. A certain kind of rain, so it has particularity.

Sound has particularity in language that is connected within our lived experience. Like when you speak a language you're fluent in, it means you don't think about it anymore. I think a lot of times in English, we don't think about how sound makes meaning, how we have to break it down or we must get elemental with it in a way. I think that's kind of what I was trying to do in this poem, or maybe what happened in this poem was more of an incantatory quality or something like that.

SL: While you're speaking about this it makes me think of my own work and the complex feelings I have in terms of code meshing and code enmeshment. There is a musicality of certain kinds of speech that isn't within the standard accepted English.

KA: Yeah, and usage as well. I'm teaching an online course right now on the poetry and poetics of Lucille Clifton. One of the things that she does in her work is speak in a vernacular, or what we might call African American Vernacular English. It used to be called Black English, now it's called African American Vernacular. This is what I'm talking to the students about, most of whom are not African American. Although there are some people of color in the class, they are not the majority of the class. I'm trying to talk to them about how this vernacular has its own rules as a language. It has its own way of behaving. One of the ways that it behaves is its usage of the verb "be." There are two things that happen in this vernacular. One is when the verb "be" is eliminated completely and is more colloquial. The other is when it's doubled in order to create emphasis. For example, the phrase "What it is, is," you've heard this phrase right? It's really emphasizing the presentness of things. Or in the case of the past tense, a doubling of past-tenseness in the phrase, "What had happened was."

SL: Yes! I just said that the other day to a friend "What had happened was"!

KA: You're really saying, "Here's the deal," or "Hey, this is what's going on." You're really emphasizing the beingness of the terms. Lucille Clifton does that in her poem "what did she know, when did she know it?" which is an incredible poem about childhood sexual abuse and it starts "What it was was the soft tap, tap into the room, etc., etc.," And it goes on. It's that use of language as a malleable and plastic form that can be molded by orality. Standard English has these kind of rules for the roles that language plays in different parts of the sentence the way it's used; repetition of a term does not play the same role that it does in Black English, or in Urdu/Hindi where you can just repeat a word for emphasis.

I'm attracted to vernacular or languages like African American Vernacular English that uses English differently. When I studied, learning Urdu, though oftentimes in Urdu, emphasis is given through repetition. Instead of saying something is very bad, you can say it's very bad, but you can also say it's bad-bad. You just say the word again to emphasize and sometimes it's not even the word itself, but you rhyme it with a nonsense word, like bad-wad or something like that. I think it's exciting to learn how other language systems use language itself. Language is a medium, right? And I mean, in journalism, or in standard prose, you'd have a copy editor who's correcting you and putting commas in specific places. However, poetry has its own rules. It can leave standard grammar behind and reinvent itself both on and off the page. I find myself veering more towards the anarchic, more towards the open, more towards the brand new, the unusual, and the unexpected.

SL: As a poet, it's like you said, being able to break that rule or use repetition, which raises another question about the oral transmission of your work and your work on the page. When you're writing, do you feel it being spoken in your body? Do you write with performance in mind, or in terms of the spoken or oral? How do you navigate the spoken work versus work that is read on the page?

KA: It's mostly always spoken, that started really early for me. I grew up listening to poetry recited in my house all the time. I know that others with my background have had this experience of poetry recited in languages that I didn't have command of. I would hear poetry recitation, or do poetry recitation in Arabic in terms of Quranic recitation. It was almost like poetry was pure sound to me first before it had any meaning. In fact, I think especially in terms of the Quran, which is scripture, so it's giving religious rules and guidelines. I think I would have liked it less if I actually knew what it meant because I would have had that connection to familiarity instead of the experience of the music of the language itself. That clarifies a real difference and it was my move towards what I thought poetry was.

SL: I love that! I also think about this in terms of how stories are told in my family in terms of breaking traditional narrative structure because the storyteller in my family doesn't necessarily say, "This is how I feel about it now looking back on it." It's more like, "I'm gonna immerse, and bring you here." In thinking about this, how do you define voice? What does voice mean to you?

KA: I think voice is individual to the human, not only because our own minds and experiences are different, but our physical bodies, the cavities that our bodies make. I mean in the singing voice, for example, one person is an alto, one person is a soprano. In the case of a singer having a lot of range, they may settle in one part of their voice. Then there are different kinds of singers.

There are people who are amazing at singing opera but probably couldn't do a different kind of singing. Do you know what I mean? I think that the voice has physical qualities as well. If our vocal chords are muscles, and the sounds of our voices have different qualities in timbre, then that impacts how voice works in the human body. I think the voice "metaphorically" as far as a poetic voice is concerned, is impacted by all of that.

I don't know if you've ever had this experience but, when you read a person's poem on the page, you imagine their physical voice based on the work. Then, when you encounter them, you think, "Wow, I didn't think they were gonna sound like that." They're either bigger physically and have a deeper voice, or they're small, birdlike, and have tiny little voice, all of which you've imagined differently. So, I think that's something very interesting, and I think it's just that every human is very individual, physically and experience wise.

If you think of our ancestors—who they were, what our physical form was—now has been just created by generations of combinations, history, and DNA that made us the unique manifestation of flesh and sound that we are. Our bones, our muscles, how tall we are, how big our ribcage is, all those things that go into making sound are created in that way. Then I guess you could argue, although I know less about it, that the brain is the same way, like who we are as humans. Are we immortal spirits that just shine through from the ether into these fleshly forms that are made for us? That is possible. Or it's equally possible that our personalities, our relationships, and language is also constructed in some way by the physical brain, the tissues of the brain and how it works. It's one or the other, it's probably a combination of both.

SL: Is there anything I did not ask you that you'd like to add as we end?

KA: I'm really interested in how the physical voice and/or the sound of a poem is impacted in collaborative work between two people. I've never done collaborations, but I know many people who have. Of course, *Sappho's Gymnasium* by Olga Broumas and T Begley is one of my touchstone books, and that's a collaboration. My friend Josh Davis is publishing collaborative poems right now with Allison Blevins. I think one book is coming out immediately and then there's another one that was just accepted, but what does that mean for the creative artists involved? How do you disappear into a work that is shared between two people? Like I said, I've never been either brave enough or egoless enough, maybe, to really do that and sublimate myself. I've always wanted to be in charge of my own stuff. I think it takes a certain kind of awesomeness to be able to say, "Okay, we're going to do this poem together as a group or as a duo or whatever." I'm interested in that.

SL: I do a lot of different collaborations, but it's never with my poetry. It's more like "Hey, let's have these conversations via audio clips and exchanges." But to the degree that it would be we're gonna sit and do a poem together? I don't know...

KA: And yeah, I dance, or used to. Anyways, and dance is always a collaboration. You usually don't do it by yourself, although I guess there's people who do that too, but I never did.

SL: What type of dance? I'm curious.

KA: It was a modern dance. I was trained in ballet but danced in a company that was directed by Andres and Marguerite San Millan, two dancers from the Alwin Nikolais company, so I guess, maybe a little inspired by that. I also trained when I did my MFA, I did my minor concentration in dance. Normally when you do your MFA at NYU, you take a series of workshops as the main curriculum and then a series of electives in literary theory, literature, or craft as electives. But I didn't want to do that, I already had an MA in English prior to entering my MFA so I did my secondary concentration in dance. And I did it at the Gallatin School at NYU, which is the School of Individualized Study. It was dance, but it was within the context of various other disciplines. I worked with Ann Axtmann, who was using dance as a part of social and political movements. I did another class with Lanny Harrison, who taught dance and performance in the context of contemplative practices and psychotherapy. I would do it again in a heartbeat. I'm 51 years old, so I can't do all the things physically I used to do. But dance is a vital part of my creative practice, both on and off the stage.

Kazim Ali *is the author of multiple books including the novel* Indian Winter *(Coach House Books, 2024). Poetry collections include* Sukun: New and Selected Poems *(Wesleyan University, 2023),* Inquisition *(Wesleyan University, 2018),* Sky Ward *(Wesleyan University, 2013), winner of the Ohioana Book Award in poetry, and* The Far Mosque *(Alice James Books, 2005), winner of Alice James Books' New England/New York Award. He is an accomplished translator of Marguerite Duras, Sohrab Sepehri, and Ananda Devi among others. He has taught at several universities across the country and is currently a Professor of Literature at the University of California, San Diego.*

Morowa Yejide

"Blasphemy"

With these words I blaspheme. Because I'm a writer, and by nature I care less about what others think than about the happenings in my head. So, I say this now. Decipher it how you must.

I'll start in the middle, out here in the badlands. That's where the blood and guts are. Where birth and destruction reign. Because everyone is busy running and jockeying and jousting and trying to survive the fray. There is the vigilance against destruction of social media platform and profile. There is the tireless culling of reviews and choices and picks scraped from the bottom of riverbeds like fool's gold. The old Zulu flank the new. Balkanized groups born of aged interests shift alliance for proximity to fire and gaze. The stench of decomposing egos and ripe arrogance chokes the air.

And there is no Writing Life for me. There is no cabin in a stand of three-hundred-year-old trees. No roaring fire. No antique typewriter or mahogany desk. There's just my life and how writing fits into it.

I check the chinks in my armor and prepare to escalate. Because beyond the boundaries of one battle there lies a larger one, and my family within it. We are man, woman, and three boys—a tribe of five reading cloud formations and checking the direction of the wind; raw and exposed to the elements. Because my sons look like Emmitt, Trayvon, Michael, and the others. Because my husband looks like Rodney, Dante, George, and the others. I make deals with God and use anger, fear, and hope—three inexhaustible fuels. I commune with long-dead writers and tap out tidings, epistles, and prophecies.

I wipe the blood spatter from my face and return to the combat zone. Because my triumph lies not in the beginning or the end. My victory is in the middle; a teller whose only weapon is in the telling. In the dark I strike a match to thought and scroll words on the walls of oblivion. Some say they have lived the realms I've written. Herein is my manna. Herein is sustenance for my ages.

SL: Can you tell us about this page and why you chose it? How does it represent your practice?

MY: This page is really born out of a stream of consciousness that I think many writers may have had. When you're trying to write, we're all writers we can say, but we don't all write under the same conditions. *Blasphemy* is really about the fact that, when we're running around at events, conferences, doing book signings, craft classes, and fiction workshops, what's often never discussed are the conditions under which some of us have to write. What I mean by that is the extreme conditions of racism. The worry that I have for my children is not the same that another writer might have for her children. It's something nobody wants to talk about.

Everyone's so busy putting on their best face and putting their best foot forward. All of that's necessary, but at the same time, there are certain realities that plague us. I think writers, myself in particular, write out of everything that impacts my life and the lives of people that I care about. *Blasphemy* is about taking a moment to unload the burden of the things that are constantly pervasive when you're trying to be positive and trying to be creative.

It's not just the historical things that go on, but that those things are still impacting us today. Then, mix in between that, you have the toxic social media environment, which I find more and more of a real hindrance to creativity. You have so many people creating and presenting a digitized self and just scrolling, going through sound bites, and not really reading through anything. They are taking the surface title of things. All of this goes against what reading, writing, creativity, and critical thinking is all about. That's something I think is desperately needed in the world today and needs to be revived so we can all get back to our human selves of thinking for ourselves and talking to each other, and really looking at each other and it meaning certain things. So that's, I think, what inspired *Blasphemy*.

SL: I especially love the lines "...there is no mahogany desk for me. There is no cabin in the woods and the stand of 300-year-old trees." Can you talk about how that impacts how you define voice or how you've come to know voice? How have you come to know voice against the battle of the digitized gaze, especially in the online landscape where people are performing writing life or their creative lives. Have these factors helped you to further sharpen your idea of what voice is for you and your work?

MY: I think for me it didn't really help sharpen. Not having the opportunity to go off for retreats. I never had the luxury of doing that and having all this free time to write. My life is writing and all of the things that impact my writing in my life. I made peace with it. I think there's a lot of mythology around being a writer, but it's really about the work; whether that's with a roaring fire, or in my case, at the dining room table while dinner is in the oven, during my lunch break on a job, or at three o'clock in the morning writing out notes. Whatever that looks like, that's what it is. My voice came out of that experience. Largely out of me just doing my best to embrace the situation that I found myself writing in and the conditions I found myself writing under.

SL: I've not quite heard anyone put it that way, in terms of the realness. When you write and when you think about your voice or the page itself, do you have an audience in mind? I know the question deals with thinking about performance in mind. What's in your process as you're thinking or planning your words, then thinking about how they will be received through the ear and through the body?

MY: I feel that it was always a benefit that I was able to shut everything out while I was writing. I wrote for the landscape and the world that I was trying to build. The characters became the standards that I was trying to reach in writing. I have a very insular world when I'm writing, and the audience is not something I think about. I'm usually fixated on the concepts and the themes. If anything, I'm concerned about how clearly those come across on the page. Later, of course in the editing stage, then that becomes more important. How clearly is this coming through? In my view, if you're writing for an audience or trying to endear some segment of the population, you've already lost the war because writing to me is really an art form. It's a way of expressing our humanity, our lives. The ages that we've been through. The ages that we imagine, the experiences, and how those experiences impact us.

I think all artists in one medium or another, whether painters, song writers, or writers of books, all tune into the life of the universe. I think that's what we're trying to reach when we're doing our art. Even with a one page, even if it's in frustration as it was when I penned *Blasphemy.* It's that desire to reach that higher meaning that's above the fray of so many things that are not important.

SL: As we wrap, what else would you like to add? Is there a question I didn't ask you that you would like to think about or pose an answer to?

MY: The thing I would close with is everyone has their own path. Every writer has their own path. Every book is different. Every paragraph is different. Every sentence is different. Every word is different. That's the beauty of each of us. We all have our own way of expressing and no two ways are alike. I think if I would leave anything, it would be to embrace that path and travel it.

***Morowa Yejidé**, a native of Washington, DC, is the author of the critically acclaimed novel* Time of the Locust, *which was a 2012 finalist for the PEN/Bellwether Prize, long listed for the 2015 PEN/Bingham Prize, and a 2015 NAACP Image Award nominee. Her most recent novel,* Creatures of Passage, *was shortlisted for the Ernest J. Gaines Award for Literary Excellence and a 2021 Notable Book selection by NPR and the* Washington Post. *She lives in the DC area with her husband and three sons.*

IV.

"...not complete until it is performed....

It's not just enough to have words."

Tanure Ojaide

Lynn Kozak

From *Iliad* 16.727–77

Hektor ordered Kebriones, his awesome charioteer, to strike the horses and drive them back into battle, straight at Patroklos; and Patroklos on the other side jumps down from his chariot to the ground with his spear in his left hand, and with his right hand he picks up a jagged piece of marble rock, his hand wrapping round it, and he makes a throw, really puts his weight behind it, the kind of throw that no man can avoid for long, and it is not in vain because it hits Kebriones, Hektor's awesome charioteer, who's holding the reins, the sharp rock hits him right in the middle of the forehead, and the eyebrows, they can't stand up against this rock: the whole skull just caves in, and his eyeballs fall out, his eyeballs fall out to the ground, lie in the dust at his feet; and then he falls, he falls like an acrobat or like a tumbler headfirst out of the well-made chariot, and the life left his bones; and oh Patroklos, you really wanted to make fun of him, didn't you? Now Patroklos, he comes running over and he says: "O *popoi*, did you see how graceful this man was? I mean, he was like a diver; I mean, if we were all, right now, on a boat on the fishy sea, even in a storm, this man, diving like this, he would fill our bellies with delicious oysters; I mean, that's how well he just dove off his chariot onto the plain; I mean, who knew Troy had such great divers?" That's what Patroklos said, and now, like a lion, you sprang, Patroklos, you sprang towards the corpse of Kebriones like a lion who goes into the sheepfold even though he's already been hit in his chest, and his own courage is gonna kill him; that's how you sprang, Patroklos, onto the hero Kebriones' corpse; and Hektor, Hektor is on the other side, and he gets down from his chariot to the ground, and so now, now these two clash over the corpse of Kebriones; like wrangling lions, up in the mountains, two lions, both starving, over the corpse of a dead deer; that's how these two masters of the war-cry now fought over the corpse of Kebriones, Menoitios' strong son, Patroklos, and shining Hektor, just desperate to cut each other's flesh with the pitiless bronze; and now Hektor grabs hold of the head, and he won't let go, and Patroklos, he's got the feet on the other side; so now the whole battle, from both sides, happens all around the corpse of Kebriones; like when the east wind and the south wind crash into one another up in the woods, in the deeps of the mountains, and all the tall trees there, the oak and the ash and the tall cherry, all of them with their branches outstretched and tall clatter together with the wind's force and scream as the branches break in an unholy sound; that's the kind of sound that came now as the Trojans and the Danaans clashed over the body of Kebriones, wanting to cut each other down, and not one of them thought about deadly fear; and so many spears fixed in the ground, sharp spears, all around the body of Kebriones, and arrows flew, jumping off their strings, and rocks came raining down, clattering off the shields of men, all around the corpse of Kebriones; but Kebriones, he just lay there in the whirlwind of dust, massive in his mass, and he had forgotten all about chariot driving.

PB: Lynn, I've got to ask about this project, because it's so unique. Basically, you're standing in front of a very receptive audience—and reciting—or retelling—an English language version of the *Iliad*. Tell us what happens in *Previously on the Iliad*.

LK: I had written a book a few years earlier that was arguing that in the *Iliad* you could understand ancient epic and some of the techniques of ancient epics as a function of serial narrative (*Experiencing Hektor*, Bloomsbury, 2016). What does it mean to be able to keep a long narrative in mind for both an audience and a performer, with breaks, over a long period of time? I wanted to test this out by doing a serial performance of the *Iliad*.

I've discovered through previous performances that I can remember quite a lot of text if I'm actively translating it, so I never write out a translation in English. I just translate it over and over again from the Greek, and if I only work from the Greek text, I can remember about an hour of text. Actually, I can remember more than that because I also did a longer chunk of the *Odyssey* that was about two hours, so I can remember quite a lot of text if it's an active translation process. I just started performing one night at this bar not too far from campus, and I was really shocked at how many people showed up. I think the first night we had something like 60 or 65 people, and it really grew over the series. I think it was 28 or 29 weeks in total, so we started in January, and we finished in August. We really built a community around it. Some people would come every single week, some people made friends at the bar coming to these performances, some people would bring snacks. It was wonderful to see what happened organically around it, that I certainly didn't expect.

PB: So let me just delve into that process a little bit because it's quite extraordinary and yet, of course, in some ways I think it reflects ancient practices.

LK: It's a cognitive mystery to me because I haven't memorized the Greek or the English, exactly, so if you asked me to recite the Greek I couldn't write or recite the Greek, and I couldn't come up with the same English version every time either. The way it would work is Monday nights we perform. On Tuesday, I would sit down with the next chunk of Greek text and do my first translation pass, looking words up and figuring out the grammar. Wednesday we would sit down with the director for the first time, and I would try to read in English from the Greek having done that translation work the day before. And then I would get up on my feet, and we would rehearse Thursday, Friday, Saturday, and I would just be looking at the Greek text and translating from the Greek every time that we ran through a section.

Sometimes directors would want me to fix a phrase or a certain way of saying things. so sometimes the English would get fixed in small phrases but then sometimes it wouldn't. So, like I said, it's almost impossible to describe what the process is like and what exactly I have memorized. But overall, the memorization of my lines was not bad, because I was dropping between five and ten lines a week, which is really not a lot (out of between 400 and 650 lines). There were a couple weeks where I really messed up and dropped a huge chunk, but for the most part, it was pretty much line for line. But this method of memorization did mean there was flexibility, and one of the reasons I wanted to do the performance this way is because I had translated both epic and tragedy for performance before for real actors, and then often found it frustrating when I heard the actor say something that I just didn't feel quite right about or where I didn't quite like the translation. When I'm doing it, I can change it in that moment, I can go with what feels right or I can comment on it or talk about my frustration with translating that bit, so it gives me more leeway as the translator/performer.

PB: I noticed that you did use epithets which you modernize. For instance, "that's what she said." It would be a point of reference to a poetic style, and yet it's also very colloquial at the same time.

LK: Yes, Joseph Shragge set that in the first week, when he directed me. It became one of the formulas that started to get a community response, and so it was interesting how my own formulas and my own language choices became fixed in their own way. Another example is talking about having nice shin guards, where it was just easier to put it in language that I knew would be more easily understood in the oral-aural situation because talking about the Greeks as "well-greaved," which is how most people translate that word, is not going to necessarily resonate with the contemporary English audience when they hear that word.

PB: And part of your work too, as I understand, is to make connections between ancient texts and modern television, popular culture shows, and characters. Tell us about that.

LK: I work on reception, so I'm interested in how contemporary culture takes on ancient stories. So, for example, I've worked on the television show *Hannibal* because it responds directly to the *Iliad.* But I would say that I'm more interested in just having a contemporary conversation around the *Iliad* or around ancient tragedy.

I'm still addicted to these texts and these stories and so I think, for me, doing this project was just a way for me to get even closer to the *Iliad*. I've read it so many times, I've worked on it, but embodying those characters and actually saying all those words and telling the story myself—getting to tell the story as some combination of myself and the *Iliad*'s narrator and the Iliadic characters—it's just an incredible experience. It's wonderful getting to teach the *Iliad,* but actually getting to tell somebody the *Iliad* and getting to bring them into that experience with you—it was just a real thrill for me. It's better than *Game of Thrones*.

PB: Could you replay that little scene, those 34 lines, as you do it on *Previously on the Iliad*? This is the scene where Patroclus kills the charioteer of Hector. Hector loses 11 charioteers—they're kind of like the red shirt security guys on *Star Trek*.

LK: I talked about red shirts in my book on the *Iliad*. I haven't memorized this passage. I purposely didn't look back at the Greek to transcribe this because I wanted to keep the orality from my performance and not obsess over its fidelity to the Greek. But I can read it now. It's one of my favorite passages, one of my favorite deaths. I had a show called *My Favorite Deaths* that featured this one—I just like how self-contained it is. It's the death of Kebriones, and I'm just going to go into it.

***Lynn Kozak** works on archaic and classical ancient Greek literature, as well as its receptions, translations, and comparisons with contemporary texts. From January-August 2018, Kozak translated and performed the whole* Iliad *in weekly serial instalments, as part of an FRQSC-funded project "Previously On...The Iliad"; all performances are available to view on YouTube. They also performed a version of the Apologoi from the* Odyssey *as part of the 2019 Festival Interculturel du Conte.*

Carolyn Finney

"Memory Divine"

"Home" has always been an overwhelmingly enticing, all-consuming, magnificent idea for me. As someone who was adopted as a baby, I struggle with the weight of the word: to me, it implies a sense of ownership, of claiming, of belonging, of recognition, of relationship, of being claimed, of being wanted, of being seen—of knowing—that I have found, in parts, elusive. When I eagerly left "home" at eighteen, it was always the place I returned to with feelings of both desire and trepidation. This "home" was where my parents who raised me resided and where I found out that I was not kin in the biological sense. This "home" was where I looked for myself everywhere, every day and came up wanting. This "home" was filled with contradictions that I'm still wading through in an effort to make sense of, well, everything. But this "home" was also the only place I knew that I could return to with some degree of certainty that I would be welcomed. I cannot say that I thought the land was extra special or exceptional at that time (except that it was), but it was the only place in my life that felt like a certainty, a kind of north star in a world that did not know how to see me (and that I did not know how to see). For better and for worse, I became myself on this land. So many "firsts": experiencing loss, falling in love, being denied, wrestling with anger, feeling humiliation, facing fear and losing, facing fear and winning, creating new worlds. And dreaming, so much dreaming. Day dreaming wasn't just something I did; on this land, it was a state of mind, a state of being. It was an out of body experience I had within my brown body. And that body became something more, too, as I ran, swam, biked and climbed my way through a life I wasn't sure I had earned, but was desperate to prove myself worthy of. And all the while, as I dreamed and flew, my parents toiled in the background, their dreams fading as their children grew.

By the time my parents left our home in 2003, I had moved at least twelve times and had spent the better part of five years backpacking in Africa and Asia, ultimately finding respite in a village in Nepal for a year and a half. By 2003, I had pursued an acting career for eleven years and returned to school where I ultimately completed three degrees. By 2003, I had married and divorced, and married and divorced again. By 2003, I had become so practiced at throwing my heart out in the world in my search for home that I almost didn't notice that I was about to lose the only home that I had ever known. As my parents were getting their picture taken in front of their cherry tree, I was working on my doctorate and looking for stories of us on the library shelves and coming up wanting. Again. As I watched the story of my parents on that land fade to black, I decided to tell a different story. It was time to hold myself accountable.

SL: Tell us about this page. What was it that spoke to you in terms of choosing it? How does it represent your practice? Also, because you write across different genres, and you're an artist who has worked on a stage, I am curious about how this page and your practice connect to all of that fullness.

CF: I chose this piece, in part because it was practical. There are past pieces that I could have chosen that are much more compact, and simple, but I wanted to choose a piece that was recently published. I also feel that this essay addresses broad themes I'm particularly drawn to—belonging, place, identity and representation. And because of my academic training as a geographer, I think a lot about the concept of place.

Over the last 15 years, I've been working to create a public platform asking myself the following question: how can I tell stories about questions of race, difference in relationship to the landscape, belonging, and identity? These are topics that are really challenging for us to have conversations about in the United States. Which is why I always start with the story of myself and my parents on the land. I do that because we're all biased about how we think about these things. I always want to make sure to put my bias on the table. Having a bias is neither bad nor good; it's just a way of knowing.

Telling that story, in part, makes my bias clear for everyone to see. I think one of the characteristics we all share is how we respond to things as human beings, influenced by the emotional lives that we all carry around with us. I always think we all have experienced some form of trauma in our lives simply by being alive on a daily basis. I don't care where you're from, or what you look like, the act of being human and dealing with daily life is always there. The other truth is that there's always land underneath us, and we need land to survive. So, I wanted to get at that. I'm driven by this idea of home because I've never felt quite at home anywhere. That's a longer conversation about what it means to be adopted, raised by people that you may not be genetically related to, and the challenges when trying to find that information.

How do I think about relationships more broadly, and what counts as a good relationship? What does it mean if I think beyond human-to-human relationships? And what does *that* mean? I've only come to this in the last few years because I found that in my work, this is the story people wanted me to talk about more than anything else, no matter all the other stories and histories I share. They want to know more about my personal story. Which means, whether I want to or not, I'm constantly digging deeper, peeling back the onion skins of my experience to see what it is that I'm trying to get at for myself, not just for everybody else.

Deep down, I know there's healing. There's healing that I need, that others need, and that the land needs. I must be honest about that and part of what I was sharing in my piece was the sense of my own struggle over belonging. Thinking about home. Thinking about how I've moved around so much, as an adult. What does it mean to feel like one is connected? I think there's a lot more I could say about that, and what does *that* mean? Can we actually ever heal those tender places in order to move forward? This is what I do all the time, talking about "a thing" and being the "thing" itself. Engaging with people in organizations and communities who ask me to come in and talk or write about all of the above all the time. Consequently, there's emotional labor involved, along with the intellectual work. And this has become part of my practice.

I'm always in it, the practice. And I don't know if you meant it this way, Shanta, but it is the practice of doing the work. I am an artist-scholar-in-residence and storyteller at Middlebury College, but there's also the practice of asking myself: how am I a better human being? How am I able to set down the things that weigh me down in order to be open to what's emergent, new, and possible? I'm asking other people to do that. So, I say it honestly, authentically—how am I doing it? What does that look like for me?

And sometimes, it's hard. I'm digging down, looking at my past, trying to understand certain things so that I can release them. I don't want to ignore it, and I don't believe anything ever goes away simply because you wish it away, because wherever you go, there you are. I'm trying to involve that in the practice of working with other people in groups and communities. If I ask you to be vulnerable, I have to be vulnerable. What does it mean to lead with my heart? And that doesn't mean you tell everybody everything. It just means to question: what does it mean to put your story out there? I believe my healing is embedded in my practice.

SL: I'm very curious about the concept of voice, and orality and does it play a role in everything you're talking about in terms of healing and grief. Also, how do you define orality? When you're composing on the page, do you think as a public speaker, as an artist, across all your modalities? As someone who's done very stage centered, do you compose with orality different in mind than on page? Or how do all of these play together?

CF: Oh my god, nobody has ever asked me that, and it's such a great question. Only somebody else who does some similar kind of work gets that! I almost want to take my time with this question, like the way you would with something juicy that someone gives you to eat. I don't want to eat it fast.

In terms of orality, I think a lot in rhythm, the rhythm that I speak in. I do a lot of interviews, so I'm all over the place. And I rarely give a straight answer to a question, but if you stay with me long enough, I know I'll get there. A good question sends my mind a poppin' and the circuits hoppin'!

I always invite interviewers to share the transcript with me so that I can help capture a certain kind of rhythm. I also read it out loud and ask myself, does this sound like me? For three years, I wrote a column four times a year for the *Earth Island Journal*. When I was writing my 700-750 words, I had to read it over and over because there'll be something in the rhythm of the sentence that conveys what I'm trying to share. If it doesn't come out quite right, then I know I have to go back in to revise it which may be different than someone else's approach. I call myself a writer, but my first love, the first place where I stand comfortably, is in orality. I lead with thinking, "How does it sound?" And then I ask myself, "how does it *feel* when I've said the thing and does that *feel* right?"

An editor can help with the grammatical errors I may have made. However, sometimes, it's challenging because editors who are really strict and want to adhere to more traditional sentence constructions often want to flatten out the rhythm, and I have to push back.

I have to push back just enough, because if I don't, I lose what is me and my words. I don't think something being well written is only about what kinds of words you used, or whether you get your grammar in all the right places with your periods in the right place, your apostrophes in the right place. I think those things are quite secondary. I mostly think about, who is the voice that is speaking? Sometimes the voice challenges us, you know? I think about Alice Walker's *The Color Purple* and what I felt when that book first came out and my aunt gave me a copy.

When I encountered those opening pages—about a young black girl who hasn't had any formal education, and it's all in her voice—my whole world tilted. I was a voracious reader when I was young, and I never read anything like that. That book made me work, aside from the fact that it was amazing to hear that a young Black girl could be at the center of a story. That matters, too, right? But it also made me work at being able to *listen* differently, mentally, and hold the words differently. What that did was open, within me, an ability to hear a different way that English could be spoken and imagined. That main character in *The Color Purple*—her dream life told me so much about who she was, the rhythm of who she was, how she is in the world as a body and a spirit. I'm always thinking about that.

There's an exercise that I learned from somebody here in Vermont named Peter Forbes, who used to run the Center for Whole Communities back in the mid-2000s, late 2000s. I ended up being a facilitator at that center. We would have these circles where we'd be in a yurt, and there'd be a question posed to a circle of 20 people. We would talk about it for 45 minutes to an hour. Meanwhile, during this process, he'd write down what we were saying, then he'd read it back to us. He had structured it in an almost poetic form. I learned how to engage in that process as I watched him do that, and I now do it for groups all the time. I love it and I love seeing them go!

I take their words and play with them. I can repeat themes, move them around, but I always try to answer the question: what was the core feeling? Was it an idea? What's the rhythm of what the group is saying? When I am doing this exercise, I'm listening. I tell the group that I can't talk, I can't be part of the conversation in the usual way. I have to tilt my head, which is my way of signaling that I'm listening. It's a really good practice that pushes me to ask, how do I hear and how do I listen? And to discover and recognize that how we listen and how we hear things aren't always the same thing.

Then I have to bring this practice of listening to the written page in preparation for it to be spoken. Once I've fine-tuned what I've written, I read it out loud, softly to myself first, to feel the piece. And then I share it with the group. I love watching how my words land on people. I feel both trepidation and excitement. Here's the thing: the act of reading is often done in privacy. If I am reading something, in private, I can respond or not respond to what I am reading. But when I say the thing to you, especially for the first time, I can see how it's landing. This also means I can adjust and adapt my reading to the audience. Or I should say, *with* the audience. Do I need to slow down? Do I need to repeat it? Because when I repeat, it is because I could feel something in the room when I said it the first time, so I'm just gonna say it again.

Now, there's all the room in the world to play with it. I know you can play with writing too, I'm not saying you can't. I am just saying that for me, this is a call towards orality. It gives me freedom, spaciousness, and it's multi-dimensional in a way that writing doesn't necessarily fulfill for me, even though I really like to write. For me, it's within the orality that I find the magic.

SL: Sometimes I'm imagining I'm talking to Oprah, even when I am writing certain things. I write it like I would say it to Oprah. That, in a way, is thinking of words on a stage and on a page, and then, as you have talked about, one must consider the question of how the words *feel*. How they land in the body? I want to wrap up with this last question, what is voice for you? How do you define voice, especially across everything you do?

CF: How would I define voice? Hmmm... When I was a kid, my parents said that they would always find me talking to myself.

Now, I will admit that as an adult, I still do. I just don't do it around people! As a kid, I would have conversations. But I would say more often than not it was because of what was going on in my head. I needed an outlet, and everything needed to come out. I needed to be able to give it breath. There was something powerful and necessary about putting it out there—taking it out of my head to give it room to become something else, something more. Maybe to manifest, to transform, to give me some freedom because I was worried about things all the time. I was thinking about 500 million different things, the way kids often do. On one level, I think voice is a place of freedom.

When I was a teenager, I got into musical theater. I didn't have a great singing voice, but it was good enough, and I just loved performance. But by the time I was 19, when I got my first paid acting job doing dinner theater in upstate New York, I developed nodes on my vocal cords. So, when you hear me now usually sounding hoarse, it's because of those nodes on my vocal cords. Basically, I was using my vocal cords incorrectly. So, my ability to sing and feel comfortable about it sort of disappeared. I have issues around my voice in that way, but not so much in terms of speaking. There's something about the freedom, the ability to articulate my inner self to the world that I can no longer find in singing, but can find in speaking.

My experience of speaking is fluid, emotionally connected and, when I'm really present, emergent. Whether it was when I used to do theater and had to read a script or when I get up in front of somebody to give a talk that I have given some version of before—I never say the same word in the same way. That doesn't mean that the intention isn't the same. But my voice might be different on that day, for whatever reason. And the audience will be different. And the moment is always different. Each new moment becomes a place of exploration that the concept of voice gives me as well. It takes me on a journey every time, even if it's the story about me growing up. I've told that story hundreds of times. But it's never exactly the same when I tell it.

My voice is in relationship to the story, and the story is something that I feel deeply because it is something that's part of my spirit. It sits in my body in a very particular way and the voice is just trying to express that. Some days, the voice may be reticent. Some days, the voice is emotional. Sometimes the voice is just tired, right? Some days the voice is talking to Oprah and having a sister-girl moment. Some days, the voice is talking to a roomful of young students. Some days, I'm just trying to talk to my parents. Some days, my voice is just trying to find its way.

I often think: what if I lost my voice, what would that mean? I remember in high school, I had the flu and got laryngitis the week after. I found that challenging. But if I seriously lost the ability to use my voice permanently, I don't know what I would do. I would survive, but it is really scary to me because how am I free? How would I express myself? Where do my thoughts go and my imagination go, you know? All the stuff that lives in this big noggin, where does it go? If I don't have the voice, and it's how I connect with people, how would I connect to others?

Voice, for me, is about relationships and connection. It's how I connect in the world. It's how I connect when I'm talking to strangers, especially because I travel a lot, mostly alone. I live alone and when I go out in the world, my voice is how I connect. So, asking me not to speak? It doesn't mean I can't be quiet. It just means that speaking is my pathway to potential relationships and connection. And if I didn't have it, oh boy, I'd have to do some deep digging to figure out how to get there otherwise.

Writing for me is also a place that I can connect. But again, I know it's not true for all writers and people who write. For me, there's a kind of one-sidedness to writing because once I've written a piece, I give it to you to read, you'll read it or you'll not read it, and I may never get any response from you at all about it. I'm not judging the process so much as trying to understand it. There is no immediate gratification. But if I'm speaking to you, even if you don't say anything, there's still something happening at that moment. I can say for myself, I know it's filling a void even if just for a minute. Perhaps your voice joins the chorus, and then we're in it together, but you're in it anyway. Your heart is beating. You're in the room, and I'm experiencing that your heart is beating.

I want to say one more thing, just because I can't help myself! About three or four months, right before COVID hit, I was giving a talk, somewhere in the Midwest. I think it was at a university in Minnesota. For the first time, the person who invited me out said we're going to have two people signing because we have somebody in the audience who is hearing challenged.

I've never had this experience before, working with sign language interpreters. I got really nervous because I'm a fast talker. These two women—the women doing sign language—were going to be switching on and off, because I was going to be talking for about an hour.

I was aware that they were working hard—they were breaking a sweat, right from the start. When I finished my talk, I apologized and explained that I tried to slow down. But when I'm in the moment, I tend to go off script, because I'm responding to the audience. What was so wonderful was my interaction with the young man who was hearing challenged. He came up to me afterwards. He had some good questions and told me that he still got most of it. I left there thinking about the privilege of hearing. And listening isn't only what you can audibly hear or write because he was engaged. My awareness was stretched, because it didn't mean that I needed to be silent. I don't even think it meant that I needed to judge myself for relying on my voice. It just meant I had to think differently about how my voice can hold and take up space.

You know, it's been a few years and I'm still thinking about it, how he still got a lot of what I was saying, despite my inability to slow down. I am reminded, through his wisdom and experience, that my ability to communicate and connect is not solely reliant on my voice. I can ask myself the question: how is my spirit emanating? How is my spirit received? And how does my spirit connect? I think it's about engaging and extending our whole selves—the hands, the expression, the eyes and our heart. We feel it—as the oracle from *The Matrix* says from "Balls to bones." And that is where the magic is giving room to fly.

Carolyn Finney, PhD *is a storyteller, author and a cultural geographer who is deeply interested in issues related to identity, difference, creativity, and resilience. Grounded in both artistic and intellectual ways of knowing (pursuing an acting career for eleven years and backpacking around the world before returning to school to complete three degrees), she is passionate about interrogating our past and dreaming a future that is liberatory, just and green. Along with public speaking, writing, media engagements and consulting, she served on the National Parks Advisory Board and is the author of numerous publications, most notably her first book,* Black Faces, White Spaces: Reimagining the Relationship between African Americans and the Great Outdoors *(2014). She was a Fulbright Scholar, a Canon National Parks Science Scholar and has received two Mellon Fellowships, including a residency at the New York Botanical Gardens. She is currently working on her second book and is a scholar/artist in residence in the Franklin Environmental Center at Middlebury College.* ***"Memory Divine" is an excerpt from a longer piece with the same title by Carolyn Finney, originally published in*** **A Darker Wilderness** ***ed. Erin Sharkey (Minneapolis: Milkweed Editions, 2023).***

Remica Bingham-Risher

"At Northside Skatepark"

The men are boys, the boys are men,
        they are screaming
obscenities and love overwhelms them.

My boy is a fire,
        helmet wrapped in flames.
They invent ways to one up each other—

pulling barrels and battlers
        into the space.
They are not kind to one another

or themselves but they persist
        swift as mistakes, coming
and disappearing. The concrete

is stronger than their bodies—
        some ride broken, some break—
what balance it takes to slide

over rails and stairways,
        to hold dear what hurts.
They tarry between what the world

wants for them and their own thirst:
        to care less or adore everything unseen:
the air that carries them,

the children nearby beckoning,
        the music only some can hear,
It's hammering and reckoning.

PB: Remica, what role do you think orality plays in your composition and in your practice?

RBR: The answer is twofold. It plays a huge part in the way I compose poems, because I consider poetry as it is: an oral and aural art, as hearing and speaking are concerned. I'm always thinking about sound and how that might work in the poem to ground the reader, but to also move the reader down the page. This poem is about boys skateboarding at a skatepark, so you have to be swift in places.

I'm always thinking about whatever the *thing is* I'm writing about. It's musical the way the skateboarders intertwine themselves. I was thinking about that in particular, what *kind* of music they make.

I don't think of performance as in how it will be read aloud on the stage a whole lot. I think that's part of my natural composition to think about how a reader might come to the poem. I'm not from a performance background as a poet. I'm a poet of the page first, but very intimately and deeply concerned with the way I translate work off the page. I'm always thinking how well I can compose and build enough music into the poem that it translates off the page no matter who's reading it.

PB: How would you describe the source of your voice?

RBR: A great many things have lent themselves to it. I have a book of prose coming out, and it is really a rumination of how I came to the writing life. A lot of the things I ended up asking myself in those essays first is, why do you do it like this? Who are my influences? I interviewed poets for a long time in my career and ten of them are highlighted in that book. Part of the genesis of my voice is reading and then trying to embody the voices of others that just really arrested me. Tim Seibles is a mentor of mine, and hopefully he will be included in this book. I was introduced to Tim on the page first and was immediately taken with what happens sonically in his work. Then I saw him read and I thought *crap, I didn't know it could get better!* Patricia Smith is another poet that shows up in that collection of essays. If you know anything about Patricia Smith, she's kind of the goddess of performance, but also, really and truly, has become a goddess of *form*, and formal convention. Her poem "Motown Crown", which is a crown of sonnets, is a series I'm always trying to emulate in some way sonically. All the reading that I did, all of the studying of poets that I did, helped me consider what I wanted from my own voice.

Also, just a bunch of soul music. I come from a house that would play music every Saturday morning when you were cleaning, and it's still the house that does that every Sunday while you're cleaning. My son was on the way to school the other day, and he's sixteen. Some days he's singing the latest rapper. But the other day I caught him singing UB-40's "Red Red Wine." I was like, what kind of eclectic kid are we building here? But music, especially the narrative in music, holds its place in our lives so firmly. So, the narrative in poems, and leaning on that music and rhythm in poems is the genesis of my voice.

Remica Bingham-Risher's *work has been published in* The New York Times, The Writer's Chronicle, Callaloo *and* Essence. *She is the author of* Conversion *(Lotus, 2006) winner of the Naomi Long Madgett Poetry Award,* What We Ask of Flesh *(Etruscan, 2013) shortlisted for the Hurston/Wright Legacy Award and* Starlight & Error *(Diode, 2017) winner of the Diode Editions Book Award and finalist for the Library of Virginia Book Award. Her memoir,* Soul Culture: Black Poets, Books and Questions That Grew Me Up, *was published by Beacon Press (2022). Her newest book,* Room Swept Home, *is a work of poems, historical and family photographs (Wesleyan University Press, 2024). She is the Director of Quality Enhancement Plan Initiatives at Old Dominion University in Norfolk, VA, where she resides with her husband and children.*

Carol Moldaw

“Dinner Guests”

When wanting to walk, I circle the apple trees
behind our house until suddenly done

digging at gopher holes the dogs flop down,
crumbs of earth clinging to their paws like cake.

I might accelerate or change direction
as I round a lap at the dilapidated barn.

My repetitions have worn a path in the grass
and now I follow the path I unconsciously made.

I remind myself to look up at the mountain.
The blossoms took me by surprise at first

although the buds didn’t flower all at once
but arrived like dinner guests, in lulls and bursts,

each bearing similarly beribboned gifts
the way guests used to, and now flocks of them

are already drifting off in flurried gusts
the way we tended to, when we were guests.

PB: Carol, before recording, you said you started out as a lyric poet. I'm wondering how your journey has changed from that beginning. How do you see lyricism as a component in your work?

CM: I still think of myself as a lyric poet. Two main components of the lyric are sound and image, and I'm always driven by aural and pictorial qualities as I write. Sometimes now, though, I also pursue a more complicated or abstract train of thought. I enjoy syntactically complex sentences that extend over a number of lines and an awareness of the relationship between line and sentence is important to me. That changes the quality of the lyricism, though the sentence and line might end together with a crystalline—lyric—image. The path there is just a little different, sometimes convoluted.

PB: When I think about the complications of your poems, I'm wondering to what extent you think about a poem being *heard,* rather than be seen on the page. How do those two components relate?

CM: Just as I like to think of the line and sentence in conjunction, the way a poem is heard and the way it appears on the page go hand in hand for me. I think the way a poem appears on the page should be instructive; reading it, you should be able to hear the way it's meant to sound. And reading it aloud, the lineation and stanza pattern should be relevant and revelatory. Lineation and punctuation are great aural tools.

The shape of the line and stanza shape are significant to me; they are the first things I want to "find" when I'm starting a poem. I feel each nascent poem has a shape it's meant to inhabit. I tend to keep line lengths and stanzaic patterns consistent throughout a poem; I want variations to justify themselves, to feel necessary. When the line length is consistent, variation in sentence length adds another level of complexity. When line lengths vary, breath comes into play in a different and interesting way.

How a poem sounds, how it looks on the page—I can't choose between them. They both need to feel right and work together, whether in counterpart or harmony.

PB: Certainly "Dinner Guests" illustrates that. Is that something you've cultivated? Or is it just a result of maturation?

CM: I hope that as I've matured my ability to use language supplely and intricately has grown, but it's probably more the case of one thing leading to another, than a consciously cultivated plan. One grows from one's frustration with oneself, by trying to go beyond one's limitations.

PB: Can you talk about how the tradition has made this journey, or made this path unconsciously followed?

CM: Studying prosody with Robert Fitzgerald significantly influenced my poetics. I don't consider myself a Formalist poet—I don't see how I could—but understanding poetry in terms of its meter, sound patterns, and other technical aspects, and putting that understanding into practice (and more practice) changed everything for me. It also changed the way I read. Poems speak to poems, over languages, ages, and languages. So, I guess I think of tradition as an ever-renewing wellspring. It isn't important to me to follow tradition, but it is important to me to have tools that I can turn to use.

Carol Moldaw *is the author of seven books of poetry and a novella. She has received a Merwin Conservancy Artist Residency, a National Endowment for the Arts Creative Writing Fellowship, a Lannan Foundation Residency Fellowship, and a Pushcart Prize. Along with Turkish, her poems have been translated into Chinese, Italian, Portuguese, and Spanish. A volume of her selected poems, translated into Chinese, is forthcoming from Guangxi Normal University Press in Beijing in 2025. She lives in Santa Fe, New Mexico.*

Steven Reese
Translated from the Spanish of Roberto Manzano

"Grateful Now"

The contents of a day turned out on their stretch
of ground, what do you see where you see? Not the trail
of green fragments, the eyes of fish,
not the statue's curves in the air?
You don't hear a silence, a stubborn din?
When the turning, green
volume of the trees closes overhead,
within are the seeds, and then fruit:
it happens—It's living—and below sometimes is a child
cracking almonds, and the dry, sweet smell
of childhood rises, and outside, under the sun,
a bloodline's sweaty blouses and shirts
swelling with place and voice:
record them with eyes time has sharpened,
wave on wave weaving your footsteps
and you are only that: a living mound, a restless
mass, and each twig that sounded
made you a low shrub, then tree, from where will you come'
if you don't come from another, others, everything?
Be grateful now, it is time, and put together the planks
as they suit your subjects:
in the luminous space gather the stones
of your simple monument: for what do you pass
when you pass? Hectic and inexorable you go by
and you live only when you add your waters to the river's.

PB: Talking about voice, Steve, obviously with the translator there's even more complexity, because there's the translator's voice, and then the poet's voice that you have to somewhat intuit and render. Tell us about that process.

SR: Well, I think it can be daunting from one angle. I mean, I think it can be a source of frustration. Shelley is famous for saying how impossible translation is because of the way in which the sound of language contributes to meaning. But the problem, if you want to look at it as a problem, is much larger than that because I think one of the things this poem says—it brings up the word voice—is that the sources of voice are everywhere, multiple. They come from place, they come from history, they come from others around you, the come from a lineage, they come from so many sources. So when you factor that in, then to translate voice in the sense that your book is using that word, into the voice of another language seems really impossible.

But of course, I think a lot of translators—I'm one of them—see this as an invitation or an enticement. Because really, you're entering into and trying to bring that voice over with some measure of authenticity, fidelity. You're entering that complex web of associations, forces, sources, as best you can. And for a translator, that's enormously exciting. For me to start translating Manzano's poem was to start trying to understand Cuban history, to start understanding where Manzano came from, who his friends are, all sorts of things. And that can do nothing but expand you and excite you if it doesn't just completely discourage you with its overwhelming complexity.

PB: I love the idea that this is an invitation into the poem, and its many iterations and sources. Has translating had that kind of influence on your own poems?

SR: Yeah, I think it has because whether you're conscious of it or not, the idea of language itself as a translating tool becomes just one of the gears that start working naturally in your mind. So, my own poems, I think, started to pay attention to the process of translating whatever it is, sensory data, emotional content, into words, starting to pay attention to that in a new way. And you know in Manzano's poem, all of these things—trees, bloodlines, places, sounds—all these things are voices that end up being recorded. You know, the poem says, "record these things with an attentive eye." So, I think I naturally started to gravitate toward an idea of writing that was essentially, I know this is not new, but essentially translation and language as this very singular medium that does its best to render huge webs of phenomena, and inevitably reduces it even while it sings it. So yeah, I think it has crept into my poetry writing mind inevitably.

PB: Steve, you've also taken many poems and set them to music. Sometimes adjusting, altering, augmenting the actual words of the poem, and sometimes keeping all the words. Does that relate to the act of translation and this way you're talking? Or is that a different activity altogether?

SR: I don't think it's a different activity altogether. Because in moving poems over to songs, it depends upon the kind of song that you're producing of course. So, in some ways, many times for instance, it will amount to introducing regularities into the poem, so that they coincide with the regularities of a musical form. I need four beats here, the poem's not giving me that, I need to make an adjustment. It is a matter of taking the original text and finding a rhythm for it that suits this other form.

Now when you're translating of course, you're not constricted by musical measure. But I think you are constricted by what you hear in the original text and trying to produce something that has a musicality corresponding in some way to the original. So, when I make a song out of a poem, I'm trying not to distort the poem out of its original being but to make it sing a different kind of singing. And I think translation is just that. You know, if I were completely faithful to the poem, I'd just rewrite it in Spanish. I would just reprint it.

PB: As in Borges, a perfect translation of *Don Quixote*, you know, is a copy of the text.

SR: Exactly, exactly. So yeah, so you have to find a singing that will suit the song you're making, but that certainly has its ground in the original text.

***Steven Reese** is author of three books of poems and translator of* Synergos: Selected Poems of Roberto Manzano *(Etruscan Press, 2009). His poems, prose, and translations have appeared or are forthcoming in* Poetry Northwest, Green Mountains Review, Artful Dodge, West Branch, *and other magazines.*

Nin Andrews

"The Portable Pussy"

Wherever I go, I carry a pussy with me. How, you might ask, but I and the pussy are not one and the same being, so carry it I must. Asleep or awake, depending on who else is in the room, it talks to me. Honestly, much too honestly, really. I am so relieved when those who hear it pretend not to. Or perhaps they imagine they are only hearing things. On rare occasions the pussy gets carried away. Then it sings off key or starts composing poetry. Of course, most don't suspect (or so I hope) that it's the pussy and not I who sings, or how difficult it is to carry a pussy everywhere I go, much less listen to its running commentary when all I wish for is silence. A little relief. I've even sought medical advice, but the doctors insist the pussy is all in the mind. I need only stop thinking about it, and the pussy will vanish forever. So I have been thinking about not thinking about the pussy. But I have my fears. If the pussy is in my mind, alongside my thoughts, what if the thoughts leave first? If I have to pick between a pussy and a brain, which will it be? After all, who can choose between the player and his flute? The sea below and the sky above? How can I ignore *the gullies for the torrents of the rain and the path of the thunderbolt? And who am I to command the waves: thus far and no further shall you come.*

NA: I often think of my poems as little boats, and when composing them, I wonder if they will sink or float, swamp or sail.

The boat I had in mind in this case was female sexuality, but that term is dull and clunky. I decided to use the word, pussy, instead because it encapsulates both the topic and my issues with it, i.e. my discomfort and our cultural discomfort. And it also creates tension

At first, I worried that the pussy might create too much tension. Like the name of God, perhaps it should not be said aloud. To dial it down, I chose the form of the prose poem, of a very flat prose poem, with simple syntax and diction so it would appear familiar, unthreatening, and safe. Maybe even a little prim and proper.

While writing, I pretended I was talking about the most mundane topics: what I do during my days or what I carry, as if it were a purse, keys, maybe an umbrella in case of rain. I then talked about what a pain it is to carry such things. Women often complain about their purses, their lives, how heavy or annoying they've become.

But then, to close the poem, I wanted to at least attempt to answer the question, what do you do with female sexuality? Or with the pussy or the poet that is prattling away in your head? And what if they are the same? I used the book of Job to answer the question, and also *not* to answer the question posed—as God does so beautifully in the book of Job.

When I first read this poem aloud, some audience members gave me a hard time. I remember one young man who stood up and shouted, "You can't use that word, pussy, in a poem. You just can't write like that!" A few women agreed. Certain topics, they suggested, were best left alone. "They're just taboo," an elderly blonde informed me. I thought of Tiresias who was blinded either by Athena for seeing her bathing naked or by Hera for revealing that women enjoy sex more than men. And I thought how you CAN say pussy in a poem. That is the beauty of poetry. You can say almost anything—if you say it well.

At that time, I was reading to Ohio Bible belt audiences, and I was made aware that I might be pushing a little too hard on certain buttons. Also, when I first wrote this poem and test-drove it, I found that kind of response very helpful because it showed me how close to the wind the poem was tacking, and how easily it could tip over. At that point in its genesis, the pussy was a bit livelier. Wearing a pink tutu and taking opera and dancing lessons, it was preparing for its debut on stage. The ending was not from the Old Testament.

Changing course, I chose to limit the pussy's ambitions and extracurricular activities so it merely sang softly and wrote poems, and one could imagine not noticing it, certainly not seeing or hearing it. It could dwell underground, as women's sexuality so often does. I called on the Bible to help me out with my conservative audience members. And to give a nod to the patriarchy.

Nin Andrews' *most recent book is* Son of a Bird *(Etruscan, 2025). She is the author of six chapbooks and 6 full-length poetry collections including* The Last Orgasm *(Etruscan, 2020) and* Miss August *(CavanKerry, 2017). Her poems have been featured in numerous publications including* Ploughshares, Agni, The Paris Review *and four editions of* Best American Poetry. *She has won two Ohio individual artist grants, the Pearl Chapbook Contest, the Kent State University Chapbook Contest, and the Gerald Cable Poetry Award. She is also the editor of a book of translations of the Belgian poet, Henri Michaux, titled,* Someone Wants to Steal My Name.

Jeff Diteman

"Fire Sails Through My Body"

Finite humankind has eyes on towers
everyone is obviously rusted
iconic confessors ask to dissect
such hype and howling

Here galactic immersion tremors man
harks on a stethoscope by torchlight
his girl is seeded broken as the phonemes
uttered when tipsy

Along come men glossed with fear of lepers
daughters of chrome pure hyperdemocracies
hypotheses drown and foreign empires roam
buzzing everywhere

A democracy! Just a mustard seed.
Peasant ankles varicosed with the birthweight
humming testosterone licking its dentures
finally alone

Fire sails through my body like a pirate ship

SL: I don't know if it's because I've been diving into a lot of sci-fi lately, but this feels so sci-fi inspired. Why don't you start by telling us a little bit about this piece, why did you choose this poem?

JD: This piece is a homophonic mashup translation. It's a mashup in the sense that I worked with two other existing poems. I started with a poem by Sappho, fragment 31, and I used Sappho for the sonic scaffolding of the piece: I took the sounds of Sappho's fragment, mapped them out with the international phonetic alphabet, and charted all the sounds there. And then I attempted to overlay them with the semantic content from another poem, a French poem called "*Il y a dans le fond quelque chose qui beugle*" by Raymond Queneau; It's a piece from 1965. So, we're already spanning, you know, two and a half millennia in this exchange.

You take the ancient Greek, and it's "*phainetai moi kênos îsos theoisin*," etc., then that becomes "Finite humankind has eyes on towers." This is part of a larger project where I'm taking this one poem by Queneau, and I've transformed it in 43 different ways. I've created 43 different translations of it using different constraints and strategies and genres. I've turned it into a sonnet, into a sestina, into a palindrome, into a short story, into a letter to the editor, and all sorts of different things. And this is one of them. This one is one of my favorites, especially in terms of the voice.

I think that what makes this piece so interesting is precisely the use of the sonic patterns—the meter, and the phonetic patterns—that come from Sappho, because she was such a master of that. And that is often lost in translations of Sappho. In a sense, this is a translation of what is one of the most fascinating elements of Sappho, which is the sound. It also contains elements of Sappho's meaning as well because Sappho's piece is about a sort of a rumbling feeling in the body, a surging of energy through the body that arises in response to feelings of powerful jealousy. For all the pieces where I did a mash-up with the Queneau piece—I've done a few others, with a Mayakovsky for example, with a Catullus—every time I did, I tried to choose a piece that also had this similar theme, because the Queneau piece is "*Il y a dans le fond quelque chose qui beugle,*" that's the refrain and the title. And "beugle" means "bellow," like "mooooo," there's this sound deep inside.

There's something deep inside the earth that comes rumbling up in this poem. And in the Sappho piece, too, there's this sense of rumbling.

SL: There are so many layers to this. And it leads me to ask about orality, especially because you speak several languages. How does orality or voice play a role in your composition and your translation? If voice or orality play one role in one language, do these play the same role in another language in terms of how you're working with language on the page?

JD: As a literary translator, I'm constantly preoccupied with the question of voice because that is what makes a literary translation an interesting thing to read. To me, what makes any given author distinctive in their original language is the patterns of the ways in which they respond to expectations, whether they adhere to standard language, whether they interject it with dialect or vernacular, or whether they interject it with totally surprising elements. How do they adhere to expectations and defy expectations? And that interplay, that tension, is one of the sites of the distinctiveness of an author's voice. I'm always thinking about that when I translate.

You and I work together on Ammarialú Posso Figueroa's book, and we have all these conversations about voice, right? There will be different characters who speak in different voices, and we try to capture that. It's very important to read any translation out loud, before calling it finished. It has to sing with an orality. The oral language comes first. In the history of language—in the development of language—oral language predates written language by millennia. Of course, that's also true for poetry. In a sense, by engaging with writers on the level of voice, we're getting back to something kind of primordial, I think, in poetry itself.

I'm a musician, and if I were to set a piece of original writing to music, I would want my translation to be able to fit over that same music. I think about things in terms like that. I'm a person who counts syllables when I'm translating. I sometimes make sound maps of things, using color coding and all kinds of strategies.

SL: This adds another dimension to the question, because you mentioned that you're a musician, have you ever married the music to what was on the page? When you're doing your translations, do you think about how it will be performed on a stage? As you're engaging in translation, do you do it with both in mind—how it is on the page and how it will be heard when it is in the air, or resting into the audience members' bodies?

JD: For many years, I was more focused on writing original poetry. When I was attending a lot of poetry readings and open mics, I was primarily concerned with sound and with creating a sonic and an emotional experience for the audience. There's a twinning that goes on between that kind of experience and the sound that you're trying to produce in a reader's head, even if they're not reading it out loud. That concern never goes away.

I had the good fortune to attend a slam poetry workshop in the Czech Republic in 2004, led by Mark Smith, a pioneer of the slam poetry scene in Chicago in the 1980s. In the workshop, Mark talked about how the last thing you want to do as a poet is get up in front of an audience quivering behind an eight and a half by eleven sheet of paper, reading meekly, and never making eye contact, and all that. A lot of poets do that because we're introverted people. We're more comfortable in our solitude and all that, but Mark emphasized the theatrical dimension of poetry. That is something that has really stuck with me, both with my work for the page and work that I've done for the stage. Think about Mayakovsky. Think about these poets who just, even if it is just on the page, something thrills you through it. There's an experience that goes with that, and that can come from quiet poetry as well. It doesn't have to be loud, but it has to sing.

SL: I think you bring up a very important point, the question of the preservation of an original voice versus your voice. When you come across someone else's work, and you want to preserve their voice while keeping your voice out of the way, how do you parse that? As someone who has done many years of translation across many different cultural backgrounds, how do you navigate this terrain? Because you're not just navigating your voice, you're navigating several voices... thousands upon thousands!

JD: You know, that question, it makes me think of a kind of a fundamental split or dichotomy in terms of writing itself. There are some writers who display their mastery through their ability to navigate and express different voices. Writers like Ken Kesey or Anne Carson, who, when you're reading them, you never know where you're going to go or what voice you're going to hear. And there are so many distinctive voices, and they all come across with this purity. Then there are other writers like Franz Kafka, who, no matter what story he's telling, no matter what character it is, there's always this same Kafkaesque dreamlike monologue going on. Kafka has this super distinctive voice, you always know it's Kafka.

Maybe that's a useful dichotomy through which to think about things like translation, because a translator has to be a mimic in a certain sense. A translator must be willing to get their own voice out of the way, be extremely sensitive to the voice of the original author, or that of the characters, or the author's own polyphony. I think that translators sometimes make good writers because of that, because if you practice the craft of translation over and over and over, you become extremely sensitive to the subtleties of register, the subtleties of expression, and voice. You're thinking about it all the time. I'm thinking about it even in technical translation, in academic translations; I'm not just trying to convey the messages, I'm also trying to convey something about the style. That sensitivity is a tool that all writers can use.

SL: How does your approach to translation fit within the tradition of translation? I know that translations in and of themselves have inspired a lot of controversy, a lot of discussion. There have been certain eras in which translators have taken lots of liberties and we're returning to a moment where we are taking a more careful approach with different considerations. How does your approach fit within tradition and genre of translation?

JD: I'm translating in the twenty-first century, I'm translating in the age of Google, I'm translating in the age of globalization and multiculturalism. Things are very different now than they were 100 years ago for translators and for publishers. When Willa and Edwin Muir had to translate Kafka, for example, they had to adhere to certain expectations from the publisher. That imposed a lot of constraints on what they could and couldn't do in terms of reproducing the author's original voice. I think that for quite a while, in the twentieth century, translations tended to be more domesticating—that's a term that we use in the industry—they tended to adhere more to the expectations of the target audience and to be less concerned with absolute fidelity in terms of style and in terms of content.

There are eras in translation, like *les belles infidèles* in seventeenth-century France, where it was a trend to just completely transform things. If you look at the translation history of the *1001 Arabian Nights*, you see the most extreme examples of that kind of domestication. All of that came under a lot of fire during the cultural turn in translation studies, under the influence of theorists like Lawrence Venuti, who said we shouldn't be translating this way. This kind of domesticating work is abusive to the text, and it does a disservice both to the author and to the audience. Instead, we should be challenging audiences with the foreignness of the foreign.

I operate somewhere in between Venuti and the more extremely creative translators who just want to transform things. For me, it depends on the project. I described my Queneau project where obviously, what I'm doing involves all kinds of infidelities to Queneau, I'm taking his poem and transforming it in lots of different ways. That's appropriate for that project, because Queneau himself was a great transformer, both of other people's texts and his own.

He wrote the *Exercises in Style*, which has 99 different transformations of the same little story, and he demonstrates the power of multiplicity in style through that. So, my transformations of Queneau are very much in a Quenellian spirit.

On the other hand, on a current project that I'm working on, a novel from 1844, that is being translated into English for the first time—a collaborative translation—I'm tending toward a very high level of fidelity. The whole team agrees that we want to bring across the author's original intent, the author's original message, and the author's original voice for political reasons, for reasons of historical scholarship. It's a first translation, you don't want to take too many liberties with that kind of text. I'm guided by the purpose of the text and in translation theory, we call that *skopos*—we ask, what is the purpose? I will vary the level of intervention and creativity, or originality, I guess, that I bring to a translation project, depending on the purpose.

SL: I believe you left breadcrumbs to this next question throughout your different answers. So, we'll wrap with this: how do you define voice? You can approach this by thinking about how you define voice for yourself versus how you define voice as you approach it as a translator.

JD: I've been thinking about this question a lot. Voice is something that arises from a series of different tensions, the tension between standard language and unexpected, idiosyncratic or vernacular language. The tension between universals and particulars. I think that voice is what makes good writing worth reading. It is of paramount importance to study different voices with open-mindedness. Being someone who works with a lot of international texts, being someone who works with texts from Spanish speaking traditions—from Colombia, from Mexico, from Peru—and then also working with French writing, both from France and from the francophone Caribbean, I am not afraid to create translations that are a little bit surprising to the contemporary English-speaking reader's ear. I think that readers now are ready for surprising, new, distinctive voices, and I think that's one of the reasons our project with Amalialú's work is successful. The reason that people have started to show so much interest in it is because the original writing is excellent, and partially because of our approach, which is to preserve the distinctiveness of that voice without glossing it over. Because that voice, what does it do? It sings in Spanish, right? And if you want to make a song in English that's a translation of a song in Spanish, you can do that, right? "*Quizás, quizás, quizás,*"—"Perhaps, perhaps, perhaps," you know, we translate songs all the time. Why can't we translate short stories that have song-like qualities using some of those same strategies? Why shouldn't a story from Colombia sing with some of the same cadences as those Latin rhythms, right from Colombia? I listen to Colombian music when I'm working with Amalialú's work.

I think that there's a narrative about voice where we have the saying, "finding one's voice." There's this myth that you've truly arrived as a creator—whether as a visual artist or a literary artist—when you've found your voice. The dichotomy I was talking about earlier about the distinction between having a particular voice and having a mastery of a multiplicity of voices, immediately problematizes the very idea of finding one's voice or having one voice. I have struggled to find my voice as a poet. It turns out that I have found my voice as a poet by doing things like the "Fire Sails Through my Body." I think that's how I produced my very best poetry, and it is original poetry. But it's good because of its openness to other voices and letting other voices flow through me and through the interplay of chance and intention.

Jeffrey Diteman *is a literary scholar and translator working from French and Spanish to English. His poetry has appeared in* Meat for Tea, Past Simple, *and* Drunken Boat. *His translations have been published by* Harper's Magazine, Le Monde, Latin American Literature Today, The Massachusetts Review, *and* McSweeney's, *with translated novels released by Deep Vellum and Restless Books. His research interests include translation studies, cultural hybridity, experimental poetics, feminism, and postcolonial theory.*

Tanure Ojaide

"Remembering"
(for Ezekiel)

The day the farmer lost all his harvest to locusts
the day the herdsman lost all his cows to rinderpest

the day the fisherman lost his boat and nets to a storm
the day there was a total eclipse of the sun

the day fire left dry leaves to burn out green ones
the day water failed to quench the burning thirst

the day the wind refused to blow away smothering fumes
the day the earth opened up a bottomless pit to another world

the day the muse thrashed the minstrel
the day the minstrel was struck dumb

the day the goat refused to eat yam leaves
the day the parrot refused to eat corn

the day the drums refused to beat for the dancer
the day the iroko was struck down by lightning

the day erased from the memory of celebrations
the day gone down without a record of its hours

the day all the gates closed to the fugitive
the day the crossroads refused its sacrifice

the day all the alarms refused to go off
the day the clear-eyed guide lost his vision

the day the boneless beast opened its mouth
to swallow an entire man like sautéed crayfish

that was the day of the summer solstice when in
Jerusalem and my best friend died in Sapele.

PB: Thank you for that beautiful poem, Tanure. Tell us about how that feels, to say a poem like that.

TO: You know, when you lose your best friend, and we were so close, even when he dies... you know, in Nigeria people are not buried sometimes immediately when they die and will not be buried for another month or two. And in my dreams, I was still in my teens, I was still going to places with him, as if he was alive. Just to show you how close we were. So, you expect that type of poem to capture that feeling. He was a living saint, I will say he was such a beautiful human being, always lively, always happy. And so you know what it means to lose that type of human treasure, I tried to capture it as much as I could. Especially, it was a day I couldn't forget. We were in Tel Aviv for something, then went to Jerusalem. But that whole day something was happening, and at the moment he died, I felt something was happening which I couldn't understand, and just the feeling, I hope I was able to capture it in the poem.

PB: Tell us a little bit about how you grew up with poetry as voice.

TO: Even before I went to school to learn English, to study English, of course I spoke my indigenous, Nigerian language, Yoruba. I also heard songs because my grandmother who raised me would always sing. Always, and the songs were very meaningful. So, by the time I was in high school and went to university, I was studying poetry. I felt what my grandmother was doing was singing poetry. The word for poem and song in my language are the same, so poetry is meant to be sung. Like this poem, it's almost like an oral tradition superimposed upon writing.

In fact, many of us Africans do that. There are genres where it's a satiric song. Or there are chants like the Riki of the Yoruba, or the bongo of the Zulu. Well, this one, I've just read it's almost like a chant. I think in the beginning, I tried to negotiate a relationship between the oral tradition and the written tradition. When I write any poem, I vocalize first internally. And then later, externally, and in the process of the two tests of vocalization, I feel yes, this is what I'm supposed to do.

Like in my tradition, a poem is not complete until it is performed. There's something more to it when it is performed to an audience. People listen to it. I can see your use of voice; the voice is very important. Your voice itself carries the feelings if you are trying to express ideas, or you want to express feelings. If you're writing a love poem, for instance, the voice is, I think, the greatest determinant of your true feelings. These things are part of the poem itself, which words alone don't carry.

The voice completes the poem. The poem is almost lifeless on the page. But you give life to it when you vocalize it. So, the voice itself is the destination of any composition. We are composing. How would this sound? Yeah, if we're in the west, it's almost the same. So, voice in the African tradition, and I think also in the Western tradition, it's very important in bringing out the essence of the poem. Not the words per say. The voice that comes out of it. What people hear you say. That's the beauty of the poem. The repetition, the inflection of your voice is the tonality and the pitch. All these things matter a lot. So, voice again I will say is very crucial to poetry.

Tanure Ojaide *has been the Frank Porter Graham Professor of Africana Studies since 2006. He is the author of twenty poetry collections and nine scholarly books. His poetry awards include the Commonwealth Poetry Prize for the Africa Region (1987), the All-Africa Okigbo Prize for Poetry (1988, 1997), the BBC Arts and Africa Poetry Award (1988), and the Association of Nigerian Authors Poetry Award (1988, 1994, 2003, and 2011).*

Angelique Palmer

"twirl: when the tornado spoke to the damage."

Ain't it grand the wind stopped blowin'

Learned to do the twirl fresh
off my first exhale
Yes, twirl,
circle-motion
gyrate,
roundhouse
kick to the throat
like I'm 'sposed to

This here is
natural.

I twirl, that's my money, kid.
That's my get lifted.
When they
put enough dirt
in my skirt; when they
gave up a good enough gray
to challenge me, I got to
thinking;
getting smart with my shit
-got to being about being the music of it.

I been invisible or
night time.
I like this
cover of dark
lanterns made busy; brown
liquor
burning
throat. That's that
SWISH
them boys learned from my hips.
Watch me!

I spin
hard

SL: How do you define voice?

AP: What voice is to me? Sometimes it's new in my body. Most of the time, I can say something, and it belongs to someone else. It belongs to an ancestor; it sounds like my Mom. Even the timbre and tonality of voice are different, for different occasions. Voice is on demand. I can demand different things. I can demand it be gentle, visceral, thunder, or conjure. I can use it to whisper a spell that heals the ache in a wound. I can use it like a large, brilliant sickle to hammer down and amputate the infection. If I can use my voice in different ways, then voice becomes what you demand of it.

With the latest project I worked on, I demanded that my voice heal me. In healing me, perhaps it is evidence to someone else that you were never alone. We went through the same, or very similar experiences and you were never alone. You're not doing it wrong. You're not crazy, quit gaslighting yourself girl! We're good! Here's how we heal. I did that by saying to myself, "Here is how I heal."

I'm a kindergarten teacher and a poet. I love the dichotomy of those two things. On some days, I demand my voice to help my little friends know it's okay to make a mistake. We made a mess and now we clean it up. Or, that went out of the lines, let's try again next time! Sometimes, my voice is gentle in that way. Sometimes, it's the booming thrum of vocal cords that alerts those same children I love dearly, "You have made a mistake you're not allowed to make again. Not on my watch." Those things can happen on the same day, an hour apart.

My voice is both.

I've used this same voice to seduce lovers. I've used it to dismiss them. I've also used it to beg them to stay. I have begged people to stay with me, and I'm not proud of that. But it has happened. I heard myself do it. And because I heard myself do it, it is part of my history. It was my voice, and I heard it, so that means I'm gon' reckon with it.

I have used this particular voice to heal in front of a large audience of the community. That gathering of human souls listened. You could hear a pin drop. That was frightening.

SL: What did your body feel like as you're talking about these different modes of begging someone to stay, seducing someone, or dismissing them? Or even when you engage publicly in your healing. What's that feeling like in your body? Those modes and ranges?

AP: It's different kinds of energies. I joked with a coworker recently that my brain is not just two sides: left brain, right brain. There's an entire committee sitting up there building on stuff, vetoing stuff, having arguments, throwing chairs sometimes. It's not pretty. But it's happening, and those energies are processed in that way.

In that specific (public) moment it was electric, and completely frightening. I was frozen, and I met that with something, and I used this voice, to harken back to what I was talking about, what I was gifted with, and summon some courage. To deliver this healing that I knew I was called to do.

It's Two-Headed: it is both angry and happy. It's happy you're here, and angry that you decided to show up without calling.

SL: Speaking of orality and voice, it seems like what you're talking about manifests in different spaces. Sometimes just yourself, or sometimes communal. When you're composing, are you thinking about those different spaces? How does composition and orality come to you?

AP: If it's a poem I probably needed to write it, I needed to get it out of my head, my heart, or my body. If I read it and was like "Ooohhh!" then it's probably going back in for performance. I don't love being called a performance poet, or even a slam poet all the time. I know that it's accurate. When that happens, I think that's what doesn't allow people to evolve. I'm starting to understand why people who left the slam scene, also started to distance themselves from it. Oftentimes they'd say, "That's not all I can do," not to shun that part of themselves.

Slam is what I did, and I was good at competitive poetry. At least for one brilliant moment on the final stage in Albuquerque, New Mexico, I got it all the way right. A couple of times, I got real damn close. So, that's where I come from. "I am a poet who slams," is what I would always say. I am a poet who brings her poems to competition.

But you know what? Sometimes my formula doesn't work in rooms. Sometimes my telling of the truth and being myself will not work for that particular set of randomly chosen judges.

SL: What do you think is the difference between the poet who slams, versus the slam poet?

AP: I don't think that a "slam poet" exists. I think these are people who either use performance pieces, monologues, or poems to be in competition. Sometimes they use the competition to edit their work. Sometimes they use competition to garner jobs. Slam does that for people.

SL: Do you see yourself as having transitioned out of that role? There was a long time where I never read poetry in public because I thought I had to do that...participate in slam poetry. And I didn't (and don't), have that voice, so I rarely, if ever, read my work publicly many years ago.

AP: I don't have that voice either. I've been successful in competitive circles. Without having *that voice*. I don't have that, that's not my forte. Sometimes it would feel disingenuous to me. Even if I've written a persona piece. I've written a persona piece in the voice of a tornado. I'm not a tornado, but I know it's a genuine piece to me. If I had to walk around pretending to be something just to score well, I don't think I would be credible or successful. I don't think I have *that voice.*

I remember asking a mentor a long time ago, "Why can't I win any slams?" I don't know why it became important to me, but it suddenly became important to me to win slams. He said, "Talk to them. You're talking about them. Talk to them." That's when I got better at it, and that's what I'm good at.

I think that's the difference with most people who are successful in those circles. They talk *to* the audience in verse, in rhyme, in free verse. In large booming voices or even in the gentle voices. That approach helps them to be successful in those areas.

SL: How have you seen your definition of voice change? How have you seen that shift over time?

AP: There's an organization that organized a lot of different slams and festivals that went out of business in 2018. In 2018, I started to hear people say that "She's maturing. Angelique is getting too old for this." I don't believe that. That's bullshit.

But I did feel different around that time.

I loved watching those festivals come up. The big circus tents come up, three days later they disappear, but you still have that feeling. It imploded. It fell in on a lot of us who believed in it [the slam poetry scene], harder than we probably should have. That's when my feelings toward it changed.

Currently I'm helping someone to compete in The Womxn of the World Poetry Slam. In the past, this has been an amazing memory for me. This poet and I sat down to talk about her goals, and we ended up talking about my past experiences. I say that to say my voice has changed. It's arcing. It hasn't hit a pinnacle. You don't get onto the next season of your life without settling the arc. I think I felt like I was done right around that time. With proving myself to other people. But it was more than likely proving myself to myself. Since a lot of things went right in one instance, I thought, "Well that's a fluke, and I have to do it right this time."

It wasn't fun anymore.

Instead of trying to prove that I'm not a fluke, I started proving that I am a writer. I started working on healing. Then the world closed. We had a whole pandemic. I sat with myself. That's how my voice CHANGED-changed. I didn't get to hear other people's thoughts on my voice. I didn't get to hear other people's voices in conversation. That sometimes is what slam does, in terms of conversation. I didn't hear that anymore because we were all shut into our own spaces for a while. I got to hear my own voice the way I wanted to hear it. It's my on-demand voice. I started demanding what I needed from my own voice.*

* Since this conversation, Angelique began to compete again. She bested all the femme poets in the DC area to represent Washington DC at the 2023 Women of the World Poetry Slam or WoWps. Competing at WoWps again in 2024, Angelique finished the competition ranked 19th out of 96 poets. In terms of reflecting more on her experiences within slam poetry, Angelique shares, "I think I was quite bitter about feeling pushed out of the competitive arena. Two things: that was a myth that only lived in me. Secondly, I made my own lane, one that is fiercely loving, fiercely creative, fiercely protective, and fiercely competitive. This too has made me a better writer."

Angelique Palmer *is a performance poet, Kindergarten Teacher, Spoken Word instructor at Wilkes University. She is in her first year of a three-year term as Fairfax County Poet Laureate. A finalist in the 2015 Women of the World Poetry Slam, she's currently ranked 19th among the top 96 competitive poets in the world. Her first full-length book,* THE CHAMBERMAID'S STYLE GUIDE, *debuted on Sargent Press in 2016. Her second book is the 2021 follow-up* ALSO DARK *on Etruscan Press. The New Orleans native, and Florida State University Creative Writing graduate has called Fairfax County home since 2017.* ***"Twirl: when the tornado spoke to the damage" is an excerpt from a longer poem by the same title.***

Philip Metres

"Cell/(ph)one: A Simultaneity In Four Voices"

Instructions for use:
Tear out this page, and then cut into four columns and give to four readers. Have the readers perform their monologues together, reading through the text twice. Line breaks are slight pauses. Space breaks indicate silences. Improvisation is welcome.

1. [Cell/phone]

You are wanted. You are not
alone. You are wanted. You are
not alone.

Someone needs to answer me
now. Someone needs me
to answer now. Someone
needs me alone and no one else
to answer now.

A watch. A phone. I watch.
I wait for you. For you alone. I
text. I cell. I tower above alone.
I satellite. Alight, I roam and I
charge, working this self own.

I am wanted. I have to take this
call. I have to take
this call. I have to take this
call. I have to take this call.

(repeat)

2. [Breaking Convo]

Hello?
Hey—
How ARE you?
How are YOU?
Huh? [Hold up finger]

What's up?
What?
Hold on.
Say it again.

Hello?
Hey…
How ARE you?
How are YOU?
Huh? [Hold up finger]

What's up?
What? [Turn head away]
Hold on. hold on.
Say it again.
NO!!!
NO!!! NO!!! Hell no!!!
Yes, I can hold.

(repeat)

3. [Guantanamo]

Please pass this on
to my wife.
Tell her it's time
for her to move on.

I will never leave
Guantanamo.

She must understand
I am not abandoning her.

That I love her.

But she must move on
with her life.

She is getting older.

But I will never leave
Guantanamo.

That I love her.

But she must move on
with her life.

(repeat)

4. [Intercept Message]

The number you have reached
has been disconnected. If you
need help, hang up and dial the
operator.

Please hang up and try again.

The following tones are for the
deaf community.

Dilililiilililllililiiililli

The number you have reached
has been disconnected.

Dilililiilililllililiiililli

Please hang up and try again.

Da da da da da da

Please try again.

Da da da da da da

(repeat)

"Cell/(ph)one: A Simultaneity In Four Voices" is a poem that is within the full collection, *Sand Opera* (Alice James Books, 2025). Courtesy of the poet.

SL: I would love to hear more about this page, why did you choose it?

PM: I chose a poem called "Cell/(ph)one: A Simultaneity In Four Voices," which is from *Sand Opera*. I chose it because it speaks to something that I've longed to try to create in poems—a sense of polyvocality. And since it's a poem that's literally meant to be performed by four different people simultaneously, it creates a unique experience for an audience. It's a very different poem read on the page versus being heard and seen. It has "instructions for use":

"Tear out these pages, then cut into four columns for four readers. Have the readers perform their monologues simultaneously, reading through the text twice. Read line breaks as slight pauses. Space breaks as silences. Improvisation is welcome."

This poem began as a satire of the noise that we find in public space, where people aren't really listening to each other. But it has a political dimension insofar as we're a society that likes to tweet but not listen. We like to share our posture, but we find it much more uncomfortable to try to deal with someone else's reality. First voice says "You are wanted. You are not / alone. You are wanted. You / are not alone. // Someone needs to answer / now. Someone needs me / to answer now. Someone / needs me alone and no one / else to answer now." etc. That's a kind of or almost the inner thoughts of someone talking on the phone. The second voice is simply someone acting out a conversation with someone. "Hello. Hey, how ARE you? You what? Huh? What's up? Hold on. What? Say it again. What's up? What? Hold on. What? Say it again. " etc.

The fourth voice says, "the number you have reached / has been disconnected. If you need help, hang / up and dial the operator. // Please hang up and try again. // The following tones are for / the deaf community. // The number you have reached has been disconnected. Please hang up and try again." Etc.

But it was with the third voice that the poem found its gravity, its politics, its reason for being.

I read a story in the *New York Times* about the time a journalist went to Guantanamo Bay Prison. One of the prisoners asked the journalist to send a message home:. "Please pass this on to my wife. / Tell her It's time for her // to move on. I will never leave / Guantanamo. She must understand // I'm not abandoning her. That I / love her. But she must move on // with her life. She is getting older. But I will never leave // Guantanamo. That I love her. // but she must move on / with her life."

What began as a sort of satire, a send-up of the noisiness of our public spaces and our inability to listen to each other, veered into the theme and subject of *Sand Opera*. The book explores the War on Terror, despite the noise of our society's distractions. We're constantly distracted by everything going on around us, and we're not present for them. We can't hear them. Literally, we can't hear them. I chose this poem, partly because of the way in which this poem is trying to interrogate the monological aspects of a lyric, and to surprise us with the kinds of noise that we encounter in daily life.

SL: I would also argue there's an inability for us to hear ourselves as all in this cacophony, right?

PM: Yes, that's a wonderful thing to say. When I perform it, I often just find three people at a reading venue to perform it with me. One of the things that's always a challenge for people is to read the poem as a simultaneity. They often stop at first, because it's hard to try to speak when other people are speaking. I encourage them to just perform their piece and try not to be distracted by the noise. But what you're saying is really powerful. Of course, one of the reasons why we go to poetry is that it is often that still small, silent voice that enables us to hear ourselves better.

SL: When you constructed this or composed it, did you have performance in mind? Did it just come to you? You mention that it started off as a satire and then landed in this other place. Can you talk a little bit about that along with how you compose? Are you composing with orality in mind?

PM: I conceived this piece as a script that was meant to be performed. I noticed that in the process of putting it in a book that I had some hesitancy about adding it, because there's a tension between the oral and the literary. But I embraced it instead of saying, "Oh, this isn't a 'poem.'" I said, "Why can't it be a poem?" Forced myself to expand my notion of what a poem is and what it can do, and to enter into this more performative sense of what a poem is about.

One of the questions you're asking is about the relationship between those two things. I would say that certainly in all the poems that I write, I'm trying to listen to each poem's individual music, its architecture, its sound. This one was on the outside rim of the galaxy that is my poetry—and that's partly why I chose to share it with you. Interestingly, I often start readings with this poem, partly because It's a shock to an audience. It clears the space and the way for what is to come. By creating noise, it actually clears space. I don't know why that is, but It's partly because it defies so many expectations about what we think of poetry readings.

SL: Speaking for myself having tried to do this on the page, polyvocality is challenging. One can illustrate this in performance, but it's not always easy to really show that on a page. In terms of structure, it's incredibly difficult! What is your advice, especially for poets who are already out in the world doing their poetics? How can they expand and play with voice a bit, especially in the ways that you have with polyvocality?

PM: As someone who has been academically trained, I had all these rules built up in my head about what was appropriate, right, or poetic. I'm very grateful that I got exposed to the avant-garde traditions that constantly push the boundaries of what we consider poetic, or what we consider possible for poetry. I think reading widely and voraciously and seeing what people have tried is always an encouragement. Also, to draw upon other arts as well. One should not just see poetry as the "be all and end all," but also explore the way other practices work. One of the many influences on this poem was the beginning to a play where I saw a whole bunch of characters talking at the same time. Then they stopped talking all at the same time, and then they went into their roles. That always struck me as such a powerful gesture on the theatrical stage. I wanted to bring that into a kind of poetry reading and a poetry situation.

Philip Metres *is the author of twelve books, including* Fugitive/Refuge *(Copper Canyon, 2024),* Shrapnel Maps *(Copper Canyon, 2020),* The Sound of Listening: Poetry as Refuge and Resistance *(University of Michigan, 2018),* Sand Opera *(Alice James, 2015), and* I Burned at the Feast: Selected Poems of Arseny Tarkovsky *(Cleveland State, 2015). His work—poetry, translation, essays, fiction, criticism, and scholarship—has garnered fellowships from the Guggenheim Foundation, the Lannan Foundation, the National Endowment for the Arts, the Ohio Arts Council, and the Watson Foundation. He is the recipient of the Adrienne Rich Award, three Arab American Book Awards, the Lyric Poetry Prize, and the Cleveland Arts Prize. He is professor of English and director of the Peace, Justice, and Human Rights program at John Carroll University. He lives with his family in Cleveland, Ohio.*

Damon Honeycutt

"Horizon Line...Dusk"

"Horizon Line...Dusk" is the fifth movement of a string quartet titled *Children of the Final Sun*. Courtesy of the artist.

SL: It's an interesting experiment to ask someone to play just one page of a music composition. I'd like to start by having you tell us about this page and this piece of music you chose. Why did you choose it? And how does it represent your practice?

DH: This is the fifth movement of a string quartet called *Children of The Final Sun*, and it has a poem attached to it. This movement is titled "Horizon Line, Dusk."

I chose this because this was the first movement I wrote, even though it's the fifth movement in the piece. It's a series of chords that came to me in a meditative state based on journal writing. The string quartet is a sonic representation of my time when I was dancing. One can say it is a self-expressive sonic mythology. It is/was a sonic narrative about my experience allowing me to reflect upon what I did, where I traveled given that I've traveled and performed dance in over 20 countries around the world. Based on what I saw and thought during my meditative state, it felt like music was the more apropos voice for the experiences that I had.

SL: Why don't you read us the first page, you mentioned that it was accompanied by a poem.

DH:

It was dusk.

The continent was behind him and he wept for he knew he might not ever return there.

The land he wants traveled to the City he helped build and destroy was that his back

On the bow of the vessel, all there is all he sees are a sea of stars within the void,

meeting at the horizon of events.

The horizon line always is... from where we travel from, to where we go to... to the vantage point all look for, but look up, the stars are your navigation... it is there that you will find your way.

sailing low, before the dawn.

SL: What is interesting is that you might not claim the title of poet, but I know enough about your work that it would be apt to add that title, poet. Given that you are a multifaceted artist—there is the embodiment dimension of your work through both your dance, Kung Fu practice...you are a swordsman, a composer—how does orality or voice play a role across all your modalities? Is it different when you're composing versus working through movement versus working through other things? What are your thoughts on that?

DH: If I take orality as just a concept of voice and in reflecting on my martial arts training being Kung Fu, or Chinese martial arts, a lot of my teachers that I had didn't speak the same language as me. So, the orality, the voice, became the movement. The articulation of it became accents of rhythm enhanced through my experiences with the Peking Opera. During my time with them, they would vocalize rhythmic noises. Those rhythmic noises would be in the form of gongs or percussive instruments that would accent movements. It became a language much in the same way a lot of other music traditions of the world are communicated. For example, the Tabla are an excellent representation of that, where you use the voice to communicate different techniques on the instrument.

Taking those concepts and putting them into written form, I had to find a way of translating my physical movement experiences into western notation. I had to really think outside the box. I had to put myself in a different state. Basically, I had to throw ideas at the page, then create aggregates of notes on that page, and allow them to cohesively come together in an intuitive fashion. Of course, all of this is embodied through meditative and introspective practices. So, it wasn't necessarily chance operations or aleatoric. However, it had a lot of synchronicity that I think would be mysterious to a lot of people.

SL: Based on your answer, it feels like voice and orality become unified, whether you are working in movement, through the body, through writing, or through your composition. Given that you gave an introduction to one of your compositional pieces, how is your work received differently on the page and in performance? Now, I know, in this case, we're talking about individuals who are going to be playing your work based on how they read it. Are you always composing as if, for example, someone is going to be moving your piece or responding in some way, even if they're responding with instruments? You also have performed your work around the world. How do things shift for you in terms of how it is received on a page versus on a stage? Also, are you able to talk a little bit about how it shifts in cultural contexts as well.

DH: That's a lot to unpack. When communicating on the page within a compositional piece, I always have to think that I'm not there. Whatever they get as this tome of written things has to communicate what it is. And then of course, in music, we have our languages of dynamics and techniques.

We listened to my string quartet, so in dealing with just string instruments, are they going to play harmonics? Are they doing pizzicato? What's the dynamic range of them? Do I want to articulate their bowing? These are all concepts I can represent on the page. That being said, those *are* the things I do put on there.

I also like to engage metaphorical context or give the musicians instructions like, "Play this section of music as if you're in a hurry to go somewhere." I've also tried to embodied movement paired with sound. Another piece I wrote, a sax quartet, has actual physical movements within the composition. It instructed that they turn to the right or turn to the left while performing the composition. That was an interesting experiment in and of itself. However, giving a player who's playing an instrument something that is a kinesthetic instruction, you could say, might have them approach their own technique differently. It is my joy as a composer to see how individual their approach is with that kind of metaphorical direction, in addition to how it's performed on the stage.

When people watch musicians play music that has that kind of instruction in it, the performers themselves move very differently because they feel individual freedom in that expression. I'm not so high strung on like, "You must play it this way, or that way." If they are able to embody the metaphor, the art will speak for itself. I don't have to be the artist to show up to tell them what to do.

SL: I'm curious about another question, have you seen your music being played, your composition? Have you experienced it?

DH: Yes, a few times.

SL: How did that feel for you? Also, is it normal to include kinesthetic instructions, I've not quite heard of a composer doing that. It reminds me of some of my experiences with dance, where a choreographer is choreographing movement. Are the kinesthetic instructions pulling from your choreography and Kung Fu?

DH: I guess so. A lot of kung fu movements are metaphors. Like, "Parting the horse's mane," as a movement. That movement comes from Tai Chi, and you ask what does that mean, or "Needle at sea bottom." Or you have metaphors like, "We have to hear the wind in your kicks."

For us who study this, we get that, we know what it means. Even if you look at the word, Kung Fu, hard work over time, that is a very basic understanding of the term. But really, I like Mark Salzman's definition, which come from his book, *Iron and Silk*, a memoir where he says, and I paraphrase, 'To have skill which transcends surface beauty.' And so, you have this polishing effect of going through things over time. I feel that gives the individual—no matter where they're at in the journey, or the spectrum of technique—an audience to engage with the work. I am always honored by seeing my piece performed and it is highly emotional because I must surrender my work to them. I also must witness them go through my piece, succeed or fail at it while they engage with it. And that's always a very unique and beautiful experience.

SL: How do you define voice, especially as an artist who works across so many mediums? Does your concept and definition of voice change depending on what medium you're working with? You mentioned something about giving over a page, giving over work, and you're not there, but your voice is very much there. This alongside the voices articulated through other voices. Whether we're talking about instruments, bodies, or something else, because I know you also have a legacy with the dance company Pilobolus's S*hadowland* that is still being performed. How do you define voice and how it shifts across these modalities?

DH: There are different legacies with *Shadowland*. What was interesting about *Shadowland* is that we were making shadows, so you are not really seen on stage all the time. That's kind of an interesting, non-attachment that we talked about a lot among the dancers.

I didn't even think about it until now, but with the *Shadowland* concept, it's creating bodies out of that one thing, and creating multiple things in a gestalt, right? I guess, taking that metaphor, and then putting it towards my music, once I hand it over, it is with a hope that the performer is open, and receptive enough to think for themselves within the piece. And, again, work with the piece of music that's in front of them with their technique, not make it about their technique.

My compositions have technique in them, but I'm not making it so technocratic that it's about that technique that I used to create them. I don't say to the players, "Oh, you have to have these absolute articulations," or "You must have these absolute defining dynamics," or "You must use only these types of bowings." The player has their own way of interpreting those that might be more efficient. I like to keep my composition open, especially for the ones who will be playing it. This creates space for them to be able to have a dialogue with the work.

SL: So, with all these layers, how do you define voice if you were to define it based on all of those things?

DH: Voice is the personal way that I would engage with any situation of art making that's open to dialogue rather than just speaking with conversation, rather than saying, "I found my voice and this is what it sounds like."

Damon Honeycutt *is a versatile artist who cultivates martial arts, dance, writing, and music composition. Honeycutt has worked with dance companies such as Scapegoat Garden, Nai-Ni Chen, and Pilobolus. He has traveled to over 20 countries performing in venues that range from the 2009 Royal Variety Performance in the presence of HM The Queen, Komische Oper Berlin, Folies Bergère, and the 79th Annual Academy Awards Ceremony. As a composer, Honeycutt has composed and had his music performed by Chatham Baroque, The Power String Quartet headed by Jennifer Choi, The Delgani String Quartet, Ensemble Entelechron, and Ken Thomson's Saxophone Quartet. Honeycutt has an M.F.A. in Music Composition from The Vermont College of Fine Arts, an M.A. in Conscious Evolution and Integral Studies from The Graduate Institute, and a B.F.A. from the California Institute of the Arts. He is now a father, educator, theoretician, and retired adventurer.* ***"Horizon Line...Dusk" is the fifth movement of a string quartet titled*** **Children of the Final Sun.**

Books from Etruscan Press

Zarathustra Must Die | Dorian Alexander
The Disappearance of Seth | Kazim Ali
Son of a Bird | Nin Andrews
The Last Orgasm | Nin Andrews
Drift Ice | Jennifer Atkinson
Crow Man | Tom Bailey
Coronology | Claire Bateman
Viscera | Felice Belle
Reading the Signs and other itinerant essays | Stephen Benz
Topographies | Stephen Benz
What We Ask of Flesh | Remica L. Bingham
The Greatest Jewish-American Lover in Hungarian History | Michael Blumenthal
No Hurry | Michael Blumenthal
Choir of the Wells | Bruce Bond
Cinder | Bruce Bond
The Other Sky | Bruce Bond and Aron Wiesenfeld
Peal | Bruce Bond
Scar | Bruce Bond
Until We Talk | Darrell Bourque and Bill Gingles
Big Time | Rus Bradburd
Poems and Their Making: A Conversation | Moderated by Philip Brady
Crave: Sojourn of a Hungry Soul | Laurie Jean Cannady
Toucans in the Arctic | Scott Coffel
Sixteen | Auguste Corteau
Don't Mind Me | Brian Coughlan
Wattle & daub | Brian Coughlan
Body of a Dancer | Renée E. D'Aoust

Generations: Lullaby with Incendiary Device, The Nazi Patrol, and How It Is That We | Dante Di Stefano, William Heyen, and H. L. Hix
Ill Angels | Dante Di Stefano
Aard-vark to Axolotl: Pictures From my Grandfather's Dictionary | Karen Donovan
Trio: Planet Parable, Run: A Verse-History of Victoria Woodhull, and Endless Body | Karen Donovan, Diane Raptosh, and Daneen Wardrop
Scything Grace | Sean Thomas Dougherty
Areas of Fog | Will Dowd
Romer | Robert Eastwood
Wait for God to Notice| Sari Fordham
Bon Courage: Essays on Inheritance, Citizenship, and a Creative Life| Ru Freeman
Surrendering Oz | Bonnie Friedman
Funeral Playlist | Sarah Gorham
Nahoonkara | Peter Grandbois
Triptych: The Three-Legged World, In Time, and Orpheus & Echo | Peter Grandbois, James McCorkle, and Robert Miltner
The Candle: Poems of Our 20th Century Holocausts | William Heyen
The Confessions of Doc Williams & Other Poems | William Heyen
The Football Corporations | William Heyen
A Poetics of Hiroshima | William Heyen
September 11, 2001: American Writers Respond | Edited by William Heyen
Shoah Train | William Heyen
American Anger: An Evidentiary | H. L. Hix
As Easy As Lying | H. L. Hix
As Much As, If Not More Than | H. L. Hix
Chromatic | H. L. Hix
Demonstrategy: Poetry, For and Against | H. L. Hix
First Fire, Then Birds | H. L. Hix
God Bless | H. L. Hix
I'm Here to Learn to Dream in Your Language | H. L. Hix
Incident Light | H. L. Hix
Legible Heavens | H. L. Hix
Lines of Inquiry | H. L. Hix

Rain Inscription | H. L. Hix
Shadows of Houses | H. L. Hix
Wild and Whirling Words: A Poetic Conversation | Moderated by H. L. Hix
All the Difference | Patricia Horvath
Art Into Life | Frederick R. Karl
Free Concert: New and Selected Poems | Milton Kessler
Who's Afraid of Helen of Troy: An Essay on Love | David Lazar
Black Metamorphoses | Shanta Lee
Mailer's Last Days: New and Selected Remembrances of a Life in Literature |
J. Michael Lennon
Parallel Lives | Michael Lind
The Burning House | Paul Lisicky
Museum of Stones | Lynn Lurie
Quick Kills | Lynn Lurie
Synergos | Roberto Manzano
The Gambler's Nephew | Jack Matthews
American Mother | Colum McCann with Diane Foley
The Subtle Bodies | James McCorkle
An Archaeology of Yearning | Bruce Mills
Arcadia Road: A Trilogy | Thorpe Moeckel
Venison | Thorpe Moeckel
So Late, So Soon | Carol Moldaw
The Widening | Carol Moldaw
Clay and Star: Selected Poems of Liliana Ursu | Translated by Mihaela Moscaliuc
Cannot Stay: Essays on Travel | Kevin Oderman
White Vespa | Kevin Oderman
Also Dark | Angelique Palmer
Fates: The Medea Notebooks, Starfish Wash-Up, and overflow of an unknown self |
Ann Pedone, Katherine Soniat, and D. M. Spitzer
The Dog Looks Happy Upside Down | Meg Pokrass
Mr. Either/Or | Aaron Poochigian
Mr. Either/Or: All the Rage| Aaron Poochigian
The Shyster's Daughter | Paula Priamos

Help Wanted: Female | Sara Pritchard
American Amnesiac | Diane Raptosh
Dear Z: The Zygote Epistles | Diane Raptosh
Human Directional | Diane Raptosh
I Eric America | Diane Raptosh
50 Miles | Sheryl St. Germain
Saint Joe's Passion | J.D. Schraffenberger
Lies Will Take You Somewhere | Sheila Schwartz
Fast Animal | Tim Seibles
One Turn Around the Sun | Tim Seibles
Voodoo Libretto: New and Selected Poems | Tim Seibles
Rough Ground | Alix Anne Shaw
A Heaven Wrought of Iron: Poems From the Odyssey | D. M. Spitzer
American Fugue | Alexis Stamatis
Variations in the Key of K | Alex Stein
The Casanova Chronicles | Myrna Stone
Luz Bones | Myrna Stone
In the Cemetery of the Orange Trees | Jeff Talarigo
The White Horse: A Colombian Journey | Diane Thiel
The Arsonist's Song Has Nothing to Do With Fire | Allison Titus
Bestiality of the Involved | Spring Ulmer
The Waw | Jacqueline Gay Walley
Silk Road | Daneen Wardrop
Sinnerman | Michael Waters
The Fugitive Self | John Wheatcroft
YOU. | Joseph P. Wood
Leaves Borrowed from Human Flesh | Abigail Ardelle Zammit

Etruscan Press Is Proud of Support Received From

Wilkes University 

Ohio Arts Council 

The Stephen & Jeryl Oristaglio Foundation

Community of Literary Magazines and Presses 

National Endowment for the Arts 

Drs. Barbara Brothers & Gratia Murphy Endowment

Founded in 2001 with a generous grant from the Oristaglio Foundation, Etruscan Press is a nonprofit cooperative of poets and writers working to produce and promote books that nurture the dialogue among genres, achieve a distinctive voice, and reshape the literary and cultural histories of which we are a part.

etruscan press
www.etruscanpress.org
Etruscan Press books may be ordered from

Consortium Book Sales and Distribution
800.283.3572
www.cbsd.com

Etruscan Press is a 501(c)(3) nonprofit organization.
Contributions to Etruscan Press are tax deductible
as allowed under applicable law.
For more information, a prospectus,
or to order one of our titles,
contact us at books@etruscanpress.org.

www.ingramcontent.com/pod-product-compliance
Lightning Source LLC
Jackson TN
JSHW040824100825
89125JS00008B/13

9798990767812